Nature and the Numinous in
Mythopoeic Fantasy Literature

CRITICAL EXPLORATIONS IN SCIENCE FICTION AND FANTASY
(a series edited by Donald E. Palumbo and C.W. Sullivan III)

1 *Worlds Apart? Dualism and Transgression in Contemporary Female Dystopias* (Dunja M. Mohr, 2005)

2 *Tolkien and Shakespeare: Essays on Shared Themes and Language* (ed. Janet Brennan Croft, 2007)

3 *Culture, Identities and Technology in the* Star Wars *Films: Essays on the Two Trilogies* (ed. Carl Silvio, Tony M. Vinci, 2007)

4 *The Influence of* Star Trek *on Television, Film and Culture* (ed. Lincoln Geraghty, 2008)

5 *Hugo Gernsback and the Century of Science Fiction* (Gary Westfahl, 2007)

6 *One Earth, One People: The Mythopoeic Fantasy Series of Ursula K. Le Guin, Lloyd Alexander, Madeleine L'Engle and Orson Scott Card* (Marek Oziewicz, 2008)

7 *The Evolution of Tolkien's Mythology: A Study of the History of Middle-earth* (Elizabeth A. Whittingham, 2008)

8 *H. Beam Piper: A Biography* (John F. Carr, 2008)

9 *Dreams and Nightmares: Science and Technology in Myth and Fiction* (Mordecai Roshwald, 2008)

10 Lilith *in a New Light: Essays on the George MacDonald Fantasy Novel* (ed. Lucas H. Harriman, 2008)

11 *Feminist Narrative and the Supernatural: The Function of Fantastic Devices in Seven Recent Novels* (Katherine J. Weese, 2008)

12 *The Science of Fiction and the Fiction of Science: Collected Essays on SF Storytelling and the Gnostic Imagination* (Frank McConnell, ed. Gary Westfahl, 2009)

13 *Kim Stanley Robinson Maps the Unimaginable: Critical Essays* (ed. William J. Burling, 2009)

14 *The Inter-Galactic Playground: A Critical Study of Children's and Teens' Science Fiction* (Farah Mendlesohn, 2009)

15 *Science Fiction from Québec: A Postcolonial Study* (Amy J. Ransom, 2009)

16 *Science Fiction and the Two Cultures: Essays on Bridging the Gap Between the Sciences and the Humanities* (ed. Gary Westfahl, George Slusser, 2009)

17 *Stephen R. Donaldson and the Modern Epic Vision: A Critical Study of the "Chronicles of Thomas Covenant" Novels* (Christine Barkley, 2009)

18 *Ursula K. Le Guin's Journey to Post-Feminism* (Amy M. Clarke, 2010)

19 *Portals of Power: Magical Agency and Transformation in Literary Fantasy* (Lori M. Campbell, 2010)

20 *The Animal Fable in Science Fiction and Fantasy* (Bruce Shaw, 2010)

21 *Illuminating* Torchwood: *Essays on Narrative, Character and Sexuality in the BBC Series* (ed. Andrew Ireland, 2010)

22 *Comics as a Nexus of Cultures: Essays on the Interplay of Media, Disciplines and International Perspectives* (ed. Mark Berninger, Jochen Ecke, Gideon Haberkorn, 2010)

23 *The Anatomy of Utopia: Narration, Estrangement and Ambiguity in More, Wells, Huxley and Clarke* (Károly Pintér, 2010)

24 *The Anticipation Novelists of 1950s French Science Fiction: Stepchildren of Voltaire* (Bradford Lyau, 2010)

25 *The Twilight Mystique: Critical Essays on the Novels and Films* (ed. Amy M. Clarke, Marijane Osborn, 2010)

26 *The Mythic Fantasy of Robert Holdstock: Critical Essays on the Fiction* (ed. Donald E. Morse, Kálmán Matolcsy, 2011)

27 *Science Fiction and the Prediction of the Future: Essays on Foresight and Fallacy* (ed. Gary Westfahl, Wong Kin Yuen, Amy Kit-sze Chan, 2011)
28 *Apocalypse in Australian Fiction and Film: A Critical Study* (Roslyn Weaver, 2011)
29 *British Science Fiction Film and Television: Critical Essays* (ed. Tobias Hochscherf, James Leggott, 2011)
30 *Cult Telefantasy Series: A Critical Analysis of* The Prisoner, Twin Peaks, The X-Files, Buffy the Vampire Slayer, Lost, Heroes, Doctor Who *and* Star Trek (Sue Short, 2011)
31 *The Postnational Fantasy: Essays on Postcolonialism, Cosmopolitics and Science Fiction* (ed. Masood Ashraf Raja, Jason W. Ellis and Swaralipi Nandi, 2011)
32 *Heinlein's Juvenile Novels: A Cultural Dictionary* (C.W. Sullivan III, 2011)
33 *Welsh Mythology and Folklore in Popular Culture: Essays on Adaptations in Literature, Film, Television and Digital Media* (ed. Audrey L. Becker and Kristin Noone, 2011)
34 *I See You: The Shifting Paradigms of James Cameron's* Avatar (Ellen Grabiner, 2012)
35 *Of Bread, Blood and* The Hunger Games: *Critical Essays on the Suzanne Collins Trilogy* (ed. Mary F. Pharr and Leisa A. Clark, 2012)
36 *The Sex Is Out of This World: Essays on the Carnal Side of Science Fiction* (ed. Sherry Ginn and Michael G. Cornelius, 2012)
37 *Lois McMaster Bujold: Essays on a Modern Master of Science Fiction and Fantasy* (ed. Janet Brennan Croft, 2013)
38 *Girls Transforming: Invisibility and Age-Shifting in Children's Fantasy Fiction Since the 1970s* (Sanna Lehtonen, 2013)
39 Doctor Who *in Time and Space: Essays on Themes, Characters, History and Fandom, 1963–2012* (ed. Gillian I. Leitch, 2013)
40 *The Worlds of* Farscape: *Essays on the Groundbreaking Television Series* (ed. Sherry Ginn, 2013)
41 *Orbiting Ray Bradbury's Mars: Biographical, Anthropological, Literary, Scientific and Other Perspectives* (ed. Gloria McMillan, 2013)
42 *The Heritage of Heinlein: A Critical Reading of the Fiction Television Series* (Thomas D. Clareson and Joe Sanders, 2014)
43 *The Past That Might Have Been, the Future That May Come: Women Writing Fantastic Fiction, 1960s to the Present* (Lauren J. Lacey, 2014)
44 *Environments in Science Fiction: Essays on Alternative Spaces* (ed. Susan M. Bernardo, 2014)
45 *Discworld and the Disciplines: Critical Approaches to the Terry Pratchett Works* (ed. Anne Hiebert Alton and William C. Spruiell, 2014)
46 *Nature and the Numinous in Mythopoeic Fantasy Literature* (Chris Brawley, ed. Donald E. Palumbo and C.W. Sullivan III, 2014)
47 *J.R.R. Tolkien, Robert Howard and the Birth of Modern Fantasy* (Deke Parsons, 2014)

Nature and the Numinous in Mythopoeic Fantasy Literature

CHRIS BRAWLEY

CRITICAL EXPLORATIONS IN
SCIENCE FICTION AND FANTASY, 46

Series Editors Donald E. Palumbo *and* C.W. Sullivan III

McFarland & Company, Inc., Publishers
Jefferson, North Carolina

Poetry from Ursula K. Le Guin *Buffalo Gals and Other Animal Presences,* copyright © 1987 by Ursula K. Le Guin, is reprinted by permission of Curtis Brown, Ltd.

LIBRARY OF CONGRESS CATALOGUING-IN-PUBLICATION DATA

Brawley, Chris.
  Nature and the Numinous in Mythopoeic Fantasy Literature / Chris Brawley.
    p.   cm. — (Critical Explorations in Science Fiction and Fantasy ; 46)
  Includes bibliographical references and index.

ISBN 978-0-7864-9465-1 (softcover : acid free paper) ∞
ISBN 978-1-4766-1582-0 (ebook)

  1. Fantasy literature—History and criticism. 2. Holy, The, in literature. 3. Mythology in literature. 4. Ecocriticism. I. Title.
  PN56.F34B56 2014
  809.3'8766—dc23   2014018797

BRITISH LIBRARY CATALOGUING DATA ARE AVAILABLE

© 2014 Chris Brawley. All rights reserved

No part of this book may be reproduced or transmitted in any form or by any means, electronic or mechanical, including photocopying or recording, or by any information storage and retrieval system, without permission in writing from the publisher.

Cover photograph by Michele Cornelius © 2014 iStock

Printed in the United States of America

McFarland & Company, Inc., Publishers
  Box 611, Jefferson, North Carolina 28640
    www.mcfarlandpub.com

For my mother

Table of Contents

Preface ... 1

Introduction. Fantasy: Recovering What Was Lost ... 5

One. "Quieting the Eye": The Perception of the Eternal through the Temporal in Coleridge's *The Rime of the Ancient Mariner* ... 27

Two. The Ideal and the Shadow: George MacDonald's *Phantastes* ... 48

Three. "Further Up and Further In": Apocalypse and the New Narnia in C.S. Lewis's *The Last Battle* ... 71

Four. The Fading of the World: Tolkien's Ecology and Loss in *The Lord of the Rings* ... 93

Five. Affirming the World that Swerves: The Alter-Tales in Algernon Blackwood's *The Centaur* and Ursula Le Guin's *Buffalo Gals and Other Animal Presences* ... 119

Six. "A daisy is nearer heaven than an airship": The Utopian Vision in Algernon Blackwood's *The Centaur* ... 123

Seven. "Yes. You can keep your eye": Ursula Le Guin's *Buffalo Gals and Other Animal Presences* ... 145

Eight. The Sacramental Vision: Perceiving the World Anew ... 178

Bibliography ... 189

Index ... 195

Preface

This book has as its origins a near life-long search into the nature of mythopoeic fantasy and its particular religious hold on readers' imaginations. This interest started out as an investigation of standard authors in the field, mainly authors such as George MacDonald, C.S. Lewis, and J.R.R. Tolkien. What was of particular interest to me was how these authors' works *felt* so religious but yet there were no overt references to any specific religions in their works. A loose connection was made between religion and the functioning of the imagination when I came across Coleridge's *Biographia Literaria* and saw how his theories came to life in his poem *The Rime of the Ancient Mariner*. The idea of the poet or writer as a *Creator* or *Maker* in a religious sense seemed to be made explicit in Coleridge's work, and when I researched the critical approaches of MacDonald, Lewis and Tolkien, they seemed to be echoing in their own way Coleridge's distinctions between the primary and secondary imagination.

The religious connection was made more explicit when I encountered the works of Rudolf Otto, in particular *The Idea of the Holy* (1919). Otto's term the numinous, as an indescribable feeling that gives one a sense of awe, made perfect sense when I applied his ideas to mythopoeic fantasy; it seemed as if this was the quality of *wonder* which many fantasy critics point to as one of the defining elements of mythopoeic fantasy. Through Otto's work, I also found that the numinous as a concept was not necessarily relegated to the field of religion studies but could also apply to literary works as well.

Up to this point, however, the research was nothing particularly new or groundbreaking. There is much research devoted to trying to pinpoint the religious elements in authors such as MacDonald, Lewis and Tolkien. For me, what was new was the connection I was starting to make between the numinous in mythopoeic fantasy and its ability to offer the reader a new way of perceiving nature, that these authors were, in their own way, environmentalists; they all seemed to perceive nature sacramentally in their own lives and used the vehicle of mythopoeic fantasy to convey this religious sensibility towards nature to their readers.

Thus making connections between mythopoeic fantasy and ecocriticism came quite naturally, but an even more specific direction appeared when I encountered Lynn White's essay "The Historical Roots of Our Ecological Crisis." Arguing that Christianity bears "a huge burden of guilt" for environmental destruction seemed to contrast with what mythopoeic fantasists such as MacDonald, Lewis and Tolkien were trying to achieve in their writing. Christianity was their canvas to paint new worlds to engage the reader with the wonder of *this* world and to see the sacramental vision. So how could White's ideas (also shared by many other environmentalists) run so counter to these great mythopoeic fantasists? The first few chapters of my book are my attempts to make sense of all this.

It was my original intent to publish the work dealing solely with the connections between authors whose religious backgrounds were somewhat similar. But then, what could be done to expand the research beyond those mythopoeic fantasists who shared a similar religious ideology? Why was it that I had sensed the numinous in both Tolkien and Ursula Le Guin, an author who was more influenced by indigenous religions and Daoism than Christianity? What would it be like if I violated or rethought boundaries and wrote about writers like Le Guin or Blackwood, who seemed more akin to each other than to Lewis and Tolkien, even though they are not categorized together? It was for this reason that I adopted Kathryn Hume's idea of fantasy as an "impulse" in literature and not necessarily as a genre unto itself. Perhaps I am at fault for not avoiding the pitfall of what Marek Oziewicz (and others) refer to as the "baggy theory" of fantasy, but I genuinely believe that in order to understand how the numinous functions properly within mythopoeic fantasy, it is best to cast our nets widely.

The violating and rethinking of boundaries also brought my book within the discussions of postmodernism and posthumanism. Critic Patrick Murphy says that the greatest contribution postmodernism gives to writers is "the interrogation of foundational assumptions." This interrogation has informed my entire book. Having as my starting point a broad definition of fantasy, as that which departs from our consensual views of reality, I was able to paint broad stokes and make connections between authors who are both traditionally lumped together (MacDonald, Lewis and Tolkien), and some who are not (Le Guin and Blackwood). And finally I made these connections because they are the authors I have always loved, and the ones I believe make the strongest statements (fictionally and non-fictionally) for viewing the world sacramentally. The list of authors I *could have* used is obviously endless, but my hope is that my book will open up further avenues of exploration between why readers are drawn to literature that violates our consensual views of reality and, perhaps more importantly, challenges the ways in which we engage with the natural world around us.

Introduction
Fantasy: Recovering What Was Lost

"The whole secret of the study of nature lies in learning how to use one's eyes"—George Sand, *Nouvelles Lettres d'un Voyageur*, [461]

With the cinematic adaptations of such popular fantasy works as J. K. Rowling's Harry Potter series, Tolkien's *The Hobbit* and *The Lord of the Rings*, Lewis's *The Chronicles of Narnia*; or to the creative genius of Lucas's never-ending *Star Wars* saga, Cameron's *Avatar*; or to the latest superhero to hit the screen, it seems that fantasy has resurfaced as a major mode of expression in the popular imagination. Perhaps what is most intriguing about this is that fantasy is not only embraced by a small clique of devotees, nor is it aimed simply at children. The gap between the child and the adult has apparently been bridged by fantasy, and one may find many adults as eager to indulge in the pleasures of it as any child. This validates J.R.R. Tolkien's familiar evaluation of the genre: "If fairy-story as a kind is worth reading at all it is worthy to be written for and read by adults" ("On Fairy-Stories" 67).

However, with this admission, certain questions must immediately be addressed: why are children and adults interested in fantasy? And, why is the genre experiencing such a resurgence? Is fantasy a mere form of escapism, or is there something of intellectual value within this mode of expression? What does it *do*, if anything, for us or to us?

The purpose of this book is to try to address the question of what fantasy *does* for those of us who read, watch or study the genre. The answer will be twofold. First, drawing on the works of scholars and writers in the field of fantasy, as well as scholars in the field of religious studies, it will be argued that fantasy acts as a form of myth, which by its revisionist and subversive nature, allows readers to experience a religious feeling of "awe" which is the core of all major religious traditions. Second, by exploring critics in the field of Ecocriticism, the feeling of awe which is experienced in a fantasy has the ability to reshape our perceptions of the natural world and can challenge us to rethink our relations with the natural world. Once this twofold critical perspective is set up, the book will then proceed to analyze works by authors whose work in the field of fantasy best highlight our concerns.

The Fantasy Critics

Before preceding any further, it is important to attempt to define just what fantasy *is*. Any cursory study of critics will point out the difficulties, if not impossibilities, of such an undertaking. For our purposes, the focus will be on two critical theorists whose works advance the present thesis, Kathryn Hume and Rosemary Jackson. In her critical study *Fantasy and Mimesis*, Hume shows that many definitions of fantasy suffer from exclusivity, focusing on fantasy as a separate genre identified by elements such as text, audience, author or reader. This isolation of certain elements of fantasy, for Hume, is too limiting. Due to Hume's important contributions to our study, we will adopt her inclusive definition of fantasy as one of two impulses which inform all fiction. The first impulse is that of mimesis, which tries to imitate reality as closely as possible, so much so that others may easily identify with it. The other impulse, fantasy itself, is defined by Hume as "any departure from consensus reality" (21). It may seem that this definition of fantasy suffers from the opposite of exclusivity, being overly inclusive and allowing for works from the ancient world up to the present day to be considered "fantasy." It could also be argued that this definition fails to maintain any distinction between the boundaries considered important by critics in the field, such as those between fantasy and science fiction or the horror story. However, because of its very inclusiveness, her definition is the most effective for this study and the most applicable in terms of capturing the full range of mythopoeic fantasy's potential.

Probably the most useful insight in Hume's discussion of fantasy is her answer to the question of how fantasy is used. She posits four basic approaches to reality which literature, either mimetic or fantastic, addresses. It will be important for later discussion to briefly outline these approaches. The first approach to reality is the *literature of illusion*. Works in this category attempt to offer an escape from the complexities of life and the overall boredom of the everyday world. Whether they be pastoral texts, such as *Wind in the Willows*, which offers an idyllic Eden free from responsibility, or the adventure story in the *Wizard of Oz*, where the reader is encouraged to identify with the main character, these texts disengage the readers from the ordinary world in order to offer them comfort. According to Hume, these books "offer us roses without thorns and pleasures without payment" (55).

The next two approaches to reality are related, being two ends of a continuum, the *literature of vision* and the *literature of revision*. While they both aim at engaging the reader, the literature of vision attempts to disturb readers by taking them away from a secure sense of reality and positing a new one for them to contemplate. Authors such as Beckett, Kafka, and Vonnegut all employ fantasy to show how reality can be limited.

On the other end of the continuum lies the literature of revision. This type of literature takes the vision further by not only offering a vision of a different reality, but comforting the reader with a "plan" or way to actively engage the new reality. Some examples Hume uses here are reactionary dystopias such as Orwell's *1984*, Zamiatin's *We*, and Huxley's *Brave New World*. According to Hume, "Literature of revision allows people to escape from their culture's imperfect systems of authority based on reason, and lets them experience other possibilities for ordering experience, whether religious or utopian" (123).

Often the literature of revision is didactic, whether on a human or cosmological level, offering the reader a possible course of action to improve some existing condition. For example, when Hume discusses C.S. Lewis's *Space Trilogy*, she sees it as a form of cosmic didacticism: Lewis is attempting to revise morality in order to bring it into accord with his Christian cosmological worldview. Of course this is what readers also experience in the world of Narnia, as will be seen in chapter three. Hume says that Lewis "takes theological doctrines which have gone dead for most Westerners, strips them of their immediate connotations and contexts in order to evade our stock responses, and then makes their inner dynamic vivid again, attempting to reimpress us with the wonder of it all" (118). The emphasis on "reimpressing" and "wonder" will be key themes as to how fantasy functions with respect to the authors discussed in later chapters.

Introduction

The last approach to reality that Hume discusses is the *literature of disillusion*, which aims at disturbing the reader's vision of reality and fails to offer any alternative program for revision. This type of literature offers up the disconcerting admission that reality is finally unknowable. In this chapter, Hume explores works such as Carroll's *Alice in Wonderland*, Burroughs's *Naked Lunch*, and Golding's *The Inheritors*. Whether these texts employ dream frameworks, drug experiences or psychosis, the visions are always perspectivist in the sense that reality is only a form of subjective interpretation (Hume 125).

The purpose in briefly outlining Hume's definition of the literary approaches to reality is not just to applaud their accuracy, but also to suggest more precise ways that the tradition of mythopoeic fantasy may fit in our argument that fantasy is a veiled religious activity, and that it can revise our perceptions of the natural world. Based on her inclusive definition of fantasy as "any departure from consensus reality," the selections Hume draws upon are considerable, leaving little engagement with specific texts. Hume does spend time discussing Lewis, especially the *Space Trilogy*, in terms of the literature of revision, but the other authors who are the focus of the present discussion require more careful consideration than she provides (Hume 117). Although *The Lord of the Rings* is referred to on many occasions, Hume seems to place Tolkien's work within the literature of illusion. She suggests his work is a "literature of desire," a desire to turn one's back on the world, to escape it, and to ponder the idyllic beauty of Middle-earth as a form of wishful longing (59). Her contention that these works of illusion are "crippled myths" and that Tolkien "fans" find life unsatisfactory is to miss the fact that Tolkien, like Lewis, is rather writing literature of revision, allowing his readers not an escape from reality but urging a rediscovery of it, especially in its deepest religious form (66).

This work aims at adopting Hume's categories of literature but adapting her application of them by placing mythopoeic fantasists not within a literature of illusion, which offers readers escape, but within the literature of revision. What these authors are attempting, in both their fiction and in their criticism of fantasy, is the employment of mythopoeic fantasy as the appropriate means, in fact the only means, to help readers respond to their world religiously, seeing the world not as it *is*, but the world as it was *meant* to be seen (Tolkien "On Fairy-Stories" 77). This literature of revision endows the reader with a sacramental vision of the world, not only as it exists in the fantasy novel, but metaphorically as a means of recreating his or her own world once the book has been put down.

In treating certain fantasy authors within the literature of illusion, Hume fails to acknowledge these authors' unique visions. In discussing this literature of illusion, Hume believes that because there is no universally accepted mythology or religion, fantasy offers a secular form of what was once the domain of the religious. I would argue the contrary, that these fantasy authors are mythopoeic, that is, they are attempting to recreate (*mythos*="story"; *poenin*="recreate") a new mythology in order to infuse readers with the sense of the transcendent which is no longer accessible, for many people, in religion.

This approach owes a debt to recent scholarship on the defining of mythopoeic fantasy as a useful term in dealing with texts which revise perceptions of the natural world in a sacramental manner. In particular, Marek Oziewicz's work *One Earth, One People: The Mythopoeic Fantasy Series of Ursula K. Le Guin, Lloyd Alexander, Madeline L'Engle, and Orson Scott Card*, defines the term mythopoeic fantasy as "a unique literary expression of a worldview that assumes the existence of the supernatural" (4). Oziewicz traces the origins of this term to Tolkien and Lewis who, although they never actually agreed on an exact term, certainly had in mind a religious origin to the works they read and wrote. Although for the purposes of this work, the term mythopoeic fantasy will be used, I disagree with Oziewicz's use of the term "supernatural." As Brain Attebery states in his Foreword to Oziewicz's text, the term "supernatural" doesn't seem to apply to certain authors whose approach is more non-theistic in nature. Considering that this work deals with authors such as Le Guin and Blackwood, we must be careful in using the term supernatural. So, by mythopoeic fantasy, what will be meant are those authors who are employing fantasy as a subversive mode of literature to revise our perceptions of the natural world; and, the distinguishing feature of these authors is going to be an inculcation of a certain religious or mystical "feeling" of the numinous in the reader.

Kathryn Hume's contention that the function of literature is to impart a meaning-giving experience is especially appropriate for these mythopoeic authors (170). Their desire is to offer their readers new perspectives and, most importantly, for these readers to respond with feeling and emotion, both in the created world of fantasy, and in the revisioning of their own world. Hume argues that fantasy creates meaning structures for readers, in much the same way that the historian of religions Mircea Eliade argued that ancient cultures imitated mythic patterns to create reality (191). For Hume, however, the readers who do not have these meaning structures are not able to experience any form of the numinous, inwardly or outwardly. This respect for the transcendent is what is at the heart of the mythopoeic imagination, is in fact what mythopoeic authors hope to implant in their readers, and will be discussed in subsequent chapters. What is important in all these works is the emotional response to them, a response that most of these authors would agree can not really be put into words at all.

Further contributions to the present project emerge from the works of Rosemary Jackson. In *Fantasy: The Literature of Subversion*, Jackson draws upon Tzvetan Todorov's definition of the fantastic as the "absolute hesitation" on the part of the protagonist and the reader in the face of the unexplainable (27). Making a distinction between the marvellous, that which has a supernatural explanation, and the uncanny, that which has a natural explanation, Todorov argues that the fantastic exists in-between these two categories, disturbing the main character as well as the reader as to the true nature of a perceived event. Todorov's classic example of a text that embodies this "hesitation" is a story by Jaques Cazotte titled "Le Diable Amoreux." In the story, Alvaro is in love with Biondetta who is, in fact, a devil. However, the uncertainty throughout the text experienced by Alvaro as to the true nature of Biondetta leaves him unsettled, disturbed. As Jackson states, "He is split between a primitive faith in the possibility of supernatural events occurring (Biondetta as Devil) and a deep incredulity that there is anything other than the merely human (Biondetta as woman)" (29). The uncertainty that is experienced by Alvaro, and consequently by the reader, is exactly the "hesitation" that Todorov posits as the key to defining the purely fantastic.

In her definition of the fantastic, Jackson draws on Todorov while employing a model similar to Kathryn Hume's "impulses." Jackson's categories are the mimetic and the marvellous. For Jackson, as well as Hume, the mimetic is the deliberate attempt to imitate something in the "real" world, while the marvellous, or Hume's "fantasy," is the creation of an alternative, or secondary, world which has relation to our own only in a metaphorical or symbolic way. Jackson's argument, however, is that the truly fantastic has no confidence in either the mimetic or marvellous representations of the world; it straddles that thin line between the two, serving only to disturb the protagonist or reader and failing to provide any true comfort in the nature of perceived reality. This is where her influence by Todorov becomes evident. For Jackson, moreover, fantasy is a *subversive* mode of literature which "traces the unsaid and the unseen of culture: that which has been silenced, made invisible, covered over and made 'absent'" (4).

What interests us the most in Jackson's analysis is the category of the marvellous, as it applies to our mythopoeic fantasists. Although Jackson's concerns are largely with the fantastic as she understands it, and not with the marvellous, it is worth analyzing her critical comments on the marvellous in the hopes that they will shed light on our particular interests. While Jackson argues that the impulses which inform both the fantastic and the marvellous are similar, they have separate functions. The fantastic, by subverting such unities as character, time, and place, seeks to disturb or unsettle the reader, while the marvellous seeks to comfort the reader. Jackson states that such creations as Middle-earth or Narnia are compensatory, making up for a lack by presenting some version of an "ideal" world that readers can escape into. These texts, for Jackson, are backward-looking, expressing nostalgia for the sacred which cannot be found within the nature of the truly fantastic (9). According to her definition, such texts are not fantasy, but belong to her category of the marvellous. The portrayal of the ideal, in the form of the created secondary world, is what these authors use as their tool to investigate the "real" world. The secondary worlds, however, are only indirectly relevant to our own. According to Jackson, "This secondary, duplicated cosmos, is relatively autonomous, relating to the 'real' world only through metaphorical reflections and never, or rarely, intruding or interrogating it" (42). It is this idea which must be challenged.

If mythopoeic authors fulfill Kathryn Hume's criteria for the literature of revision (a point on which she would not entirely agree), we must now consider Jackson's contributions to our study. In employing the term "subversive" for fantasies which disrupt unities of character, space, and time, Jackson is accurate; however, I would further use the term for those works she identifies as marvellous, the works by the authors used in the present study. For these authors, their works are meant to be subversive, both in the sense of disturbing or unsettling the reader, and in the sense of engaging the imagination in the created secondary world, so that the "real" world can be transformed as the result of the re-vision initiated in the encounter with the fantasy world.

Jackson mistakenly views the marvellous as a form of escapism, a term which most of our authors would disapprove. A desire to escape the world only to be comforted in a fantasy landscape is *not* at the core of the mythopoeic imagination. What concerns our authors is the desire to use fantastic elements subversively to reorganize and recombine normative modes of perception in order to revision the world in a more sacramental way. As C.S. Lewis so eloquently puts it, in this type of fantasy, "we do not retreat from reality, we rediscover it" (*On Stories and Other Essays on Literature* 90).

These mythopoeic authors achieve a sense of rediscovered reality through a subversion of ordinary modes of perception. Jackson adopts Freud's idea that fantasy relates to an earlier, magical or animistic pattern of thought where distinctions between self and other are blurred or break down. She states that in fantasies this same process occurs: "Generic distinctions between animal, vegetable, and mineral are blurred in fantasy's attempt to 'turn over' 'normal' perceptions and undermine 'realistic' ways of seeing" (49). I would argue that Jackson's arguments are accurate, and that they not only apply to her limited definition of fantasy, but that they are a major concern also of authors within her category of the marvellous, whom this discussion has called mythopoeic. A good example would be Tolkien's Ents in *The Lord of the Rings*. The Ents are trees which have the same abilities as humans; they can walk, talk, think, and act. However, through the use of the imagination, which is able to fuse both the human and the tree within the story, these creations are truly subversive. The Ents, and their subsequent actions, are not meant as escapes from reality, but vehicles for the imagination to rediscover trees in the "real" world, to remove from them what Tolkien refers to as the "drab blur of triteness or familiarity" so that they can be seen anew, as living beings ("On Fairy-Stories" 77). This ability to see the world in a different way is what Tolkien referred to in his 1947 essay "On Fairy-Stories" as one of the four major functions of fantasy, "recovery."

For our purposes, Tolkien's concept of recovery fits nicely into our thesis that mythopoeic fantasy aids in our revisioning of the natural world. As stated above, Tolkien's creation of the Ents in *The Lord of the Rings* is a result of the imagination's ability to fuse two separate categories, the tree and the human, into one literary construction, the Ent.

Fantasy: Recovering What Was Lost

According to Tolkien, this is the function of the sub-creator, an artist who is imitating God's original creative act. Sub-creation requires an act of subversion, a reordering of our normal modes of perception. The result of this reordering, which Tolkien terms "Enchantment," invites the reader to a religious view of the world. So the question must now be asked: what is the value in this literary subversion? Merely to entertain? To help us escape the world around us? On the contrary, at the center of this activity is the more self-aware engagement in the "real" world through which comes a rediscovery or a "recovery" of its divine nature.

As a philologist, Tolkien was well aware of language's ability not only to express ideas about our world, but also to superimpose abstractions onto concrete reality. For example, we have the word "tree," and an abstract conception of it, so that whenever the word is mentioned, a preconceived notion appears in the mind. While language's importance is vital for us to communicate and understand our world should not be denied, one should be wary of its representation of reality. One of the negative aspects of language is that it allows for the "appropriation" of the world, a sense that reality is somehow "known." Since trees are all around, and we have a word and a conception of them, we risk losing the individuality of each tree, that sense of childlike wonder that is closely allied to the religious imagination. What Tolkien refers to as a "veil of familiarity" has been placed before our eyes, and we cannot see the world in its truest, most deeply religious, sense ("On Fairy-Stories" 77). Referring to this act of appropriating reality, Tolkien states, "They have become like the things which once attracted us by the glitter, or their colour, or their shape, and we laid hands on them, and then locked them in our hoard, acquired them, and acquiring, ceased to look at them" ("On Fairy-Stories" 77).

Recovery, for Tolkien, is seeing the world not as it seems to be, with our appropriations, but the world as it was meant to be seen and truly is, specifically within the nature of the sacramental vision. For Tolkien, what fantasy does is to help lift that "veil of familiarity" and allows us to "clean our windows" so that we see the world clearly, and religiously. I would argue that this concept of "recovery" (Hume's "revision" and Jackson's "subversion") is vital to the understanding of the mythopoeic authors discussed in the present work. In their various books, these authors are employing the imagination in an attempt to provide the

Introduction

reader with a vehicle for perceiving the world religiously. The result of seeing the world this way is that "we should look at green again, and be startled anew (but not blinded) by blue and yellow and red" (Tolkien "On Fairy-Stories" 77). Tolkien's Ents are not meant for mere entertainment or to comfort the reader by providing an escape from the world of responsibility. Instead, these creations are "meditations" on the natural world, so that once the fantasy is finished, trees are viewed (recovered, revisioned, subverted) in their divine originality. This is Tolkien's central contention, that by producing a piece of mythopoeic fantasy, and by extension reading that piece of mythopoeic fantasy, one participates in the human engagement with creation itself. One becomes, in essence, a sub-creator. Once that process is realized, according to Tolkien, fantasy exhibits its most effective quality:

> In making something new, fantasy may open your hoard and let all the locked things fly away like cage-birds. The gems all turn into flowers or flames, and you will be warned that all you had (or knew) was dangerous and potent, not really effectively chained, free and wild; no more yours than they were you ["On Fairy-Stories" 78].

It is no coincidence that the authors dealt with in this project were/are deeply religious or spiritual, if in a variety of ways, some non-conformist, and their fantasies were attempts at fresh visions, so that if one were not to achieve any religious sensibility through traditional biblical texts, one could encounter this sensibility within the created secondary world.

Along with Tolkien, what our mythopoeic authors are concerned with is a certain religious "feeling" for the world, a feeling for which fantasy is only the vehicle. Many fantasy critics refer to this experience as "wonder" that of "making the impossible seem familiar and the familiar new and strange" (Attebery 3). As critics have pointed out, this sense of wonder is the defining element of all successful fantasy. In fact, one critic, Brian Attebery, refers to this experience of reading fantasy literature as "extraliterary." By this he means that the "feeling" of wonder which one receives through reading fantasy is not contained *within* the text itself but is a result of the act of imagination in which the reader participates. Concerning this point Attebery states, "It is because of some movement within one's mind, called up by the written or spoken words but not contained within them. The experience is extraliterary because it depends on the needs, expectations, and background of the reader. It defies analysis under any system of literary values" (155).

The central idea of "wonder" with its reference to a felt "experience" that is, at the same time, "indescribable," is an area for further analysis. Many authors and critics of mythopoeic fantasy point to the indescribable experience of fantasy, precisely because this is its primary attraction. For these mythopoeic authors, fantasy is emotive, associated with certain feelings, specifically religious feelings, and it is these feelings which are non-rational and cannot be directly explicated by words. In Tolkien's essay "On Fairy-Stories," he seems to agree with this indescribable quality. In discussing Faerie as a "perilous realm," he states, "I will not attempt to define that, nor to describe it directly. It cannot be done. Faerie cannot be caught in a net of words; for it is one of its qualities to be indescribable" ("On Fairy-Stories" 39).

The Religious Connection

The indescribable nature of "wonder" or "enchantment" which authors and critics refer to as the defining element of fantasy may best be understood within the context of a different academic discussion, located in the history-of-religions field. In his seminal text *The Idea of the Holy*, Rudolf Otto attempted to analyze what he considered the "core" of religious thought. He employed the Latin root "numen," coining the phrase "numinous consciousness" to refer to a quality or state of mind which has as its basis a unique, original feeling-response to the holy which he equates with God (6–7). The numinous, he argued, was that quality of "holiness" in its original meaning as that which inspires awe, a meaning devoid of our modern associations of the holy as a moral category. Otto promoted the idea that this numinous consciousness was the basis of the first stirrings of the religious imagination which, at their inception, were a form of religious dread, but later evolved into more complex, rational conceptions which informed most of the major religious traditions (14). This numinous quality, for Otto, was non-rational in that it was a "feeling" or "experiential" mode of comprehending the divine reality, and in that sense was indescribable, much in the same manner as is referred to in fantasy: "This mental state is perfectly *sui generis* and irreducible to any other; and therefore, like every absolutely primary and elementary datum, while it admits of being discussed, it cannot be strictly defined" (7).

Introduction

What Otto does admit is that the numinous consciousness can be evoked through means of symbols which objectify the numinous state of mind. These symbols act as vehicles of the numinous consciousness, concretizing it within rational forms. It is interesting to note that in discussing the numinous consciousness, Otto points to the feelings of the "eerie" and "weird" which one feels in the face of the "wholly other" (14). This concept of the wholly other is what interests us in our discussion of fantasy as it aids us in the understanding of "wonder" within fantasy literature. In one of Otto's examples, he discusses the particular dread some have of ghosts. However, what gives a sense of dread is not the thing in itself, that ghosts can be defined as "long" or "white," but exactly that sense of otherness which attracts the imagination; similarly, it is this otherness which is at the core of fantasy's departure from reality (28–29). According to Otto, a ghost fills the imagination with dread "because it is a thing which 'doesn't really exist at all,' the 'wholly other,' something which has no place in our scheme of reality but belongs to an absolutely different one, and which at the same time arouses an irrepressible interest in the mind" (29).

The recognition that the imagination is attracted to what is presented as "wholly other" is what ties Otto to such fantasy critics as Hume, Jackson and Tolkien. Hume's definition of fantasy as "any departure from consensus reality," as well as Jackson's contention that fantasy is "subversive," both highlight this act of the imagination as capturing the sense of awe (for Otto, religious awe) through the presentation of the other. While it may seem unsuitable to connect Otto's analysis of the numinous with a consideration of fantasy, Otto does mention fairy stories and fantasy as viable vehicles for the perception of the numinous. He considers the element of the "wondrous" to be a category that is infused with the numinous, in a line of thought pursued by Tolkien.

Otto argues that the experience of the numinous is non-rational, a religious sensibility only to be evoked or awakened rather than dogmatized. This is similar to mythopoeic fantasy's effort to evoke a sense of "wonder" in the created secondary world. This is that "extraliterary" quality of fantasy which cannot, ultimately, be described. However, what captures this sense of wonder is the subversive representation of the wholly other, the departure from reality which fantasy creates. In Otto's theory, the fantastic image is the "ideogram" which represents, symbolically, the numinous consciousness (24).

The fact that mythopoeic fantasy may induce an awareness of the numinous, and also have a profound effect on the world we know, is what places mythopoeic authors in our present study within Hume's literature of revision and Jackson's category of the subversive. These authors are not content with simply providing readers with a renewed access to the transcendent; on the contrary, they are also attempting to create secondary worlds to engage the reader with a new experience so that ordinary reality may be transformed through the sacramental vision. This transformation of ordinary reality is made possible through the infusion of the numinous. In short, the mythopoeic author undertakes two tasks: to instill awareness of the transcendent, and to turn that awareness back to the mundane world.

Ecocritical and Posthumanist Considerations

Certain questions must now be asked: what is the practical applicability of this approach to mythopoeic fantasy? Recent scholarship has pointed to an area which has been largely ignored by the critics of past decades, and it is to this area which some mythopoeic fantasy speaks: the environment. With a growing concern for such environmental problems as overpopulation, pollution, the ozone layer, global warming, and the mass extinction of species, it is perhaps unfortunate that literary studies have not fully responded to these growing concerns. As environmental critics have pointed out, these concerns should not be relegated to the fields of natural science. Instead, the revisioning of the relationship between humans and the natural world demands the participation of the humanities.

As a result of this growing concern for the environment, literary studies that engage environmental concerns have lately become an important area of study. Throughout the 1980s and 1990s, environmental studies began to grow and by 1993, it became a recognizable field of inquiry (in 1993, Patrick Murphy formed the journal *ISLE: Interdisciplinary Studies in Literature and Environment* which brought scholars together as a recognizable school). Within the field of environmental studies, many sub-fields began to develop, each emphasizing a separate area of interest: deep ecology, ecofeminism, and ecocriticism. The latter area, ecocriticism, is an area of literary studies which has as its basis the analysis of literature and its relationship to the natural world. The term itself was coined in 1973 by William Ruekart and, as its principles began to grow, it sought to offer "an alternate view of existence that [would] provide an ethical and conceptual foundation for right relations with the earth" (Glotfelty xxi). The desire for an "alternate view" of existence is precisely what may be found in a study of mythopoeic authors, although these authors cannot be identified retroactively as "environmentalists."

Considering the religious or spiritual backgrounds of the mythopoeic authors under study here, what is of considerable interest is the criticisms which have been directed at Christianity as the source of environmental problems, specifically the separation of God-human-nature, which for some critics lies at the root of environmental problems. In his much debated article "The Historical Roots of our Environmental Crisis," Lynn White states that our attempts at proposals for environmental care are ineffective; what must be addressed is the underlying ideologies which inform the way nature is perceived. White states, "What people do about their ecology depends on what they think about themselves in relation to things around them" (9). What people think, White argues, is largely informed by religion, specifically Christianity, which he believes "bears a huge burden of guilt" for environmental problems. White traces the religious roots of the environmental problems back to the biblical story of creation and Adam and Eve in Genesis. In the story, God creates humans as separate beings from himself, albeit in his image in chapter one, and tells them of their "dominion" over the earth. By placing Adam and Eve at the center of the story, and thereby giving them control over nature, White argues that Christianity is "the most anthropocentric religion the world has seen" (9). This anthropomorphism is what informs the Western world's view of nature and unless this view changes, he argues, the environment will continue to be exploited.

The problem of the hierarchical nature of the Western mind, the God-human-nature dichotomy, has also been addressed by the famous mythologist Joseph Campbell. In many of his works, he refers to Western mythology as participating in "mythic dissociation" (*The Masks of God: Creative Mythology* 393). Since the nature of divinity is transcendent (somehow "out there"), and man is to have "dominion" over the earth, humans are dissociated from the divine; God is not in the world, in humans, or in nature. This mythic dissociation is not to be found in

Eastern religions such as Buddhism, Daoism, or Hinduism. In fact, in these religions it is quite the opposite. In his *Power of Myth* interviews, Campbell discusses this idea of mythic dissociation as he relates the story of a lecture he attended by the famous Zen philosopher D.T. Suzuki. According to Campbell, Suzuki opened his lecture in the following manner:

> God against man, man against God
> Man against nature, nature against man
> Nature against God, God against nature
> Very funny religion [*The Power of Myth with Bill Moyers*].

Since Campbell's time, the critique of the West has gained in academic popularity within the fields of cultural studies and the overall discourse of posthumanism. Although ecocriticism and posthumanism seem fairly unlikely bedfellows, some broad stokes may be painted to underline some central concerns within both fields. Matthew Calarco defines posthumanism in *Zoographies: The Question of the Animal from Heidegger to Derrida* as "a critical investigation of human subjectivity, of the material (for example, economic, historical, linguistic, and social) forces at work in the formation of human subjects" (89). With this in mind, Caralco, and many of the authors in the present study, will argue that the human-animal distinction cannot and should not be maintained, and that our hyper-rational Western approach is a flaw. What is needed, suggests Calarco, is a revolution in thought, a paradigm-shift, a thinking of "unheard of thoughts" and a re-making of language, art, history, and religion. This fits in exactly with mythopoeic fantasy's intention of subverting normative modes of perception.

Another call for a "dissolution of the West" in recent years is Donna Haraway's *A Cyborg Manifesto* which has as its central argument the "*pleasure* in the confusion of boundaries and the *responsibility* for their construction" (150). For Haraway, the cyborg is our ontology; it is our mythology; it is that metaphor for fusion and couplings between disparate subjects and objects that have the ability to subvert our Western, dualistic thinking. Specifically, Haraway posits that the cyborg challenges the "Myths of Origin" in the Western world. "The cyborg would not recognize the Garden of Eden," she states, "it is not made of mud and cannot dream of returning to dust" (151). Thus there is no original unity within the cyborg myth but only partiality, a commitment to experience the intimacy of boundaries; furthermore, Haraway states, "we can learn from our fusions with animals and machines how not to be Man, the embodiment of Western logos" (173).

In the chapters focusing on mythopoeic fantasists who have been influenced by the Western, Judeo-Christian worldview (Coleridge, MacDonald, Lewis and Tolkien), it will be argued that even though they are writing within the Western worldview, the employment of mythopoeic fantasy as a means of capturing the sense of the numinous and subverting normative perceptions of the natural world is the end goal. It is, perhaps, these authors who may be seen retroactively as writing the new myths of the cyborg.

In contrast to the mythic dissociation inherent in Western creation myths, many Eastern creation stories posit the source of divinity as immanent, not transcendent. For example, in the Brihadaranyaka Upanishad, the Self (Purusha) was all that existed in the beginning. Once the Self realized "I AM," it became lonely and desired a mate. Since it was all that existed, it decided to split itself into two, a male and female, and through the union of these energies, humans came into existence. When the female counterpart realized the shameful nature of this act, she transformed herself into the female nature of various animals. Not content with her evasion, the male energy transformed itself into the male counterpart, and through many unions, everything was created, all the way down to the ants (Campbell *The Flight of the Wild Gander: Explorations in the Mythological Dimension* 66). What is noticed in this story is that the divine nature of the world is present within all creation, and the God-human-nature hierarchy is not present. Campbell terms this immanent ideology "mythic association" (*The Flight of the Wild Gander: Explorations in the Mythological Dimension* 195–96). Thus, chapters five, six and seven broaden the perspective of mythopoeic fantasists who are willing to both challenge the Western mythos and also employ other mythological traditions (including the Greek for Blackwood and the indigenous for Le Guin). In contrast to Christian influenced authors such as Coleridge, MacDonald, Lewis and Tolkien, Le Guin and Blackwood write from within a more mystical, more mythically associated worldview.

What Campbell, White (and many in the fields of Cultural Studies) seem to have in common, besides their criticisms of Western religious thought, is their solution to the problem. Campbell speaks of the Western religious traditions as needing to adapt to the modern, scientific worldview. What this requires, for Campbell, is a revisioning of the fundamental religious truths into more applicable metaphors. Similarly, White speaks of the need for a new religion as a way of rethinking the old. He states, "Since the roots of our trouble are so largely religious, the remedy must also be essentially religious, whether we call it that or not" (14). White points to the possibility of looking at St. Francis, whom he calls the greatest radical, in terms of his views concerning the human-nature relationship. For White, if we could rethink the major Christian tenet that nature's whole reason for existing is to serve man's needs, then we might have a chance at saving the environment (14). For Haraway, teaching modern Christian creationism should be seen as child abuse and the only solution lies with the myths created by cyborg authors, those willing to see the potential of fusions and not totalities. For Caraway, it is the thinking of "unheard of thoughts."

While Campbell, White (and others) raise fundamental issues that are important for environmental study, they do tend to overlook certain possibilities. For example, scholars have pointed out that an alternative reading of scripture shows an affirmation of creation by God, so that, far from man's exploitation of nature, man can be viewed as a "steward" of the earth (Nash 201).

Although Joseph Campbell is, for the most part, accurate in his contention that Christian mythology stresses the separation between God, humans, and nature, he also realizes that the bigger problem lies in the fact that this mythological system has lost its sense of participation in the mystery of the universe. This participation in the transcendent reality which informs the world is Campbell's first function of a living mythology. The mystical or metaphysical function of mythology, Campbell argues, is "to waken and maintain in the individual an experience of awe, humility, and respect, in recognition of that ultimate mystery, transcending names and forms 'from which,' as we read in the Upanishads, 'words turn back'" (*The Masks of God: Creative Mythology* 69). Campbell believes this mystical function to be the most important function of mythology and, without it, there can be no real mythology at all. Thus, the problem is not with Christianity as such, but its loss of a sense of mystery.

As many critics have pointed out, the roots of mythopoeic fantasy are within living mythologies, and it should come as no surprise that these mythopoeic authors are attempting to reinvigorate religious truth

Introduction

in their literary worlds. They are, in effect, trying to reproduce this feeling of awe in the face of the ultimate mystery, using such terms as "wonder" or "enchantment." Of course, it is to be noted that when Campbell discusses the mystical function of a mythology, he is heavily influenced by Rudolf Otto's discussion of the numinous and the *mysterium tremendum* which informs the religious mind (*Mysterium Tremendum* is the ultimate mystery which evokes both fear and trembling; the object of the numinous consciousness). The mythopoeic authors are attempting to awaken a dormant numinous consciousness. It should also be noted that Campbell's reference to the ultimate mystery as "transcending names and forms" is precisely that indescribable quality to which fantasy critics and authors refer.

Within the context of our discussion, it is worthwhile to reconsider the nature of the criticisms of Christianity in respect to current ecological problems. If Christianity bears a "huge burden of the guilt," as White maintains, how are we to understand these mythopoeic authors, some of whom are deeply influenced by the Christian mythology (and others, not), but are presenting alternate views of reality which subvert normal modes of perception by erasing such fundamental barriers as human and non-human? Is there anything of value within these mythopoeic authors that could address some of these basic environmental concerns? I would argue that by examining Hume's literature of revision, and Jackson's ideas concerning the subversiveness of fantasy literature, these mythopoeic authors may be placed within ecological discourse, offering new perspectives on our relations with the environment.

Within Hume's literature of revision, the fantastic impulse creates realities which not only portray a vision of a new reality but present a "plan" or "program" to revise our world to meet this new reality. Broadly speaking, many ecocritics point out that right relations to the natural world are not going to be resolved with specific programs, such as recycling or lessening our "carbon footprint," but a complete paradigm shift which includes attention to two basic principles: animism and interrelatedness. The first concept is animism. Animism assumes that the world all around us is alive, and that all beings have the ability to communicate (if we just listen). And if Lynn White's argument is correct, that Western religions such as Christianity are anthropocentric, placing "man" at the center of any dialogue, and as the only speaker, then it is difficult for modern Christianity to re-envision relations with the environment. The only way to recover our sense of sacredness in nature is to revise our attitudes regarding the human and non-human. Along with most indigenous religions, fantasy has the ability to do this. It offers the reader an animistic way of perceiving the natural world and by "departing from reality," it takes us into new realms that, while not denying reason, certainly give us a sense of awe towards the created world, a fresh way of viewing reality anew, and a way of recovering what was lost.

This way of perceiving the world is also subversive in Jackson's sense of dissolving the barriers between the human and non-human. This is where the second concept, that of interrelatedness, comes into play. By making trees walk or animals talk, mythopoeic fantasy is perhaps the most subversive art form there is. In a similar manner, environmental critics have noted that this subversion is necessary for regaining right relations with nature. If all things in the universe really are interconnected, there are many interesting questions to pose such as if there really is any boundary between the human and non-human or is this just an abstraction, a function of language? Where does one organism stop and another begin? What exactly is the nature of the subject/object relationship? By asking such questions, our most basic cultural and religious concepts are attacked, and it allows for the possibility for new ways to engage with the world. As previously stated, these questions not only need to be asked by the harder sciences like biology, but require a full engagement with the humanities, which, for this study, includes the literature of mythopoeic fantasy.

Mythopoeic fantasy offers, especially with its functions of subverting normative categories of thought (Jackson) and revising the way reality is perceived (Hume), a valid means whereby environmental perception may be addressed. It must be noted, however, that questioning the boundaries between the human and non-human does not mean that these boundaries don't exist. Of course they do. There are fundamental differences between the two categories, and mythopoeic authors never fully subvert the categories. Fantasy merely "blurs" the distinctions between the two, allowing for the contemplation and challenge of our usual ways of perceiving. In this sense, mythopoeic fantasy is much more akin to a form of play, as W.R. Irwin examines in his text *The Game of the Impossible.* Irwin defines fantasy as "a story based on and controlled by an overt violation of what is generally accepted as possibility; it is the narrative result of transforming the condition contrary to fact into fact itself" (9). Fantasy is a means whereby the author and reader willingly enter a conspiracy, a game, where what is accepted in the fantasy world is never confused with ordinary reality. One doesn't read about Tolkien's Ents and expect to see real trees walk and talk. Therefore, one must qualify environmental critiques as they apply to mythopoeic fantasy.

One must also be careful of the claim that we should dismiss reason in order to challenge the boundaries between the human and non-human. Although mythopoeic fantasy may greatly contribute to a new awareness of our relations to the environment, it never dismisses reason entirely. In fact, as Tolkien points out in his essay "On Fairy-Stories," the clearer the reason, the better the fantasy. This form of literature recognizes fact, as Tolkien states, but does not become a slave to it. As a form of subversive play, and as a human activity in its own right, fantasy challenges our most basic assumptions but never dismisses the real world. In reality, there are differences between the human and non-human, important differences, which cannot be ignored. As Tolkien states, "If men really could not distinguish between frogs and men, fairy-stories about frog-kings would not have arisen" ("On Fairy-Stories" 75).

Application

It must be noted at the outset that the authors in this study each have a distinct approach. As fantasy critics have pointed out, prior to the twentieth century, the focus of much fantasy literature was on the individual; therefore, the focus of chapters one and two will be on two works which exemplify this inner quest for the numinous: Coleridge's "The Rime of the Ancient Mariner" and MacDonald's *Phantastes*. Although not generally referred to as a major mythopoeic author, Coleridge will be included because he contributes the most important factor which later influences the subsequent authors: the importance of the imagination as a vehicle for the numinous. "The Rime of the Ancient Mariner" will be considered for its portrayal of the numinous quest as achieved through an imaginative transcendence of the self. Similarly, MacDonald's book *Phantastes* will be revealed as a quest for the numinous by the transcendence of the self through the vehicle of romantic love. So, while both works will exhibit certain dissimilarities, their primary goal is to locate the possibility of engaging the numinous within the confines of the inward self. Both authors use a revisioning of the natural world to achieve their aim.

In contrast, chapters three and four will work on a more epic scale including the wider human community. Within the two sets of material, C.S. Lewis's *The Last Battle* and J.R.R. Tolkien's *The Lord of the Rings*, the focus will not be so much on the individual but on the larger implications of the numinous as it exists in the world. Again, while the two authors share somewhat similar religious worldviews, they are not without their differences. Chapter three will explore Lewis's *The Last Battle* as it relates to concept of *Sehnsucht*, or longing, a longing which is only achieved, in this text, through the destruction of the world. A careful consideration will be given here to Lewis's revisioning of the biblical text Revelation and its implications. Although attempting to portray similar religious experiences, Tolkien will locate the numinous within his created Middle-earth, with such constructions as Tom Bombadil, Lothlorian, Treebeard and the Shire. Again, for each author a new imaginative perspective on nature is an important part of his or her method.

In chapters five, six and seven, I explore two authors whose approach to mythopoeic fantasy is more non-theistic, more mystical, and not tied directly to a specific religious worldview (as Christianity is for the others). As a transitional chapter, chapter five elaborates upon Jane Bennett's form of "enchanted materialism" as a means whereby we can transcend our Western, rational, hierarchical "dis-enchantment tales" to be enchanted again with new perceptions of the natural world. Two such authors who offer examples of mythopoeic fantasy that draws upon worldviews other-than-Western are Ursula Le Guin and Algernon Blackwood. Although many other authors, or many other works, could be used to further the present argument, Le Guin's *Buffalo Gals and Other Animal Presences* and Blackwood's *The Centaur* are exemplary in their attempt to inculcate the numinous into their mythopoeic fantasies.

Although they have varied approaches to the numinous, what these authors share is an attempt to inculcate within the reader a "feeling" of wonder both in the secondary world and, by simple transposition, a revisioning of the primary world. The most effective analytical tool for understanding these attempts is to view them within the context of fantasy critics such as Rosemary Jackson and Kathryn Hume. Mythopoeic fantasy literature departs from consensus reality in order to engage the reader in a subversive activity where perceptions of the natural world

Introduction

may be safely questioned, as a form of play. This departure and subversion is also what allows the reader to have a quasi-religious "feeling" of awe which is best understood in reference to Rudolf Otto's ideas concerning the numinous. Furthermore, the practical application of such an analysis is in its effectiveness in entering the growing field of environmental debate. While many critics find fault within the Christian religion as it relates to the environment, the fantasy worlds of these deeply religious/spiritual authors show that their worldview is not inherently antithetical to respect for the natural world. Whether they focus on the inner quest for the numinous, or they pursue the numinous in the larger community, they all share one common denominator: the need for us to see the sacramental nature of the world around us.

A Note on the Selection of Texts

Academically, the texts chosen for this study reflect postmodern concerns for a multitude of fragments; a loosely integrated meshing of texts in conversation, texts which may have never had a chance to have a conversation. Personally, the texts chosen reflect my own tastes of those works that seem closest to expressing the numinous and the need for environmental change. Of course, many others authors (and texts) could have been chosen, but I find Brian Attebery's suggestion in *The Fantastic Tradition in America* helpful. In his attempt to define fantasy, he suggests pointing to a bookshelf of personal favorites and saying, "Read this. This is fantasy." In effect, this is what I have done in the present study. I have pointed to my own bookshelf of personal favorites and said, "If you want good examples of texts which express the numinous and employ mythopoeic fantasy that challenges our views of nature, then read this ... or this."

CHAPTER ONE

"Quieting the Eye"
The Perception of the Eternal Through the Temporal in Coleridge's The Rime of the Ancient Mariner

"Art is the place of exile where we grieve for our lost home upon the earth"—Jonathan Bate, *The Song of the Earth* [73]

"O, strange is the self-power of the imagination"—Coleridge, Lecture XII [321]

"Our longing for the imagined health of the past must be a sign of the sickness of the present" (2). With this quote from *The Song of the Earth*, Jonathan Bate brings readers to an awareness of our environmental predicament while at the same time, through his "experiment in ecopoetics," posits poetry as a viable means of imagining "right" relations with the earth. The attraction which a nature poet such as Wordsworth has for modern readers involves a "nostalgia" for a time past, a time when our relationship to the earth was quite different; thus the disparity between the "fictional" past and the "realistic" present reminds us that our relationship to the natural world is perhaps one of malaise and in need of revisioning. As Bate suggests, part of the problem lies in Western cultural ideologies which subscribe to a Cartesian dualism, one which bifurcates such categories as subject/object, self/other, and culture/nature. Concerning the latter, Bate reminds readers that the word "culture" originally referred to the cultivation of land; it was only later accretions which gave it the connotation of "refinement" and thus separated the term from "nature" (5). This separation between the two terms has its modern inflection in the usage of such terms as "environment" throughout the nineteenth century. The mere fact of the word's coinage is a result of our own alienation from our environment.

Where exactly did we go wrong in terms of the environmental crisis with which we are now faced? Bate speculates that since literary forms are ways of working on our consciousness, it might be beneficial to examine our roots there (24–27). In a text such as Genesis, we become aware of how the literary form of the "Fall of Man" might influence ideology. As argued in the introduction, critics such as Joseph Campbell and Lynn White locate the origins of environmental problems within this particular myth. The text suggests, to use Campbell's terminology, a "mythic dissociation," where God is a being who is separate from the world, while humans are separate from God, on the one hand, and nature on the other hand (*The Flight of the Wild Gander: Explorations in the Mythological Dimension* 204). The text reminds us that man is to have "dominion" over the animals, and to use them as he sees fit. Of course there are alternate readings of the myth which must be kept in mind, but Bate wants us to consider how readings of these stories imply certain ideologies from which we can learn our relationships to the natural world.

There are, Bate reminds us, positive examples of relating to the earth present in other mythologies, for example, the myth of the Golden Age which is found in various traditions, most importantly in the Greek (26–27). In the Golden Age, humans existed in perfect harmony with their surroundings. Using translations of such texts as Ovid's *Metamorphosis* by Ted Hughes, Bate argues that those artists who draw inspiration from the myth of the Golden Age are poets who "listen to their source." However, the problem is that these mythologies no longer hold their value as ways of engaging imaginatively with the world. With increasing skepticism brought on by science, modern man dismisses mythic discourse as irrelevant. Not content with the symbolic intent of many of these myths, moderns are more concerned with historicity, with events that "actually" occurred. As Bate states, "the demand for historical explanations, as well as, or instead of, mythical explanations is one of the characteristics of 'modernity'" (29).

This concern for the historicity of particular events should cause us to pause and examine the relationship between cultural ideologies and language. In many oral cultures, mythologies are meditations on relationships with the natural world. The language used in the myths reflects an animistic view of the world, where gods and goddesses are associated with natural forces. In contrast, our dilemma, Bate reminds us, is that through language we can only have a "representation" of nature; to us, nature is not a living organism but an idea (63). We can only artificially recreate nature through the use of the imagination. However, this is not necessarily a problem. As Bate notes, just as parks represent a state of nature, albeit through an abstraction, they still allow us the "experience" of a recreational (re-creational) space which may aid in our understanding of our relationship to the natural world. In his book *The Song of the Earth*, Bate offers an "experiment in ecopoetics" which is "to see what happens when we regard poems as imaginary parks in which we may breathe an air that is not toxic and accommodate ourselves to a mode of dwelling which is not alienated" (64).

The "experience" of a re-creational space, where our relationship to the natural world is revised through poetry or literature, is not new but is a technique evidenced in the unique contribution of the mythopoeic authors Coleridge, MacDonald, Lewis and Tolkien. Their fantasies serve to counter arguments of the type made by Lynn White that Christianity "bears a huge burden of guilt" for environmental problems, especially in its anthropocentrism. In fact, the works of Coleridge and MacDonald engage us in the dialogue of the transcendence or annihilation of the self which brings about environmental revisioning. It is interesting to note that this is a major concern for ecocritics as well. Perhaps paradoxically, the term "environment" (from the root "environ" which means "around") betrays an obsession with self, as the environment always means what is around "us." The problem is even deeper than this. As Bate points out, the aestheticization of nature allows us to frame nature as we like it. This is why environmental groups concern themselves with "cute" animals such as the panda or dolphin, where Bate would draw our attention to the peat-bog or the earthworm, which should be taken into consideration as well (138). In order to properly revise relationships with the natural world, this anthropocentrism which entails framing nature around our image of it, must be discarded, and an awareness of the whole of nature must be embraced. It is precisely this experience of nature which the theme of the annihilation of the self engenders, as will be seen in Coleridge (and in the next chapter, MacDonald).

As many ecocritics point out, the need is to learn a new language which will offer alternatives to our normative ways of perceiving the world. As Bate states, "It may therefore be that a necessary step in overcoming the apartness is to think and to use language in a different way"

(37). Mythopoeic fantasy offers this alternative by allowing an imaginative engagement with the natural world. Bate's view of ecopoetry as a means "to engage imaginatively with the non-human," is easily extendible to the genre of mythopoeic fantasy; in departing from consensus reality and by its subversive quality, this form of literature has a distinct capacity of speaking for nature itself (199). As Bate notices, one of the reasons for ecocriticism's failure as a means of revisioning relationships to the natural world is the "silence" of nature itself; it literally cannot speak. This is in direct contrast to other critical fields such as Women's Studies or African American studies, where there are voices which may be heard. Bate says, "A critic may speak as a woman or as a person of colour, but cannot speak as a tree" (72). However, mythopoeic fantasy, with its ability to express the experience of the natural world, has the ability to give nature its proper voice. To refer to an example in the introduction, Tolkien's creation of the Ents, the creatures who are both human and arboreal, serves to speak for the trees; thus, far from being an escape from reality, Tolkien's creations are meant to recover a numinous perception of the world, one which has been lost or hidden by our linguistic appropriations. Mythopoeic fantasy, then, has an equivalent function to Bate's ecopoet who is a "potential savior of the ecosystem," not literally in the sense of saving the environment but in challenging our cultural constructs through the use the imagination.

Further features of the ecopoet are transferable to mythopoeic fantasy as well, the most important of these being the focus on the *experience* of nature. As argued in the introduction, critics of mythopoeic fantasy often refer to the quality of "wonder" or "enchantment" as its defining element, and it is this "extraliterary experience" which helps in a recovery of the numinous. To use Otto's terminology, it is both awe-inspiring and indescribable. Commenting on this role of ecopoetry, Bate states, "Ecopoetry is not a description of dwelling with the earth, not a disengaged thinking about it, but an experiencing of it" (42). This experience of the natural environment is part of the language of poetry, which is quite different from political or practical language that attempts to save the environment. Poetry, and we can now say mythopoeic fantasy, has no specific "agenda" to save the environment; it merely offers a re-creational space to experience the natural world imaginatively.

Engaging imaginatively with the environment helps us to lift the "veil of familiarity," a concept which is at the root of Tolkien and Lewis's theories of fantasy. This same idea is echoed in Bate's consideration of the process of "enframing." He states, "a poem is enframed when it becomes not an original admission of dwelling, but rather a cog in the wheel of a historical or theoretical system. To read ecopoetically is, by contrast, to find 'clearings' or 'unconcealments'"(268). To "unconceal" in this sense is similar to Tolkien's "recovery," where the moment of wonder, or in Otto's terminology "the numinous," aids in the challenging of our most cherished cultural constructions.

A borrowed phrase from Jonathan Bate's text *The Song of the Earth*, "Quieting the Eye," serves as a portion of this chapter's title precisely because it relates to how the numinous consciousness presents itself in the works of Coleridge (and in the next chapter, MacDonald): in terms of a recovery or a revisioning of our relationship to the natural world, normative modes of perception must be subverted (a challenge to the "eye"). Similarly, if one partakes in word-play, the challenge to the "eye" in these works is also a challenge to the "I," portraying the corollary theme of the annihilation of the self, a concept central to Coleridge's (and later, MacDonald's) worldview.

The theme of the annihilation of the self that is present within the works of Coleridge and MacDonald is analyzed in Otto's discussion of the *mysterium tremendum*, the object of the numinous consciousness which evokes both fear and trembling. Although Otto refers to the experience of this mystery as "absolute unapproachability," he adds to these terms "absolute overpoweringness" or *majestas*. This suggests a form of creature consciousness in which the feeling of one's own submergence, a sense of nothingness, results in a consequent form of religious humility over against an overwhelming power. Otto is careful here in distinguishing between two types of consciousness, a "consciousness of createdness" and a "consciousness of creaturehood" (20–21). In the former consciousness, that of createdness, the focus is on the creature as being "created" as a result of a divine act. If the focus is on the creature, the construct of the "self" is viewed as "real," as that which is separate from what is viewed as "other," or God. In terms of the earlier discussion of Campbell's mythic dissociation, self and God are two separate entities and, for Otto, this consciousness of createdness posits a causality of God as the creator and self as creation which, as a strictly rational conception, fails to evoke the fear and sense of awe that is experienced with the *mysterium tremendum* (20).

The latter consciousness, that of creaturehood, posits the self as somewhat illusory, and the feeling of nothingness in the face of an overwhelming power is the true source of the *mysterium tremendum*. As Otto states, "it starts from a consciousness of the absolute superiority or supremacy of a power other than myself" (21). This absolute supremacy can only be experienced with the annihilation of the self, where the finite self must be transcended in order for the numinous consciousness to be present. The eternal must be reflected in the temporal.

Coleridge (1772–1834) presents the experience of the numinous consciousness through the annihilation of the self in his poem *The Rime of the Ancient Mariner*. Although not usually referred to as "mythopoeic" by many critics, Coleridge was important in formulating a theory of the imagination, which allowed for an expression of the numinous consciousness, one which the other authors discussed in the present study indirectly drew upon in their own formulations. He also posed the problem of the annihilation of the self, one which he shares with MacDonald as will be seen in chapter two. Many of Coleridge's poems embody his religious sense of the imaginative function, but his most well known poem, *The Rime of the Ancient Mariner*, first published in *Lyrical Ballads* (1798) in collaboration with William Wordsworth, shows this most clearly.

One of the most common fallacies associated with the *Lyrical Ballads* project is the assumption that the work is the sole achievement of William Wordsworth. Although most of the poems are indeed attributed to Wordsworth, failure to acknowledge the contribution of Samuel Taylor Coleridge is a failure to acknowledge the distinct form of genius Coleridge embodied, a poet who shared with Wordsworth a deep religious feeling for life but employed a different method of achieving its expression. In his *Biographia Literaria*, Coleridge explains the differing means used by the two poets in the *Lyrical Ballads* project: whereas Wordsworth would write poems which dealt with the "natural" world, Coleridge would write poems which dealt with the "supernatural" which he stated would "transfer from our inward nature a human interest and a semblance of truth sufficient to procure for these shadows of imagination that willing suspension of disbelief for the moment, which constitutes poetic faith" ("From Biographia Literaria" 518).

Although the approaches employed by the two poets were quite

One. "Quieting the Eye"

distinct, Coleridge points out that the underlying motivations for the poems were similar; both the supernatural and natural modes were to provide an "awakening [of] the mind's attention from the lethargy of custom, ...directing it to the loveliness and the wonders of the world before us" ("From Biographia Literaria" 518). Awakening one's mind to the "wonders of the world" is precisely the sense of recovery envisioned by our present authors. Keeping the underlying themes of the poems within *Lyrical Ballads* in mind, it is interesting to examine the criticism of these two modes after the publication of the *Lyrical Ballads*. Although Coleridge's *The Rime of the Ancient Mariner* was to serve as the lead poem in the 1798 version of the *Lyrical Ballads*, reviews of the poem were not favorable; according to Charles Burney, *The Rime* was "the strangest story of cock and bull we ever saw on paper." It was, according to other reviews, "absurd, or unintelligible," or the product of a mind which resembled a "mad German poet" (Butler and Green 22). Wordsworth himself was disappointed by the poem and stated "*The Ancient Mariner* has upon the whole been an injury to the volume, I mean that the old words and the strangeness of it have deterred readers from going on" (Butler and Green 22).

The subsequent publication of the *Lyrical Ballads* relegated *The Rime* to a different position in the text; far from being the lead poem, the 1800 version of *Lyrical Ballads* placed the poem in the twenty-third position. Such a decision on Wordsworth's part allowed readers to experience the much more understandable poetry of the "natural" world before encountering Coleridge's strange "supernatural" contributions.

It is interesting to speculate on the adverse reaction of the critics and populace concerning *The Rime of the Ancient Mariner*. What was it about the poem that people disliked? What was Coleridge trying to accomplish with images such as a dead albatross, a skeleton ship with Death and Life-in Death, and spirits inhabiting dead bodies? Upon reading the *Biographia Literaria*, a much later text published in 1817, it becomes clear that behind Coleridge's poetry was an elaborate view of the imagination, and the function of the imagination was to produce fantastic images or symbols which were "characterized ... above all by a translucence of the eternal through and in the temporal" (Coleridge "Selections from the Statesman's Manual" 388). Thus, what the critics and readers failed to understand was that Coleridge's *The Rime of the Ancient Mariner* employs fantastic or "supernatural" symbols to convey

Coleridge's belief in the imagination as a primary means of experiencing the numinous.

What becomes difficult for the scholar when trying to reconcile Coleridge's theory of the imagination with *The Rime* is the question of how much of the theory was formulated by the time of the writing of the poem in 1797–8. And, if one employs the crystallized version of the theory in the *Biographia Literaria* of 1817, what version of *The Rime* should be used? The 1798 version or one that coincides with the *Biographia*?

In his "Introduction" to *Imagination in Coleridge*, John Spencer Hill provides some answers (Hill). He argues that although one must be careful in attributing to Coleridge the *full* expression of his theory of the imagination in 1797–8, certainly he was starting to question the empiricist views of the time, views that held that the imagination was merely an aspect of memory which mistakenly combined and associated disparate perceptions (1–3). In Hill's argument, Coleridge formed the bulk of his theory between 1795 and 1802. Hill examines three periods in the formulation of Coleridge's theory: 1795 and earlier, where Coleridge became interested in the theories of Platonism, providing him with a distrust of materialism and empiricism; 1795, his association with and realization of the genius of Wordsworth, especially the recitation of "Guilt and Sorrow," where Coleridge realized the connection between thought and feeling; and finally, the period of 1798–1802, where Coleridge developed portions of his critical theory, as evidenced in his contributions to Wordsworth's "Preface" to the *Lyrical Ballads* and the influence of Kant and the German Transcendentalists (Hill 17–21).

If Hill's position is correct, Coleridge would have been in the process of formulating his ideas of the imagination concurrently with his writing of *The Rime of the Ancient Mariner*. However, for the present argument, it is more appropriate to employ the 1817 version of the poem for two reasons: the added gloss and the epigraph by Thomas Burnet, which both contribute to the theme Coleridge was trying to convey; and, the fact that by its publication, Coleridge's theory of the imagination had crystallized and had been published in the *Biographia Literaria* in 1817.

According to his *Biographia Literaria*, Coleridge's conception of the artist's imaginative faculties consists of a tripartite system involving the primary imagination, which is God-like in its perception; the secondary imagination, which is the artist's echo of the primary imagination; and the fancy, a mechanical faculty which is both aggregative and related to memory. As Owen Barfield points out in his text *What Coleridge Thought*, these imaginative faculties represent a "unity in multeity," and cannot ultimately be separated; a distinction can be made but not a division. For Coleridge, underlying this tripartite system was his belief in the law of polarity, one which posited that "the duality of the 'opposite forces' is a manifestation of a prior unity; and that unity is a 'power'" (Barfield 35). For Coleridge, then, all three faculties work together; however, both types of the imagination perform a more active function than that of the fancy, and it is the imagination which mirrors God's original creation. Defining the two functions of the imagination, Jonathan Wordsworth states, "With the primary imagination man unknowingly reenacts God's original and eternal creative moment; with the secondary he consciously vitalizes an object-world that would otherwise be dead" (Wordsworth 25).

The primary imagination is an unconscious faculty which allows humans to create order in the world. It is somewhat equated with sense perception, a common element in the mind which allows it to perceive a unified, ordered world. In the primary imagination, what is perceived is the "real" world of the senses, so this function of the imagination is, at first glance, not associated in any way with Coleridge's desire to produce "supernatural" images; however, the primary imagination is also more than sense perception due to its mirrored reflection of God's own creation and ordering of the world. The primary imagination, then, for Coleridge is the closest one can get to God. This truth is embodied in Coleridge's famous lines from the *Biographia Literaria*: "The primary imagination I hold to be the living Power and prime Agent of all human Perception, and as a repetition in the finite mind of the eternal act of creation in the infinite I AM" ("From Biographia Literaria" 516).

The secondary imagination differs from the primary imagination in that it is both conscious and its activities are willed. It is the artist's echo of the primary imagination which seeks to dissolve orderings of the universe in order to recreate and combine them in new ways. As mentioned in the introduction, the dissolution of the universe is the specific goal of the subversiveness of the fantastic text, and in Coleridge's system, this is the function of the secondary imagination. By recreating and redefining the world, the artist is perceiving the world in its real significance. In this sense, it is the artist's job to revitalize the world by echoing God's creation, and for Coleridge, this could be achieved by portraying the supernatural dimensions of the world. For Coleridge, then, this secondary imagination is similar to the primary imagination, which only differs in degree, not kind. The secondary imagination, according to Coleridge, "dissolves, diffuses, dissipates, in order to recreate; or where this process is rendered impossible, yet still at all events it struggles to idealize and unify" ("From Biographia Literaria" 516).

What is clear from the above statement by Coleridge is that the primary and secondary imagination work together in the process of unifying and ordering the world in a God-like fashion. This connection between the artist and the divine is important for Coleridge because the employment of the imagination is similar to an act of faith. According to Barth, in his "Theological Implications of Coleridge's Theory of Imagination," "The imagination is in fact a faculty of the transcendent, capable of perceiving and in some degree articulating transcendent reality—the reality of higher realms of being, including the divine" (5).

Although a lower faculty, fancy is also important in Coleridge's tripartite construction. For Coleridge, the fancy "has no other counters to play with, but fixities and definites. The fancy is indeed no other than a mode of memory emancipated from the order of time and space" ("From Biographia Literaria" 516). It is a faculty which is aggregative, only being able to combine elements already associated with the real world. Unlike the active imagination which unifies, the fancy can only separate units of the world, thereby not achieving the unity which is the repetition of God's original oneness. Fancy, for Coleridge, tends to be passive and cannot produce images which "awaken" the mind in order for the sacramental vision to revise relationships with the natural world.

To properly understand the difference between the fancy and the imagination, it is beneficial to analyze passages which Coleridge believed embodied the two faculties. In his *Biographia Literaria*, Coleridge quotes a few lines from Shakespeare's *Venus and Adonis* to describe the function of the fancy: "Full gently now she takes him by the hand, A lily prison'd in a gaol of snow" (Lines 361–2). Upon examining the lines, what one notices is the simple associations between Adonis's hand: Venus's hand::Lily: gaol of snow. As the lines connote, Adonis's hand is like a lily, both white and fair; similarly, since Venus is taking Adonis's hand, the image is it being imprisoned in a gaol of snow, a symbol both of enclosure and whiteness. However, what is to be recognized in terms of the function of fancy is that the images given, whether of snow or lilies, are separate from each other, and the connection between them is aggregative. They do not allow any imaginative act whereby the reader may discover a more complex meaning; all that is apparent is what is given by the association. According to I. A. Richards, "The links between them are accidental, contribute nothing to the action; though the absence of relevant links does. Pondering the links does not enrich the poem" (79).

However, for Coleridge the imagination allows deeper associations between the images of a poem, and the imaginative impulse to unify becomes noticeable. Coleridge employs another passage from *Venus and Adonis* to exemplify the imaginative faculty: "Look! How a bright star shooteth from the sky, So glides he in the night from Venus's eye" (lines 815–816). In this passage, images are not so easily separable, but they exist as a potential unified whole which the reader forms in the imagination. For example, "Look!" allows the reader to experience a sense of surprise at Adonis's flight; "star" is a light equated with beauty, while "shooteth" connotes a sense of a flight from a heavenly "sky," one which can be interpreted as a foretelling of ruin associated with Adonis. So, all these images are associative; they work together in a unity, allowing the reader to make connection after connection, and thereby realizing the full potential of the poem. For Coleridge, then, the imagination produces poetic genius which unifies disparate elements and affects readers on an emotive level which is analogous to music: "But the sense of musical delight, with the power of producing it, is a gift of imagination; and this together with the power of reducing multitude into unity of effect, and modifying a series of thoughts by some one predominant thought or feeling, may be cultivated and improved, but can never be learned" ("From Biographia Literaria" 527).

In many of his poems, especially in the 1817 version of *The Rime of the Ancient Mariner* in *Sibylline Leaves*, Coleridge attempted to realize this imaginative unity by exploring and employing supernatural images. In *Risking Enchantment*, Jeanie Watson argues that Coleridge's fascination with the supernatural as means of conveying the function of the imagination was related to his early love of stories concerning the world of "Faerie." To properly understand many of Coleridge's poems, including *Kubla Khan*, *The Song of the Pixies*, *Christabel* or *Rime*, one must accept the connection between the supernatural, which deals with divine forces outside the natural world, and the landscape of Faery which was, for Coleridge, a "mental space." As Watson states, "the world of Faery is the world of the creative imagination, the world of feeling and intuition, the world of imaginative truth" (54). By employing the supernatural in a Faerian realm, Coleridge believed, one could imaginatively reach the numinous consciousness present in the world. This act of imagination was a form of awareness, "a state of being, an mental/emotional construct, and act of creation" (Watson 23).

Constructing the supernatural worlds employed in some of his poems allowed Coleridge, as well as the reader, to explore the consubstantial nature of existence. Coleridge believed that through artistic constructions, one could realize that all matter in the world is symbolic of the numinous. One is reminded here, again, of Coleridge's definition of a symbol as "characterized ... above all by a translucence of the eternal through and in the temporal" ("Selections from the Statesman's Manual" 388). So, by use of the imaginative faculty, the whole world could be viewed as a series of symbols that reflect the numinous. Probably the most apparent embodiment of this belief in the consubstantial nature of existence is in *The Rime of the Ancient Mariner*. In the poem, Coleridge uses the supernatural realm of Faerie to portray an allegory of how the original numinous consciousness can be recovered by an act of the imagination.

Watson offers four propositions which Coleridge, and by extension the Mariner and the reader, explore and come to terms with in the supernatural world of *The Rime*: (1) the original wholeness and unity does exist; (2) the original wholeness has been lost but can be recovered; (3) Spirit, or a means to the transcendent, is available through self-knowledge; and (4) the tale of Faerie, by its use of the supernatural and its connection with the imagination, allows the original wholeness to be recovered (65). The Mariner follows this four-fold set of propositions by traveling to the Pole (Faerie or supernatural realm), achieving a vision of the consubstantial nature of existence (original unity), and exiting the supernatural realm to teach his visions to a fallen world, one which has difficulty understanding its relationship with the numinous.

It is interesting to note that Watson's four-fold set of propositions relates to what Victoria Nelson terms the "psychotopographic aesthetic" in her book *The Secret Life of Puppets* (145). Discussing the influence of

One. "Quieting the Eye"

Neoplatonic thought on fantastic sea quests to the Poles, Nelson identifies a writer's projection of inner processes onto the geological map of the outer world; thus, the human psyche becomes a *topos* reflecting the dynamic relationship between the micro and macrocosom. In one example, Nelson points to Thomas Burnet's work *The Sacred Theory of the Earth*, in which a Neoplatonic construct underlies three subsequent earths: the first being an Edenic orb in which paradise is a lived reality; the second, our present earth which is "broken" as the result of the Fall in the Garden of Eden (thus the shifting continents); and third, a millennial earth to come which will usher in a new paradisal state after a final apocalypse. What is of special note is both Burnet's influence on Coleridge (Burnet's epigraph introduces the 1817 version of *The Rime*), and the relationship of the evolving earths to Nelson's psychotopographic aesthetic; if the inner and outer processes of the mind reflect one another, then the evolving earths relate to consciousness, both of which necessitate a final destruction before a new paradise is created. As will be argued in subsequent chapters, the apocalyptic theme is important for mythopoeic fantasists as a way of destroying present ideologies related to the earth and creating new ones. For Coleridge and MacDonald, this apocalyptic destruction is one related to the annihilation of the self.

In relation to the present concentration on Coleridge's *Rime of the Ancient Mariner*, the outward quest to the Pole is, in effect, a quest to the inward experience of the numinous. In *The Rime*, the quest is depicted specifically as a journey to the Pole which, in a literal sense, is an orienting point (as in a compass) as well as in a symbolic sense, that which is furthest away from consciousness. However, as Nelson states, "what is farthest away and most hidden is, paradoxically, always what is most important: the journey to the pole is a journey to the center of the soul" (146). The Mariner embodies this symbolic journey in that his sea voyage takes him from society (consciousness), to the unknown regions (unconsciousness), where after his "fall" in shooting the Albatross, he redeems himself by a revisioning of the world via the numinous encounter with the water snakes. Thus, as many critics have pointed out, the journey mirrors the Fall in the Garden of Eden, but in terms of the present thesis the fall is specifically directed at a recovery of the sacramental vision of nature: "If humans lost their inner vision at the fall, a journey to the pole must involve an initial failure to recognize that the journey has an esoteric as well as exoteric meaning; and this failure must produce catastrophe followed by suffering and eventual redemption" (Nelson 148).

Losing the "inner vision" as a result of the Fall is also explored in Stanley Cavell's text *In Quest of the Ordinary*. Cavell interprets the Mariner's quest as a response to Kant's *Critique of Pure Reason*, which posits that experience is constituted by appearances that ultimately we cannot know in themselves; we can only know our experience of them. Cavell argues that Coleridge's response to Kant's text in *The Rime* shows that this dimension of knowledge in fact *can* be known. In the poem itself, the gloss mentions a "line" which is crossed on the journey to the pole, and Cavell interprets this as a line below which knowledge cannot reach; thus, by the Mariner's crossing of the line, he is penetrating a realm which is both outside and other. According to Cavell, "there is something in the self that logically cannot be brought to knowledge" (48). Contrary to many critics' accusations that the Mariner's transgression is in shooting the Albatross, Cavell insists that the transgression is the crossing of the line where knowledge cannot penetrate. In this transgression, the Mariner embodies the human effort to escape the human, to go beyond what Cavell describes as language games.

Cavell warns readers in his text of the dangers of language itself: "we are the victims of the very words of which we are at the same time the masters; victims and masters of the fact of words" (169). This same criticism is echoed by mythopoeic fantasists as well, mainly that when language creates abstractions which symbolize objects but are not necessarily the objects themselves, we appropriate these objects and are said to "know" them. Mythopoeic fantasy, subversive in challenging basic categories of thought, allows one to posit a different reality to be considered. So, whether the problem is Coleridge's "lethargy of custom," MacDonald's "weary and sated regards" or Lewis and Tolkien's "veil of familiarity," the artist's job is to allow the reader a different, more sacramental orientation towards the world. The insight Cavell has into the Romantic writers may be equally applied to those of the mythopoeic imagination: "they perceive us as uninterested, in a condition of boredom, which they regard as, among other things, a sign of intellectual suicide" (7).

The idea of the fallen nature of the world, where the connection with the numinous has been lost, is embodied in the Mariner's shooting of the

Albatross. It is this shooting which symbolically represents the attainment of a self, a sense of subjectivity which, for our purposes, serves as a form of mythic dissociation which divorces the Mariner from the numinous. After having entered a supernatural landscape, one which holds spectre barks, polar spirits, Death and Life-in-Death, the mariners see the bird and declare, "As if it had been a Christian soul, we hailed it in God's name" (lines 65–66). This reference equates the bird with a higher power, a guide who helps the crew through the fog and ice. The symbolism of birds in psychological discourse is relevant here as well. According to J.E. Cirlot's famous text *A Dictionary of Symbols*, birds are related to the soul and "birds, like angels, are symbols of thought, of imagination and of the swiftness of spiritual processes and relationships" (28). The Albatross here functions as a link to the numinous, an intermediary between the Mariner and the spirit, and the act of shooting separates the Mariner from this power. As a result, he no longer is able to experience the numinous but is forced to experience the nightmares of the sea.

Attributing the shooting of the bird to a psychological model of the Mariner's emerging as an ego, Anne Williams in her chapter "An 'I' for an 'Eye'" realizes the destructiveness of leaving behind the original unity. She states that the line "I shot the Albatross" is the first use of the first person in the poem, a sign of the separation from unity, and, as a result of this action, the Albatross becomes an object which embodies the Mariner's abjection, his guilt resulting from his separation (187–88). This insight is relevant to Watson's propositions; what is experienced at this point in the poem is a sense of paradise lost as the result of self-consciousness. In forming an ego consciousness, the Mariner has severed his ties with the numinous power symbolized by the Albatross.

The effects of this severance are portrayed immediately. The Mariner no longer notices his connection with other beings, and his separation allows a more noxious view: "yea, slimy things did crawl with legs upon the slimy sea" (lines 125–26). His separation from the original wholeness and his emerging ego force him to view the world with a lack of imagination, a view in which he fails to experience the numinous consciousness. The Mariner is then forced to wear the dead Albatross around his neck which, with its substitution for a cross, implies that he must suffer like Christ. What he must learn to recover is his similar Christ-like nature, both as man and God, and this recovery requires an act of imagination.

The negative consequences of the Mariner's separation from the original unity is present within the figures of Death and Life-in-Death. Williams associates these figures with negative father and mother images, who then take the lives of the crew members (190–91). These negative images, like the Albatross, are abjects or forms of awareness of corporeality which remind the Mariner of his painful separation from the numinous. After the crew's spirits leave, the Mariner realizes how alone he is with his pain, "never a saint took pity on my soul in agony" (lines 234–35). His pain is fully realized as he notices, again, his utter difference and separation from the world around him: "a thousand thousand slimy things lived on; and so did I" (lines 238–9). Psychologically, this pain is the result of his anxiety at becoming a self and, for Coleridge, what this signifies is what happens when the imagination no longer sees its connection with other forms of existence; it is a failure to realize one's relationship with the numinous. Echoing this disassociation, the gloss points out "He despiseth the creatures of the calm."

In terms of Coleridge's own beliefs concerning the imagination, the Mariner symbolizes, at this point in the poem, a failure to realize a consubstantial perception of the world; matter for the Mariner is utterly separate from himself and instead of radiating the numinous, is similar to a vision in a nightmare. At this point, the Mariner is so far cut off from the numinous that he is unable to pray for help. He is alone on a "rotting sea" among the dead corpses of his crew, who continually gaze at him with their empty eyes. However, as nightmarish as this section of the poem is, it is also the pivotal moment when the Mariner achieves the last two propositions of Watson's argument: he realizes the availability of spirit and recovers the original unity of perception. He sees the water snakes which "moved in tracks of shining white" with their "elfish light" falling from their scales. He "watched their rich attire: blue, glossy green, and velvet black, they coiled and swam; and every track was a flash of golden fire" (lines 177–81).

One is struck immediately with the contrast of language presented before and during the sight of the water snakes. Following the images of death and the "rotting sea," the Mariner now experiences the beauty inherent in the world. He blesses the snakes unaware, and at that moment is able to pray. The curse is lifted, at this point, and the dead Albatross, which symbolized his disconnection with the numinous, falls from his neck and "sank like lead into the sea" (lines 290–1). The Mariner has re-established his perception of the world as consubstantial; he sees the beauty in all things and realizes that they are symbols of the numinous. It should be noted, however, that what this involves is not necessarily a change in the actual environment. What has changed is the Mariner's *perception* of the world. He has realized the eternal through the temporal, the numinous within the world and within himself, but what this has required is an annihilation of his prior sense of self, his discarding of past perceptions of nature, and a revisioning of a higher sense of self in relation to his engagement with the non-human. With this new form of self-knowledge, or as Williams' argument claims, his stabilizing awareness of ego, the Mariner is able to view his world with the imagination; he has realized his oneness with the "Infinite I AM."

For Coleridge, the supernatural (or world of Faerie) was an effective vehicle for displaying his belief in the consubstantial nature of existence. If the imagination is properly employed, the world does, in some sense, become supernatural; it takes on a new meaning and a new beauty. Similarly, in Williams' psychological model, once consciousness emerges, a gap forms and "the fragile 'I,' to mend the break its birth necessitates, imagines a higher realm where no such gap exists" (197). For Coleridge, this higher realm is the numinous, and after the ego has severed the tie with this ground of Being, the imagination is the only means of recovering it.

The discourse on the annihilation of the self which both Coleridge and MacDonald participate in does not necessitate that the self be totally dissolved. It is true that the self must be "annihilated" in order for there to be an experience of the numinous, but the self must reconstitute itself with a new vision of its relationship to the world. This is, again, the theme of "recovery" or "revisioning" which is at the core of the mythopoeic imagination. In Coleridge's philosophy, this sense of self and other is realized in his law of polarity, in which the self must be viewed only in relation to that which transcends the self. Concerning this lesson of the Mariner, and especially in relation to Coleridge's polarity, Owen Barfield states, "we cannot acknowledge an individual being without at the same time acknowledging that which transcends individuality" (151). Echoing this same theme, Williams argues that the Mariner participates in a system founded upon self and other and, for the purposes of our argument, acknowledging both is the only way of perceiving proper relations to the natural world.

Once the numinous moment occurs through the annihilation of the self which facilitates an imaginative perception of the water snakes, the benefits become apparent: the curse is lifted and the ship moves on its way. As the ship moves, the Mariner falls into a swoon and hears two voices which describe the Mariner's encounters. One voices states, "The spirit who bideth by himself in the land of mist and snow, he loved the bird that loved the man who shot him with his bow" (lines 402–5). These lines are important in that they set up the chain of relationship between the three images of the poem: Spirit-bird-man. In terms of Coleridge's views of the imagination and its perception of the consubstantial nature of existence, these images form the original unity present in the world. However, with the shooting of the Albatross, the Mariner breaks the connection and must exist for a time in a nightmare world, one created by his newly damaged perceptions. Separated from the oneness of Being, the Mariner learns that to properly experience the numinous, the inner eye of the imagination must open.

It would seem odd that the poem would go on to relate how the Mariner was rescued by a hermit, a Pilot, and the Pilot's boy, especially upon recalling that the Pilot's boy goes crazy and, after seeing the Mariner rowing the boat, states, "full plain I see, the Devil knows how to row" (lines 568–9). Why is this figure, who has just had an experience of the numinous by the use of his imagination, referred to as a devil? One answer might be that the true gift of the imagination is not realized or understood by many. Misunderstanding the Mariner's vision is comparable to the critics' misunderstanding Coleridge's art, for it is fairly common practice to demonize what is not understood. However, demons and devils are interesting in their own way. In thinking about the reaction of the Pilot's boy, and in thinking about the early negative criticism of *The Rime of the Ancient Mariner* and the portrayal of Coleridge as some sort of madman, it might be beneficial to keep in mind an alternative definition of devil: "a devil is a god who has not been recognized" (Campbell *An Open Life: Joseph Campbell in Conversation with Michael Toms* 28).

Interpreting *The Rime* in terms of Coleridge's own religious and artistic beliefs is not new. In his essay "A Poem of Pure Imagination: An Experiment in Reading," Robert Penn Warren offers a dual interpretation of the poem, one which coincides with the argument presented above. What must be noted is that although one interpretation is primary and the other secondary, both interpretations work together and cannot be ultimately separated. Concerning the primary interpretation, Warren states that the poem is a fable; it offers a sacramental vision of the world (the unity of the "one life"), which is the result of the mythopoeic retelling of the Fall in the Garden of Eden. Thus, the shooting of the Albatross is a violation of the religious order of the world, and it disconnects the Mariner with this order. Warren believes that this act of violence is central to the poem's meaning because it shows that here "We are confronted with the mystery of the corruption of the will" (26). This corruption of the will is the result of the Mariner's own conscious choice to exist apart from the primal unity. This act is similar to the Fall in the Garden, where Adam and Eve, by partaking of the fruit, are separated from God and the original unity present in the Garden. By their own will, they consciously disassociate from their original oneness.

Concerning the secondary interpretation, Warren points out that the poem works on an artistic level, providing an allegory of the function of the imagination. The shooting of the Albatross functions in this interpretation as a "crime against the imagination" (33). Interpreting the symbolic "clusters" in the poem, Warren connects images such as the wind, the moon, the Albatross, and the imagination, all of which are associated with the unconscious, non-rational, and sacramental aspects from which the Mariner is disassociated. As argued earlier, Warren views the episode with the water snakes as the turning point of the poem. As this episode involves the regaining of the sacramental view of the world by imaginative perception, it is no wonder that the central light of the vision is provided by the moon. In the gloss, it states "By the light of the moon he beholdeth God's creatures of the great calm" (91–92). Once the imaginative vision of the water snakes occurs, the Mariner's redemption takes place; he recognizes happiness, sees love as the motivating force in the world, blesses the creatures, and is freed from the curse. Warren states, "In the end, he accepts the sacramental view of the universe, and his will is released from its state of 'utmost abstraction' and gains the state of 'immanence' in wisdom and love" (29).

In Warren's interpretation, *The Rime* works on two levels concurrently: it portrays the religious dimension in the theme of a quest to recover the numinous consciousness which has been lost; and, it works aesthetically to convey the importance of the imagination in allowing for the vision. Warren assumes that the underlying theme of the poem is that the world is full of powers and presences not visible to the physical eye (or by the "understanding"): this is a way of saying that there is a spiritual order of universal love, the sacramental vision, and of imagination; that nature, if understood aright—that is, by the imagination—offers us vital meanings [47].

Warren's position is reminiscent of the epigraph in the later version of *The Rime* by the seventeenth century theologian Thomas Burnet; this paragraph, translated from Latin into English, offers readers the theme Coleridge intended for this particular publication of the poem:

> I can readily believe that there are more invisible than visible natures in the universe of things. But who shall explain their family, their orders, relationships, the stations and functions of each? What do they do? Where do they live? Human nature has always sought after knowledge of these things, but has never attained it. Meanwhile, I do not deny the pleasure it is to contemplate in thought, as though in a picture, the image of a better and greater world: lest the mind, habituating itself to the trivia of life, should become too narrow, and subside completely into trivial thoughts only. But, at the same time we must be vigilant for truth, and set a limit, so that we can distinguish the certain from the uncertain and night from day [Jasper 60-61].

As a mythopoeic author, Coleridge offers readers both a comprehensive theory of the imagination as well as a symbolic manifestation of this theory in his poem *The Rime of the Ancient Mariner*. In his theory, he posits the artistic imagination as that faculty which closely resembles God's original act of creation. By employing the imagination, we participate in a recovery of the original unity of the world, one which has as its root the numinous consciousness. The poem embodies the experience of the numinous in relation to a retelling of the Fall in the Garden of Eden. What must be remembered in reading the poem, however, is its symbolic import, not its literal meaning; this is how it differs from conventional interpretations of the Bible and what makes it mythopoeia (Greek *mythos* = "story" and *poiein* = "to recreate"). As Harry Slochower points out in his text *Mythopoesis: Mythic Patterns in Literary Classics*, "while mythology presents its stories as if they actually took place, mythopoesis transfers them to a symbolic meaning" (15). Thus the symbolic meaning in *The Rime of the Ancient Mariner* is that the emergence of the ego, or self, as symbolically represented by the shooting of the Albatross, is what dissociates the Mariner from the numinous; it is a symbolic gesture mirroring the Fall in the Garden of Eden, where by eating the forbidden fruit, Adam and Eve were dissociated from God and nature. The redemption, however, occurs as the Mariner is able to transcend his finite self through an imaginative act of perception which renews his vision and his relationship to all creatures. Thus the implied moral "he prayeth best, who loveth best all things both great and small; For the dear God who loveth us, he made and loveth all" (lines 614–617). It is through his perception of the water snakes that the Mariner truly experiences the sense of "awe" which is so central to the apprehension of the numinous.

The concern of the present chapter has been to understand how the imagination (especially as formulated by Coleridge) helps facilitate a revised relationship with the natural world by means of an encounter with the numinous. By its subversive nature and its departure from consensus reality, mythopoeic fantasy challenges normative modes of perception and asks us to rethink our most basic cultural assumptions concerning our world. As Burnet's epigraph points out, it is beneficial to contemplate a better world lest our minds become too narrow; if minds are too narrow, then alternative modes of perception (which many ecocritics point out are our basic needs) will never be available. It is the foundation of mythopoeic fantasy, then, to broaden our minds by helping us revise the ways in which to think about our relationships in the world, especially those non-human relationships vital to our survival. What is ultimately needed in this discourse is for an "awakening" of our minds either from what Coleridge terms the "lethargy of custom" or MacDonald terms our "weary and sated regards." Perhaps it is best to conclude with a quotation from Coleridge, a quotation which serves as a concluding thought as well as a transition to George MacDonald. The quotation repeats the overall thesis on which my argument is based:

> To carry on the feelings of childhood into the powers of manhood, to combine the child's sense of wonder and novelty with the appearances which everyday for perhaps forty years has rendered familiar ... and so to represent familiar objects as to awaken the minds of others to a like freshness of sensation concerning them ... this is the prime merit of genius, and its most unequivocal mode of manifestation [Coleridge "From Biographia Literaria"].

CHAPTER TWO

The Ideal and the Shadow
George MacDonald's Phantastes

"Man is but a thought of God"—George MacDonald, *A Dish of Orts* [4]

"For the one principle of Hell is 'I am my own'"—George MacDonald, *Unspoken Sermons* [495]

"To inquire into what God has made is the main function of the imagination" (MacDonald *A Dish of Orts: Chiefly Papers on the Imagination and Shakespeare* 2). With these words, George MacDonald (1824–1905), for many the grandfather of mythopoeic fantasy, shows his considerable debt to the formulations of the imagination put forth by Samuel Taylor Coleridge. For MacDonald, the imagination is regarded as the faculty which "images" or makes a likeness of something. It is that faculty which most closely resembles the activity of God, for just as God is the primary creator, creating the universe through his power, so the artist imitates this creative act in the formation of the secondary worlds created. Agreeing with Coleridge's distinction between the imagination as offering new versions of old truths, and the fancy as mere inventiveness, MacDonald was an important figure in furthering the function of the imagination as a vehicle to apprehend the sacramental nature of the world. By embodying old truths in new forms, MacDonald was foundational for the mythopoeic artists who attempt to revise the perception of the world by infusing it with a sense of the numinous.

Although MacDonald wrote realistic novels, children's fairy tales, essays and sermons, perhaps his theories of the imagination are best realized in his two "adult" fantasies, *Phantastes* (1858) and *Lilith* (1898). A reading of either of these books reveals the extent to which MacDonald relied on the unconscious as a vehicle for the expression of God. Heavily influenced by the German Romantics, especially Novalis, MacDonald believed that "the greatest forces lie in the region of the uncomprehended," and that the closer a piece of art was to the truly dreamlike or chaotic state of mind, the closer this piece of art would mirror God's own creative impulse (*A Dish of Orts: Chiefly Papers on the Imagination and Shakespeare* 319). When these works of art embody a sense of chaos, the emphasis is placed on the emotive rather than the intellectual. MacDonald felt that fantasy was the appropriate vehicle for the chaotic, and, if a work was successful, it would elicit a certain response within the reader. As MacDonald states, "it is there not so much to convey a meaning as to wake a meaning" (*A Dish of Orts: Chiefly Papers on the Imagination and Shakespeare* 317). What MacDonald means by this statement is that images from the imagination must work unconsciously on the reader; if the art is true to its nature, it will be associative, working more like a symbol which has many potential meanings rather than a sign where meaning is limited. This lends the reader some interpretive freedom in any text, but this is the key to the imagination's workings. What "wakes" one reader might be different from what "wakes" another (as is often the case). Thus whoever really "feels" a given story will read into it only what accords with his or her own nature. One will read one meaning, while another will read something entirely different. MacDonald here espouses his theory of art: "A genuine work of art must mean many things; the truer the art, the more things it will mean" (*A Dish of Orts: Chiefly Papers on the Imagination and Shakespeare* 317).

Lest this theory of the imagination sound too decentered, MacDonald provides the reader with an analogy which is important in understanding his concept of the imagination: music. As anyone who enjoys music knows, music has an effect on the listener, not on the intellectual level but on the emotional level. A particular piece of music lends access to the feeling-oriented dimension of ourselves but, again, as in art, no two people will agree on any "meaning" a piece of music may have. MacDonald employs the analogy of the sonata to explain this difference. Although two people may have similar feelings about a piece of music, neither would agree on any meaning. As MacDonald says, "the best way with music, I imagine, is not to bring the forces of the intellect to bear upon it, but to be still and let it work on that part of us for whose sake it exists" (*A Dish of Orts: Chiefly Papers on the Imagination and Shakespeare* 321).

MacDonald's idea of music as a means of waking up meaning is one that is discussed in Otto's treatment of the numinous consciousness. Although Otto is careful to point out that musical "feelings" and the sense of the numinous are not perfectly analogous, they do share the same emotive response in the subject, both inculcating in the subject a certain disposition of mind which includes the dimension of the non-rational. For Otto, music is an effective expression of the balance between the rational and the non-rational, both mutually penetrating one another. For example, in certain musical pieces, there is the verbal text, that which expresses natural emotions such as joy or grief. On the other hand, however, there is also the emotive or non-rational aspect of music, and it is the stress of this non-rational aspect which closely allies it with the numinous. It represents the "wholly other," and is the basis of the indescribability which is both characteristic of the religious, and for this work, the mythopoeic imagination. Music, for Otto, "releases a blissful rejoicing in us, and we are conscious of a glimmering, billowy agitation occupying our minds, without being able to express or explain in concepts what it really is that moves us so deeply" (48). The indescribable nature of the feelings brought forth in music, as in the numinous consciousness, is what is central to mythopoeic fantasy's ability to recover the sacramental vision in order to revision the relationship to the natural world.

The connection, then, between the products of the imagination, or music, or the numinous, is similar. They all are emotive rather than intellectual, and the more the unconscious or non-rational is made accessible in any of these forms, the closer one may apprehend divine truth. For MacDonald, this divine truth involves knowing what a thing *is* rather than what it *means*. For example, in his *Unspoken Sermons*, MacDonald states, "to know a primrose is a higher thing than to know all the botany of it" (*Unspoken Sermons, First, Second and Third Series* 350). The function of the imagination is to provide images which are powerful in themselves, regardless of any inherent meaning. MacDonald's belief was that this state of knowing can be "awakened" by the imagination and not by mere intellect. MacDonald found this to be the case with the fairytale, music, or even nature herself: "A fairytale, a sonata, a gathering storm, a limitless night, seizes you and sweeps you away: do

Two. The Ideal and the Shadow

you begin at once to wrestle with it and ask whence its power over you, whither it is carrying you?" (*A Dish of Orts: Chiefly Papers on the Imagination and Shakespeare* 319). For MacDonald, the answer to this question would be "no."

While MacDonald's aesthetic theories of the imagination are central to the thesis that the element of wonder is the most important defining characteristic of the mythopoeic imagination, critics have also pointed out certain flaws in his theories. In his book *Modern Fantasy*, Colin Manlove argues that there are inconsistencies in MacDonald's aesthetic thinking. Manlove believes that MacDonald has "two minds over his material," an imaginative side and an intellectual side which Manlove sees as at war with one another. For example, Manlove points out that MacDonald's attempts to theorize about the nature of fairytales is in direct contradiction to his views that fairytales are meant to be incomprehensible. How can one provide a theoretical background to a genre which has as its defining characteristic that which cannot be theorized about? The problem, for Manlove, revolves around language. While Manlove argues that language may indeed have both an emotive side and a meaningful or intellectual side, he believes MacDonald would disagree. For MacDonald, the important aspect of language is its ability to allow access to the emotional dimension, and this is the function of the fairytale. However, what Manlove points out is that the fairytales themselves cannot be separated from the language element which does imply that meaning is possible. Thus, for Manlove, MacDonald's attempts to associate the fairytale with music is faulty: while music does have the ability to affect just the emotions, language by definition also affects the intellect. Manlove concludes:

> MacDonald is what one might call a would-be "exclusive" modern fantasist: he wants to have to do with the world only as a house full of mystic symbols, and with only the unconscious and imaginative side of the mind. But though he tries to shut out the conscious selves of science and law, intellect and will, they keep coming back to interrupt the proceedings [*Modern Fantasy: Five Studies* 98].

Manlove also questions the ability of mythopoeic art to offer a sacramental religious experience. If, in MacDonald's theories, the imagination is the dwelling place of God, and the products of the imagination are symbolic of the eternal (divine immanence), how does one arrive at proof of this? Are the fantasy worlds really products of God or are they merely from MacDonald's own mind? One can never be certain. On the other hand, Manlove does admit that certain images in a particular work may awaken a sense of longing (*Sehnsucht*) for heaven. In MacDonald's case, images such as jewels, flowers, and stairs are presented as manifestations of God, and Manlove concurs that, "The images in MacDonald's fantasies must thus work sacramentally and the reader may have a form of religious experience through them" (*Modern Fantasy: Five Studies* 97).

Regardless of any flaws in MacDonald's aesthetic theories, his point still has value and what is of concern here is the defining characteristic of mythopoeic fantasy, that of a sense of wonder which may be awakened so that the divine element present in the world is recovered. The fact that many of the mythopoeic authors refer to the indescribable nature of these works shows that what is more important is not particular words used but images portrayed. In his "Introduction" to *Phantastes*, the book which "baptized" his imagination, C.S. Lewis offers what he feels is the unique gift of MacDonald, one that serves as the central element of mythopoeic fantasy:

> It goes beyond the expression of things we have already felt. It arouses in us sensations we have never had before, never anticipated having, as though we had broken out of our normal mode of consciousness and "possessed" joys not promised to our birth: it gets under our skin, hits us at a level deeper than our thoughts or even our passion, troubles oldest certainties till all questions are reopened, and in general shocks us more fully awake than we are for most of our lives ["Introduction" xi].

MacDonald's theories of the imagination have interesting consequences for the thesis that mythopoeic fantasy attempts to "revise" reality, as Kathryn Hume might express it. As with other fantasy authors, MacDonald's fantasies were not attempts to "escape" reality, but by emphasizing the emotive aspects of the genre, he was asking readers to look deeply into his world to realize the eternal through the temporal or, as he says, to think things "as God thinks them" (*A Dish of Orts: Chiefly Papers on the Imagination and Shakespeare* 27). The only proper vehicle for seeing the eternal through the temporal is the imagination, which for MacDonald is the best guide one may have:

> For it is not the things we see the most clearly that influence us the most powerfully; undefined, yet vivid visions of something beyond, something which eye has not seen nor ear heard, have far more influence than any log-

Two. The Ideal and the Shadow

ical sequences whereby the same things may be demonstrated by the intellect [*A Dish of Orts: Chiefly Papers on the Imagination and Shakespeare* 28].

This view of the eternal working through the temporal is one developed by Coleridge and shared with Lewis and Tolkien; it is the worldview which posits a combination of two types of reality, one material and one mystical, neither of which may fully account for the full scope of reality. Thus fantasy becomes an important means whereby these two realities may intersect, and, according to Stephen Prickett in his book *Victorian Fantasy*, MacDonald shows his debt to the Platonic tradition: "MacDonald is a temperamental Platonist, only interested in the surface of this world for the news it gives him of another, hidden reality, perceived, as it were, in a glass darkly" (193).

In order for the eternal to be perceived through the temporal, an act of imagination is required. For MacDonald, this was the primary function of art, to provide the reader with a means of experiencing these realities. Just as Coleridge thought that our sensibilities were dulled by the "lethargy of custom," so MacDonald thought that the boredom of everyday life could bar us from seeing the world sacramentally. For MacDonald, as with our other mythopoeic authors, art was the means whereby the sacramental vision could be awakened. This theory of art is clearly illustrated in a passage from MacDonald's *Phantastes* and deserves to be quoted in full:

> But is it not rather that art rescues nature from the weary and sated regards of our senses, and the degrading injustice of our anxious every-day life, and, appealing to the imagination, which dwells apart, reveals nature in some degree as she really is, and as she represents herself to the eye of the child, whose every-day life, fearless and unambitious, meets the true import of the wonder-teeming world around him and rejoices therein without questioning? [*Phantastes* 89–90].

Whether it is Coleridge's "lethargy of custom" or MacDonald's "weary and sated regards," what these authors share is a recognition of the way normative modes of perception limit the possibility of seeing the religious dimension which underlies the mundane world. This view is shared with Lewis and Tolkien, the latter formulating his own response to this dilemma in his argument for "recovery" as the main function of fantasy literature. As discussed in the introduction, Tolkien argued that as reality is "appropriated," we run the risk of knowing our world too well, and once the world is intellectualized, that childlike sense of wonder, which is the defining element of mythopoeic fantasy, is lost. In the view of MacDonald, the ideal reader for fantasy is one who may recover the childlike wonder of the world, the vision which allows one the ability to perceive the numinous.

It is also worth noting that MacDonald refers to this act of the imagination as having the ability to reveal nature "as she really is." It is here that MacDonald's aesthetic theories intersect with concerns for the environment. In his essay "The Imagination" in *A Dish of Orts*, MacDonald discusses the culture of imagination which he argues "must be an ordering of life towards harmony with its ideal in the mind of God" (*A Dish of Orts: Chiefly Papers on the Imagination and Shakespeare* 36). For MacDonald, his Christian ideology, infused as it is with Romanticism, reveals an immanent idea of God. One who is in harmony with nature is really one who is searching out the things of God. Again, this form of "knowing" nature is not an intellectual pursuit; instead, it is an emotive response to the natural world which engenders a certain feeling of wonder which is, according to such critics as Attebery, Manlove, and Tolkien, the defining element. This notion of the mood-engendering ability of nature is one which MacDonald believed was shared both with music and fairytales. Since nature does not just wake one thought but many, so must the fairytale in its dreamlike and chaotic images awaken many meanings. Thus for MacDonald, the less the intellect has a part in the act of perceiving, whether it be in nature or art, the more one comes closer to perceiving the numinous. Again, this is the highest function of art, to wake readers into an awareness of the numinous so the world may be revisioned. As MacDonald states, "the best thing you can do for your fellow, next to rousing his conscience, is—not to give him things to think about, but to wake things up that are in him" (*A Dish of Orts: Chiefly Papers on the Imagination and Shakespeare* 319).

It is interesting to note that the basis for MacDonald's aesthetic theories, the idea of the imagination's ability to wake up meaning, parallels Otto's discussion of the numinous consciousness. Otto defines the numen as that sense of the holy minus both its moral component and its rational component. It evokes an original feeling-oriented response which is only later associated with the moral and rational. However, as Otto states throughout his book, this numinous consciousness cannot be taught but must be "awakened from the spirit" (60). This is different from the moral dimension of religion which may be passed down from

Two. The Ideal and the Shadow

generation to generation: "what is incapable of being so handed down is this numinous basis and background to religion, which can only be induced, incited, and aroused" (Otto 60). One may wonder how this process of awakening, both for MacDonald and Otto, may be achieved. For MacDonald, it is achieved through the imagination as a means of engaging the unconscious. For Otto, it is achieved through the use of associated feelings. For example, if one posits the numinous as experience X, then one may compare and contrast this feeling with others to arrive at an understanding of what experience X really is: "In other words our X cannot, strictly speaking, be taught, it can only be evoked, awakened in the mind; as everything that comes 'of the spirit' must be awakened" (7).

One of the clearest examples of MacDonald's aesthetic theories of waking up what Otto would call the numinous consciousness is in *Phantastes*. The book traces the journey of Anodos (Greek for "pathless") through fairyland, a journey through which he must learn to let go of his ego, which seeks to possess, in order to experience the numinous. Following MacDonald's own theories that a fairytale must offer up dreamlike images directly from the unconscious, which he believed was the dwelling-place of God, the book contains episodes which are largely chaotic in themselves, at times even containing stories within stories. However, as Colin Manlove has pointed out, although *Phantastes* is the most disconnected of all of MacDonald's novels, it is bound by two connected themes which relate to the present study: the Ideal, which Anodos awakens and pursues throughout the book, and the Shadow, which Anodos acquires in a cottage inhabited by an ogress. Both of these themes relate to a reawakening of the numinous consciousness for a revisioning of the relationship to the natural world.

As Manlove argues, these themes revolve around possessiveness. The quest for the Ideal in the form of the White Lady (which is a surrogate for the divine presence modeled after Novalis's Sophie) leads Anodos to an over-reliance on the self or ego which, in turn, dissociates him from an experience of the numinous; similarly, the shadow which Anodos acquires is that projected aspect of himself which dissociates him from an experience of wonder, which is the defining aspect of mythopoeic fantasy. In effect then, both the Ideal and the Shadow must be given up in order for Anodos to experience the numinous consciousness. This sacrificing of the self or ego in order to facilitate an experience of the numinous is part of what connects MacDonald to Coleridge, since the death of the self was present in MacDonald's own theories as well as his predecessor's. As he states in his *Unspoken Sermons*, "the one principle of Hell is—'I am my own'" (*Unspoken Sermons, First, Second and Third Series* 495). As with Coleridge, this clinging to the ego is what keeps us from experiencing that which is beyond words. So, although Coleridge is considered a Romantic and MacDonald is considered a Victorian, both these authors express a distrust of empiricist or rationalist modes of thought. In their theories as well as their works, these authors look to another source of truth, that of the unconscious, which leads to the reawakening of the numinous.

The Ideal

In MacDonald's fantastic fiction, female characters often are means for male characters to achieve a higher spiritual state. Usually in the form of a wise old woman (Grandmother) or a form of ideal beauty with whom the male character must be initiated, these figures are feminine aspects of divinity, and the main hero must encounter this female in order to experience the numinous. One of the clearest cases for a progressive acceptance of the numinous is in the figure of the Ideal in *Phantastes*. In this theme, the hero, Anodos, pursues an ideal woman with whom he has fallen in love and, because of his love for her, he quests through three stages of love which are connected to Romantic Love and a form of love-death. The three stages are possessiveness, self-denial, and union upon death. Anodos must journey through these stages in order for a recovery of the numinous consciousness and a subsequent revisioning of the relationship to the natural world.

In *The Nature of Love*, Irving Singer describes Romantic Love as love which transforms selfish desires into an unselfish oneness. This unselfish oneness is viewed as a oneness with the divine presence in the form of a female. Although this love has its expression in the works of such figures as Keats, Shelley and Blake, its origins can be traced even further back in time. From Plato and the Neoplatonists, Romantic Love valued a purity which transcended sexual relationships; from Christianity, especially in the form of ecstatic mysticism, it inherited an interpersonal love which allowed one to participate in divinity; and, from

Two. The Ideal and the Shadow

Courtly Love, it borrowed the idea that the relationship between a man and woman is comparable to religious love (Singer 283). The combination of these elements into Romantic Love allowed the lover to awaken a desire for the beloved which was primarily based on feeling rather than reason and would lead the lover to an experience of the numinous.

One important feature of Romantic Love, which was especially important to Keats and Blake, was the connection between imagination and the desire for oneness. For example, Blake believed that God and man existed within each other, as well as in the world, and this oneness could only be experienced through an act of the imagination. Blake states that "through the imagination we participate in God's being as the creator of such unity" (Singer 287). This transformation occurs through a process of "sympathetic identification," where one identifies with another in the process of love and, at the same time, perceives the unity behind the appearance of the two people, as well as the unity of all things.

A key concept in this expression of unity is merging. Whether it is merging with another person, nature or God, these aspects all imply a merging into the totality of being. Since Romantic Love is a "metaphysical craving for unity," this unity can be reached through a variety of vehicles (Singer 288). Once the merging has occurred, and the unity experienced, all sense of ego is dissolved. To realize the nature of divinity present in all things is to realize that one is not an individual who is separate from the world but one who is combined into the totality of everything. It is through love that one loses this sense of self and merges into another. Love is the impetus for this experience of unity and, according to Singer, "Romantic Love—whether it is religious or secular, involving man and God or just human beings—finds its divinity in the act of loving" (293).

An important sub-mode of Romantic Love is its connection with the theme of love-death, a form of love reflected in the writings of Goethe, Novalis, and many other of the German Romantics. In contrast to Romantic Love, where the lovers are granted union, love-death affirms the position that a true union can only occur in death. In this view, death is seen as a superior state, and it is through death that an awareness of unity is comprehended. According to Singer, "The two lovers will consummate their love for one another after death in a way that nothing on earth can equal" (443).

It is significant that one of the main proponents of this type of love is the German author Novalis, a major influence on the thought of George MacDonald. For Novalis, everything experienced sensuously, whether it is nature or a human being, is a manifestation of divine love. He experienced this love with a thirteen year old girl named Sophie, who tragically died two years after they met. In his poem *Hymns to the Night*, Novalis "portrays Sophie as an emanation from God, and he celebrates the phenomenon of death as the goal for which all life has been created" (Singer 442). In MacDonald's *Phantastes*, this theme of love-death, set within the broader aspects of Romantic Love, is effectively painted in the love of Anodos for his ideal beauty.

It is difficult to summarize the plot of *Phantastes* due to its dreamlike structure. MacDonald believed that "The greatest forces lie in the region of the uncomprehended," and that true fantasy should be fundamentally chaotic with only a small surface level of coherence (*A Dish of Orts: Chiefly Papers on the Imagination and Shakespeare* 319). Thus both of his adult fantasies, *Phantastes* and *Lilith*, are filled with surrealist motifs, and the novels are more streams of chaotic images than structures containing plot lines. In *Phantastes*, the hero Anodos wakes up one morning to find that his room has transformed into Fairyland. As Manlove states, this transformation highlights MacDonald's presentation of fairyland as a projection of a different mode of reality, a "change from one mode of being to another, mirroring the collapse of the empirical mode of presentation and entry into the unconscious mind and the world it perceives" ("The Circle of the Imagination: George Macdonald's *Phantastes* and *Lilith*" 60). On his journey further into fairyland, Anodos enters a cave, and it is here that he discovers and wakens a beautiful woman in a marble tomb whom he desires to possess. She flees from him, and throughout the novel, in various adventures, sometimes adventures within adventures, Anodos pursues his "marble lady" in order to experience a love which will ultimately lead him to a higher spirituality.

The first form of love Anodos embodies is extremely possessive, a love opposite the goal of Romantic Love. Before he enters Fairyland, a small figure resembling a Greek statue appears from a cubby hole within a secretary to tell Anodos of his upcoming quest. After the figure transforms into a life-sized woman, Anodos is overtaken with the desire to possess her and reaches out to embrace her. She rebukes his advances, stating that she is actually two hundred and thirty seven years old and implying that she is his grandmother. Rolland Hein, in his book *The Harmony Within*, points out that the episode reflects Anodos's confusion between two types of desire: sexual desire (which he is now pursuing), and a joyous desire for an experience in a supernatural world (which he should be pursuing) (58). Since Anodos is in a low spiritual state, he does not see his potential for spiritual growth which contact with Fairyland can fulfill. Instead, he acts upon base sexuality which shows that the trip into Fairyland might be beneficial.

Once inside Fairyland, Anodos has experiences which further show that his love at this state is possessive. He is hunted early on in the novel by an evil ash tree who represents an all-consuming, possessive desire, and who wants to destroy Anodos. Just as he is about to be overtaken by the ash, he falls at the foot of a beech tree, which transforms into a woman, embracing and protecting Anodos from the evil ash. Through rescuing Anodos, the beech tree represents the opposite of the ash's possessiveness. She gives of herself to protect Anodos and, even though she loves him, lets him continue on his quest. These two trees, the ash and the beech, reflect the dichotomy of the two loves present in the novel: the selfish and the selfless. They also symbolize the potentials at war within Anodos's self. What Anodos does not realize at this point is that the beech tree, which values loving rather than being loved, is the spiritual goal which Anodos seeks.

When Anodos enters into a cave and discovers a lady encased in marble, he states, "What I did see appeared to me perfectly lovely; more near the face that had been born with me in my soul, than anything I had seen before in nature or art" (MacDonald *Phantastes* 36). He sings a song which is effective in releasing the marble lady, but she immediately flees from Anodos and continues her journey in Fairyland. Anodos feels that his power to awaken the marble lady is a part of his imaginative act to bring her to life, and his possessive love for her leads to his referring to her as "my lost lady of the marble" (MacDonald *Phantastes* 42).

In discussing the role of ideal beauty in *Phantastes*, Rolland Hein states, "The marble lady appears to symbolize the spirit of the Ideal, or the Perfect, and, as such, is in MacDonald's thought a surrogate for the divine Presence" (61). This idea is equated to the function of Romantic Love, in which the beloved represents a part of the lover, as well as a divine source, where all must be unified into a totality. However, as

Anodos continues on his quest, he cannot experience this totality because of his egotistic desire to possess the marble lady. In fact, this mode of love is present throughout most of the novel, and Anodos continuously sees her only as property, not a path to an experience of the numinous. What Anodos fails to realize is that true merging can only occur when the ego is denied, and the love is giving rather than taking in nature.

One of the first insights readers get in relation to MacDonald's vision of true Romantic Love, where one must die to the self, is in a story Anodos reads in the Fairy Palace. It must be remembered that MacDonald's fantasies often employ stories within stories and, in this case, what Anodos reads is, in a dream-like fashion, somewhat related to his own quest.

The story he reads centers around a figure named Cosmo, a university student who has a fascination with magic and the occult. While helping a friend judge the value of an old suit of armor in a store, Cosmo is overtaken by a desire to possess an old mirror which happens to be in the corner. He purchases the mirror and, upon taking it home, notices that at certain times of the day, a beautiful woman appears within it. This, again, is the theme of the ideal beauty, but what is revealed is an alternative form of loving. Through the suggestion of the lady in the mirror, Cosmo learns that he cannot truly love her until she is freed from the enchantment of the mirror. He is told to break the mirror at the risk of never seeing his ideal again. After much inner conflict, Cosmo finally breaks the mirror, and after subsequent adventures ends up dying in his lady's arms.

What occurs within the story is an act of renunciation, where in order to love his ideal, Cosmo must break the mirror. There is a love-death element present as Cosmo must destroy the image in order to gain a deeper love based in reality; also, he must literally die for his love at the end of the story. Thus, here, if one reads the psychological dimensions of the novel and its dream imagery, Cosmo's tale represents a similar potential as that of the two trees: a growing awareness in Anodos of a new form of love, one that is not possessive and dominating, but one which is self-denying.

This form of love which is self-denying, and connected with the Romantic love-death ideal, was present in George MacDonald's life. Viewing fantasy as an inner projection of unconscious thoughts, it is

Two. The Ideal and the Shadow

easy to see the figure of Anodos as a projection of MacDonald's own unconscious self. In a letter to his wife Louisa, he wrote: "Is love a beautiful thing? You and I love but who created love? Let us ask him to purify our love to make it more real and more self-denying" ("To Louisa Powell" 26). It was only through this self-denial that MacDonald believed that one could experience God. In fact, it is so self-denying that MacDonald often used the terms of death to convey a sense of it. In writing on what is called "daily death," he says, "We die daily. Happy those who daily come to life as well" (Lewis *George MacDonald: 365 Readings* 121). This view is also present in the Cosmo story. In the middle of the narrative, added in separately as an independent thought, it states: "Who lives, he dies; who dies, he lives" (MacDonald *Phantastes* 95). These various references to death reflect MacDonald's view that to love another is to die to the self, and it is through death that one can experience the unity of God and the world.

Upon completion of the Cosmo tale in the Fairy Palace, Anodos still has not learned the advantage of self-giving love. In fact, when he sees his marble lady again as a statue on a pedestal, many of the earlier episodes are replayed. He tries to bring her to life again with his songs and, upon his success, tries again to grasp her. She flees from him, only to be pursued through the Faerian landscape. When Anodos's attempts to capture her fail, he jumps from a rocky promontory in a suicide attempt. However, as he becomes submerged in the water, he experiences a new sense of joy. The reference to water is one of the clues that symbolizes Anodos's changing attitudes. In MacDonald's work, as well as in universal symbolism, water represents death and rebirth. More specifically, it symbolizes Anodos's loss of ego, which has, up to this point, dominated his possessive love for the ideal. Now that Anodos has experienced this loss of ego, he can fully learn the joy of a self-denying love.

For MacDonald, this self-denying love is best realized and employed in action. After Anodos survives his suicidal sea episode, he finds a cottage which is inhabited by a wise old woman. In her cottage she has four mysterious doors, all of which lead Anodos to some aspect of his former life. One of the most important doors is the door of sighs, where Anodos learns that the marble lady whom he has been pursuing is in love with a knight, Sir Percival, and the best course of action that Anodos can follow is to learn to serve his marble lady and release her. After this lesson is learned, Anodos returns to the cottage where the old woman tells him that he must go and do something worthwhile.

Now that Anodos has realized the importance of being humble and serving his lady, he sets out on many quests to prove his service. He helps two knights destroy giants who are plaguing their town, helps a girl destroy wooden men who keep her from finding her way home, and he saves sacrificial victims in a forest church service. This latter adventure is of the most importance because Anodos gives up his life for others. He dresses as one of the sacrificial victims and walks to the altar where he had witnessed the others disappear. He destroys one of the religious images and, as a result, a huge monstrous brute emerges from where it stood. After a fight, both the creature and Anodos die.

This episode clearly connects *Phantastes* with the love-death component of Romantic Love. What Anodos discovers is that death is a joyous event, and he becomes one with nature. After being buried, he states, "Now that I lay in her bosom, the whole earth, and each of her many births, was as a body to me, at my will. I seemed to feel the great heart of the mother beating into mine, and feeling one with her own life, her own essential being and nature" (MacDonald *Phantastes* 181). It is only after this literal death that Anodos has a connection with the earth. He has undergone a transformation similar to what Bonnie Gaarden describes as the Romantic spiral journey, a sort of "ethical evolution." Within this spiral journey, there is an original unity which is lost once the ego separates from what is non-ego, mirroring the dissociative process between the human and non-human. The final goal, however, is the achievement of this original unity on a much higher, spiritual level (Gaarden 6). This is the journey undertaken by the Mariner in Coleridge's poem as well. Referring to this process as a form of Christian pantheism, Gaarden says, "God's heart expressed in nature communicates to man's heart more significant truth about deity than any doctrinal system could possibly convey to the intellect" (6). It is this movement from unity to dis-unity and to a higher unity which Anodos undergoes, and it is this process which gains him access to the numinous and allows him a revisioning of his relationship with nature. In fact, in one of his transformations, he becomes a primrose in his marble lady's garden, and when she notices its beauty, she plucks it and gives it a kiss. Anodos realizes that death has brought him closer to his love than in life. In the

Two. The Ideal and the Shadow

most important passage in the book, Anodos verbalizes what he has learned in his Fairyland quest:

> I knew now, that it is by loving, and not by being loved, that one can come nearest the soul of another; yea, that, when two love, it is the loving of each other, and not the being beloved by each other, that originates and perfects and assures their blessedness. I knew that love gives to him that loveth, power over any soul beloved, even if that soul love him not, bringing him inwardly close to that spirit; a power that cannot be but for good; for in proportion as selfishness intrudes, the love ceases, and the power which springs therefrom dies. Yet all love will, one day, meet with its return. All true love will, one day, behold its own image in the eyes of the beloved, and be humbly glad. This is possible in the realms of lofty death [MacDonald *Phantastes* 181].

These final episodes, and this final speech on love, highlight important aspects of the love-death relationship in Romantic Love. In Romantic Love, as noted earlier, the emphasis is on merging, either between two lovers or with nature or God. Whatever one merges with involves a unity which is experienced between all things. Thus love acts only as a vehicle to achieve this higher sensibility. In Anodos's case, he merges with nature and, through it, realizes the oneness of the world. Because he must die in order for the merging to occur, the death imagery employed by MacDonald cannot be overemphasized. Death is not a negative state but one in which humans have the ability to realize what is higher than the finite self. It is a state which brings one closer to nature, to God and closer to the beloved. For followers of the love-death tradition, it is only in death that a true consummation occurs. This value of death is portrayed in MacDonald's text as well. Anodos anticipates the day when the death of his beloved will reunite him with her on another level.

Phantastes shows a continuous progression of love through the character of Anodos. He begins his adventures with a possessive love which reflects his physical needs. As his adventure continues, he realizes that true love can only come through a death of self, where claims to possession are supplanted by a joy only experienced by serving another. As the old woman in the cottage sings, it is better to be a well giving water than an impure cistern only receiving for itself.

Many critics have pointed out the heavy emphasis on female figures within *Phantastes*. In fact, the form of love MacDonald advocates through Anodos's quest for the Ideal is equated with feminine thought. In his essay "*Phantastes* and *Lilith*: Femininity and Freedom," Roderick McGillis states, "Feminine thinking takes us out of the self and into the joy of participating in all things" (40). This is exactly the love-death component of Romantic Love. Through loving the woman in all her fantastic forms in the novel, Anodos leaves the possessive side of himself for a love that is humble, serving and connected to God. Critic Colin Manlove argues that the theme connected with females is the renunciation of the mother figure, where to achieve unity within the divine, as well as unity with the earth, the female must be removed. Thus the final union with nature is brought about only by Anodos's willingness to give up his quest for the Ideal. However, it is this act of renunciation which allows Anodos to sacrifice his life for others and upon his literal death, "he enters that higher childhood of union with earth, of solid self with solid self, which the earlier mothers have in part prefigured" (Manlove "The Circle of the Imagination: George Macdonald's *Phantastes* and *Lilith*" 66). So, whether it is his Ideal, or the beech tree, or the wise woman of the four-square cottage, these images of the female culminate with the final encounter with the ultimate mother, mother earth.

However, final death is not to be Anodos's lot. In the last chapter of the book, Anodos awakens back to an earthly existence and finds that he has left fairyland behind. He returns to his castle and the love of his sisters, but he is still haunted by his strange experiences in fairyland. He doubts whether his adventures may be translated into common life. From time to time though, he thinks of his adventures, and even looks about for the mystical red sign, which he believes will lead him back to the four-square cottage upon his final death. The last image readers are presented with is Anodos lying underneath the shadow of a beech tree, resting. He hears a faint voice which tells him, "A great good is coming- is coming-is coming to thee, Anodos" (MacDonald *Phantastes* 185). He opens his eyes and fancies he sees the old woman from the four-square cottage speaking to him through the trees. It is these images of the mother which conclude the novel: "All images of motherhood: the earth, the beech tree, and the wise woman herself come together harmoniously at the end of life" (Wolff 108).

The Shadow

The second figure related to the theme of possessiveness is the Shadow. Midway through his pursuit of his Ideal, Anodos comes to a

Two. The Ideal and the Shadow

small hut inhabited by an old woman. Entering her hut, he finds her reading from a book certain stanzas which deal with the theme of darkness. Anodos's curiosity is activated when he sees a cupboard in the hut, and he immediately decides that he will look in it. When he approaches it, the woman, without looking up from her book, voices her prohibition: "You had better not open that door" (MacDonald *Phantastes* 56). However, as in the typical folktale motif "the forbidden thing," Anodos opens the cupboard, despite her warning. After noticing a few household tools, he sees that the back of the cupboard opens up onto the night sky. He sees a dark figure, a sort of shadow, running towards him. It immediately enters the hut, but Anodos is unaware of its exact location. He asks the shadow's whereabouts and the lady responds, "there on the floor, behind you" (MacDonald *Phantastes* 57). Anodos is perplexed as to the nature of the shadow, and why it is attached to himself. Upon asking the lady its meaning, she states, "It is only your shadow that has found you ... everybody's shadow is ranging up and down looking for him" (MacDonald *Phantastes* 57). As Anodos leaves the hut, he realizes the lady is an ogress, and he knows his shadow will have a negative effect on his subsequent adventures in fairyland.

The effects of the shadow are detailed, for the most part, in chapter eight of the book and require full attention because it is here that MacDonald's emphasis on the theme of wonder, which is the characteristic of mythopoeic fantasy, is fully developed. The first two incidents which involve the shadow relate to its ability to affect nature. Upon awakening from a rest, Anodos notices that although the flowers he had lain upon were down-trodden, the ones on which his shadow fell were "scorched," "shriveled," "dead," and "hopeless of any resurrection" (MacDonald *Phantastes* 59). In a similar manner, when the shadow actually moves to a position in front of Anodos, it shoots forth rays of darkness and "wherever a ray struck, that part of the earth, or sea, or sky, became void, and desert, and sad to my heart" (MacDonald *Phantastes* 59). Given MacDonald's emphasis on the imagination's ability to perceive nature "as she is," as a manifestation of the numinous, the shadow is that part of ourselves which cuts us off from any experience of the beauties of the natural world.

That the shadow destroys wonder is evident in Anodos's encounters with others as well. In one encounter, he sees a fairychild who has two toys which are described in the following manner: "The one was the tube through which the fairy-gifted poet looks when he beholds the same thing everywhere; the other that through which he looks when he combines into new forms of loveliness those images of beauty which his own choice has gathered from all regions wherein he has traveled" (MacDonald *Phantastes* 59). The description of these toys is largely reminiscent of MacDonald's own theories concerning the imagination, especially as it relates to the numinous. Beholding "the same thing everywhere" is the ability of the imaginative mind to perceive the eternal behind the temporal, while combining "into new forms of loveliness" mirrors MacDonald's Coleridgean views of the imagination's ability to create new forms. However, what is of interest is that once Anodos realizes the nature of these toys, the shadow embraces the fairychild, who then becomes a mere "commonplace boy, with a rough broad-brimmed straw hat" whose toys now become a multiplying glass and a kaleidoscope (MacDonald *Phantastes* 60). Again, the shadow's function is to destroy the imaginative wonder by which the world may be perceived in its most sacred manner.

What is perhaps the most interesting is that, during the course of these encounters with the shadow (and there are more), Anodos begins to welcome its disenchanting power. He states, "I will not see beauty where there is none. I will dare to behold things as they are. And if I live in a wasteland instead of a paradise, I will live knowing where I live" (MacDonald *Phantastes* 61). As many critics have pointed out, the shadow, by denying the central element of wonder, represents an intellectual or materialistic mode of perception. Its function is to destroy any numinous perception of the world and appropriate reality so that it is "known," thus negating any possibility of recovery or revision within the context of the sacramental vision. As R.L. Wolff points out in *The Golden Key*, "The shadow represents pessimistic and cynical disillusionment, the worldly wiseness that destroys beauty, childish and naive pleasures, the delight of friendship and love; it is a foe of innocence, of openness, of optimism, of the imagination" (67). It is this shadow which Anodos must lose.

There is one more important episode with the shadow which is relevant to the thesis of the shadow's ability to dissociate from the numinous: his encounter with the maiden with the crystal globe. In this encounter, Anodos travels for three days with a maiden who has a crystal globe as her playtoy. As with the previous episode with the ogress of the

Two. The Ideal and the Shadow

hut, the maiden voices her prohibition concerning the globe: "you must not touch it, or if you do, it must be very gently" (MacDonald *Phantastes* 61). Again, Anodos's curiosity proves too much. He touches the globe which then emits a sweet sound, increasing to a low harmony as he continues to touch the globe. Eventually, however, the shadow reappears and enwraps the maiden along with her globe. Although the shadow has no power to change the maiden, as with the "commonplace boy," it implants within Anodos an irresistible desire to touch the globe again, this time with disastrous results: the globe bursts and emits a black vapor which descends over both the maiden and the shadow. Distraught, the maiden picks up the fragments of the globe and escapes into the forest. All Anodos is left with are her parting words, "you have broken my globe!" (MacDonald *Phantastes* 62).

This episode is important for the present thesis because when Anodos meets the maiden in a subsequent chapter, he learns the most important lesson concerning the perception of the numinous: the death of the self. The shadow does show up in other places in the text, for example in his adventures in the fairy palace; however, it is Anodos's imprisonment in the tower which directly relates to the theme of the death of the self. After he encounters the lady of the four-square cottage who tells him, "Go, my son, and do something worth doing," Anodos comes upon two brothers who are preparing to wage a battle with three giants who are threatening their country (MacDonald *Phantastes* 144). Anodos proves to be the third knight prophesied for battle and, after much preparation, the three knights meet and battle the three giants. Unfortunately, the two brothers are killed in the battle but not until they have successfully killed two of the giants. The last giant Anodos kills, and when his pride surfaces as the result of his victory, the shadow appears again.

It is here that the shadow comes to represent Anodos's own pride and over-reliance on the ego, and it is this that dissociates him from any experience of the numinous. After defeating the giants, Anodos compares himself with the great knights of old, specifically Galahad, and as he travels through the forest, his pride increases. He then encounters a knight who has the same armor and the same horse as himself. The knight has power over Anodos and commands him to follow. As they approach an isolated tower, Anodos realizes the connection between the knight and his own shadow: "I had a terrible conviction that the knight and he were one" (MacDonald *Phantastes* 161). As Anodos enters the tower, he notices that the knight and horse have disappeared only to be replaced by the shadow which enters the tower with him. Critic R.L. Wolff notices here a change in the nature of the shadow: "the shadow, which began as the intellectual skepticism that withers the imagination, and which later becomes conscience or consciousness of self, has now become personal pride, or a misconception of one's true role in the world" (103). Whether the shadow destroys wonder or mirrors Anodos's own pride, it is MacDonald's symbol for that which bars any recovery of the sacramental vision.

Imprisoned within the tower, Anodos notices the strange properties of his dwelling: when night comes, the walls of his prison vanish and he imagines himself free, while upon the coming of light, he is once again confined to his prison. After many days and nights, Anodos finally hears a sweet song outside his prison walls. When the song is completed, Anodos opens the door to his prison and realizes he was free to leave at any point. Upon leaving, he learns that his deliverer is none other than the maiden with the crystal globe. Apparently, the song brings Anodos to an epiphany because he realizes his pride and vows to be humble and lowly, to be a mere doer of his deeds. As Keith Wilson points out in his article "The Quest for 'the Truth,'" "The girl's song invites Anodos to come from his house of pride and be united with the spirit of the earth: he must lose the overwhelming sense of self and submit himself to a benevolent cosmic force" (150).

This loss of a sense of self comes to Anodos when he realizes the delight in being lowly, stating, "I am what I am, nothing more" (MacDonald *Phantastes* 166). Upon this revelation, the shadow finally disappears. Thus the shadow has come to represent, symbolically, the disillusionment which prevents one from the recovery of the numinous in order for the revisioning of the world within the context of the sacramental vision. As Wilson further points out, the shadow "shackles him to the mundane" and "If the shadow is the foe of all delight in the natural, it is also the foe of God" (147). Once Anodos realizes he had lost his shadow, and that it is best to be humbled and lowly, he knows that with this 'death of the self' he can open to the possibility of an experience of something higher, that of the numinous. He reflects, "Self will come to life even in the slaying of the self; but there is ever something deeper and stronger than it, which will emerge at last from the unknown abysses of the soul: will it be as a solemn gloom, burning with eyes? or a clear morning after the rain? or a smiling child, that finds itself nowhere, and everywhere?" (MacDonald *Phantastes* 166).

The reference to the "slaying of the self" is what underlies the entire myth of *Phantastes*, incorporating both the theme of the Ideal and the Shadow. If these two themes revolve around possessiveness, as Manlove argues, then MacDonald's thesis posits that it is only this possessiveness that keeps one from the experience of the numinous and the subsequent revisioning of the natural world. The "death of the self" is also analyzed by Otto in his discussion of the *mysterium tremendum*. In contrast to the feeling of *majestas*, or "absolute overpoweringness," the subject feels its own nothingness in the face of this overwhelming power, and this feeling inculcates religious humility. By contrasting what he terms "consciousness of createdness," the focus on the creature as being created, with the "consciousness of creaturehood," the focus on the nothingness of the creature, Otto posits that the latter is the most effective in emphasizing the superiority of a power other than the subject. This consciousness is akin to various forms of mysticism and stresses two foci paramount to our present thesis: the annihilation of the self, and its complement, the emphasis on the transcendent as the sole reality (Otto 21).

This annihilation of the self and the stress on the transcendent unite both MacDonald and Coleridge's mythopoeic visions. Through their works, the main characters only recover a sense of the numinous when they dissolve their separate selves and see a transcendent reality over and above the mundane. In a parallel manner, it is the loss of the self which brings about the revisioning of the natural world and a participation in the numinous. Both the Mariner and Anodos are on unique quests, to gain identities which reflect a higher sense of spirituality. As Roderick McGillis states of *Phantastes*, "the quest for identity is a quest for continuous becoming, not to imprint the self on the world, but to achieve that joy which is a going out of the self" (31).

Keith Wilson argues that George MacDonald is "the most apocalyptic of Victorian fantasists," reasoning that the fundamental myth underlying *Phantastes* is *via negationis*, "the discovery of God or reality by the progressive stripping away of the veils of illusion" (141). (Wilson employs the term "apocalyptic" in its technical sense of "revealing" or "unveiling.") This is an accurate statement and is easily applicable to the authors considered in the present study, although their means of projecting these apocalyptic visions differ. For Coleridge and MacDonald, the discovery of God or reality is achieved through an annihilation of the self, and it is the overemphasis on the ego which keeps one from the recovery of the numinous consciousness. It is also that clinging to the ego which dissociates one from total participation in the environment. This is precisely the thesis argued by Neil Evernden, that the Western stress on the ego denies interrelatedness and fails to recover or revise our original relationship to the natural world. For C.S. Lewis and J.R.R. Tolkien, on the other hand, our original relationship to the natural world is not to be recovered by any annihilation of the self. Their books offer the reader apocalyptic visions on a more epic scale. It is not a transcendence of the self which gives access to the numinous, but a transcendence of the entire world. Finally, it is not *here* in nature where the numinous resides. It is elsewhere.

CHAPTER THREE

"Further Up and Further In"
Apocalypse and the New Narnia in C.S. Lewis's The Last Battle

"I think that all things, in their way, reflect heavenly truth, the imagination not least"—C.S. Lewis, *Surprised by Joy* [167]

"The goal of world destruction is world creation"—Eric Rabkin, "Why Destroy the World?" [xv]

In his review of Tolkien's *The Lord of the Rings*, C.S. Lewis (1898–1963) states, "If you are tired of the real landscape, look at it in a mirror" (*On Stories and Other Essays on Literature* 90). As discussed in the previous chapter on MacDonald, mirrors are often employed by authors to highlight what is, for the present study, the defining element of mythopoeic fantasy: the experience of the numinous as a means of revisioning our relationship to the natural world. By looking at an object in a mirror, we are viewing the same object, but in a slightly different way. Similarly, the author of a mythopoeic fantasy is drawing upon constructs presented in the "real" world, but at the same time "departing" from this reality to offer the reader a fresher, more sacred way of perceiving our ordinary world. The experience of this new form of perception aids in giving its readers a "rich significance" to what both Lewis and Tolkien argued is hidden by the "veil of familiarity." Contrary to the popular criticism of fantasy as a form of "escapism," this mythopoeic literature offers a unique way of participating in reality. As with myth, in this form of literature, "we do not retreat from reality: we rediscover it" (Lewis *On Stories and Other Essays on Literature* 90).

In fact, the common theme throughout much of Lewis's essays, particularly in *On Stories and Other Essays on Literature*, is this sense of the "experience" which mythopoeic fantasy offers, an experience which is not found in other, more mimetic works. As Lewis discovered while reading many of the works of MacDonald (*Phantastes*, for instance, "baptized" his imagination), the whole function of art is to present to the reader this experience which the more narrow ways of perceiving reality exclude. Commenting on this experience in such books as *Phantastes*, *Lilith*, and "The Golden Key," Lewis states, "They give, like certain rare dreams, sensations we have never had before and enlarge our conception of the range of possible experience" (*On Stories and Other Essays on Literature* 66). For Lewis, the specific form of literature which embraced this experience was the fairy tale. By its simple plot and characterization, the fairy tale acts as a net in which to catch something greater:

> In life and art both, as it seems to me, we are always trying to catch in our net of successive moments something that is not successive. Whether in real life there is any doctor who can teach us how to do it, so that at last either the meshes will become fine enough to hold the bird, or we be so changed that we can throw our nets away and follow the bird to its own country, is not a question for this essay. But I think it is sometimes done—or very, very nearly done—in stories [Lewis *On Stories and Other Essays on Literature* 19–20].

As many critics have argued, this elusive bird is that mythic quality within stories which embodies what Otto terms the numinous.

In his often cited chapter "On Myths," in *Experiments in Criticism*, Lewis discusses the numinous as one of the six characteristics of myth. It must be noted, however, that Lewis felt that the term "myth" was problematic in that the original Greek word meant "any story"; what Lewis is concerned with in his discussion is rather a certain "mythic quality" which may or may not be found in original myths but, more importantly, is sometimes found in literary constructions of mythopoeia, works such as Stevenson's *Dr. Jekyll and Mr. Hyde*, H.G. Wells' *The Door in the Wall*, Kafka's *The Castle*, or certain episodes in Tolkien's *The Lord of the Rings*, such as the Ents or Lothlorian. Most of Lewis's six characteristics of myth focus on the experience which Lewis felt was the most important aspect of this type of literature. The first two characteristics are that these works of the imagination are extra-literary and they do not rely on suspense or surprise. As Lewis states, they are "valuable in introducing us to a permanent object of contemplation—more like a thing than a narration—which works upon us by its peculiar flavour or quality, rather as a smell or chord does" (*An Experiment in Criticism* 43). It is

Three. "Further Up and Further In"

interesting to note here that Lewis uses the analogy of music to convey the sense of a felt experience, a reference which connects his theory to MacDonald, who similarly felt that fairy tales conveyed an experience closely akin to music. This reference further traces Lewis's theory back to Otto, who also described the numinous experience as related to the experience of music.

The third characteristic is that, as readers of a mythic work, we never project ourselves onto the characters. There is always a certain distance we create when we read about characters that separates us from their actions. The fourth characteristic is that myths deal with the fantastic, which Lewis describes as anything involving impossibles or preternaturals. The fifth characteristic is that the experience of myth may be sad or joyful, but it is always grave. The sixth characteristic, which is for our purposes the most important, is that this type of literature involves the numinous. Concerning this characteristic, Lewis states:

> The experience is not only grave but awe-inspiring. We feel it to be numinous. It is as if something of great moment had been communicated to us. The recurrent efforts of the mind to grasp–we mean, chiefly, to conceptualize–this something, are seen in the persistent tendency of humanity to provide myths with allegorical explanations. And after all allegories have been tried, the myth itself continues to be more important than they [*An Experiment in Criticism* 43].

Lewis's concern is not with any particular authors' eloquence of writing style in conveying this experience, but instead the ability of the work to present this "mythic quality" as it affects the reader. This type of myth, Lewis believes, doesn't command belief as the original myths once did, but instead is more of an exercise in contemplating a certain sense of holiness for which the metaphors of fantasy are merely the vehicle. In this respect, it is interesting to note Lewis's stress on the faulty efforts of the mind to conceptualize this quality, a further connection with the indescribable nature of "wonder" to which fantasy authors and critics refer, as well as the non-rational and indescribable aspect of the numinous experience as detailed by Otto.

The attempt to capture this sense of holiness has its parallels with Coleridge's function of the imagination as well as some of the broader implications of Romantic theory. As Colin Manlove points out in his book *The Chronicles of Narnia: The Patterning of a Fantastic World*,

Lewis participates in a "Romantic Theology," which Manlove defines as "a belief that certain images may act as temporary vessels of God, filling human beings with a longing, or *sehnsucht*, for heaven" (*The Chronicles of Narnia: The Patterning of a Fantastic World* 6). In this aspect of Romanticism, where a bridge between the supernatural and natural realms is created, Lewis and Coleridge share similar views; however, what is of more importance in the present study are their differences, which provide us with the dividing line between our first two authors, Coleridge and MacDonald, and our two present authors, Lewis and Tolkien. For Coleridge, as well as MacDonald, the imagination has its ultimate source in God, and the function of the imagination to reproduce images is both creative and active. For Lewis, on the other hand, the imagination is not directly God but only a medium whereby He may reveal himself. As Mineko Honda states, "this lack of the idea of *imago dei* in Lewis comes from his radical difference between man's life and divine life" (23). As a believing Christian, Lewis, as well as Tolkien, believed that God was utterly "other," and that although mythopoeic fantasy offers metaphors to contemplate a holiness which is related to God, God himself could never be directly known.

This sense of mythic dissociation, of God as separate from humans, is the dividing line between our first four authors. These four authors are Christian, and they are attempting to infuse their readers with the numinous in "an attempt to make us thrill imaginatively to a divine reality both near and far, both with us and other" (Manlove *Christian Fantasy: From 1200 to the Present* 163). However, Coleridge and MacDonald locate the numinous both "near" and "with us," the predominant metaphor being the annihilation or death of the self as a means of achieving the numinous consciousness; Lewis and Tolkien, on the other hand, locate the numinous as "far" or "other," the predominant metaphor being the death or fading of the world. However dissimilar the metaphors appear to be, the consistent premise is the experience of the numinous as a means of revising perceptions of *this* world.

Mythopoeic fantasy is an effective means whereby to achieve this desired effect. By departing from consensus reality, fantasy aids in transforming that reality into a sacramental vision, where the world is seen anew. As Lewis states, "this excursion into the preposterous sends us back with renewed pleasure to the actual" (*On Stories and Other Essays on Literature* 14). Critics such as Eliane Tixier have also noted the dual purpose of fantasy as a means to experience the eternal as well as renew the temporal, especially as it relates to Lewis's theories. In her article entitled "Imagination Baptized or 'Holiness' in the Chronicles of Narnia," Tixier argues that on the one hand, Lewis wants to convey a sense of longing, or *Sehnsucht*, for a place beyond our world, a place of which we may only catch glimpses in this world. On the other hand, although this longing is important, "ardent longing must coexist with an ability to recognize 'footprints of the divine' in our world" (146).

The longing for a faraway reality is embodied in Lewis's term "joy," which is equivalent to Otto's term numinous, and it is this joy which gives one the ability to experience the transcendental realm above and beyond our own. It is the sacramental vision. "In fact," Tixier states, "the normal, final consequence of anticipations of Joy, of beauty, of glory in the tales, besides waking our desires and encouraging our faith, is to enable us to see, in everything beautiful, the giver of all things, to hear the divine presence in the roaring wind or to see it in the 'cushiony moss' by a brook" (157).

As Jesse Thomas argues in his article "From Joy to Joy: C.S. Lewis and the Numinous," the influence of Otto's *The Idea of the Holy* inspired Lewis to find a comparable term to explain experiences he had in his own life. His term "joy" came to refer to this deeper sense of reality which underlies the more mundane world. It is this joy or numinous quality which is "in the background" of Lewis works, whether in his theological texts, his science fiction, or in his children's stories. The most detailed account of Lewis's understanding of joy comes from his autobiography *Surprised by Joy*. In the book, Lewis defines his experience of joy as an "unsatisfied desire," not unlike grief or unhappiness, but nonetheless a kind of desire which one would not exchange for anything else in this world. Lewis presents to the reader three imaginative experiences in his life which help one understand what he meant by the term joy. The first experience was a memory of a memory. When Lewis was a child, his brother presented to him a toy garden which was made out of an old tin and some moss. Lewis states that this toy garden was always equated with ideas of Paradise and, later in his life, when he reflected on the memory of the toy garden, he felt a "stab" or "pang," which had a profound impact on his life. Lewis describes the effect of the experience:

And before I knew what I desired, the desire itself was gone, the whole glimpse withdrawn, the world turned commonplace again, or only stirred by a longing for the longing which had just ceased. It had taken only a moment of time; and in a certain sense everything else that had ever happened to me was insignificant in comparison [*Surprised by Joy: The Shape of My Early Life* 16].

What is helpful in this account of joy is Lewis's admission that once the glimpse recedes, the world is referred to as "commonplace" again, stressing the dichotomy between the two disparate realities. Thus in this example, the two realities are mutually exclusive. In a similar manner, the second experience of joy which Lewis relates reflects the exclusivity of the two modes. Upon reading *Squirrel Nutkin* by Beatrix Potter, Lewis says that the desire was reawakened and, in a Platonic sense, the story gave him an experience of the "Idea" of autumn: "It was something quite different from ordinary life and even from ordinary pleasure; something, as they would now say, 'in another dimension'" (*Surprised by Joy: The Shape of My Early Life* 17). What is noticed here is, again, the view that ordinary reality and the experience of joy are quite different from one another.

The final experience of joy comes from Lewis's fascination with the world of Norse mythology, especially Longfellow's *Saga of King Olaf* and myths concerning the hero Balder. In his reading of these myths, Lewis felt the same experience of joy. In fact, it was this element of joy that Lewis admits was missing in his own Christianity and made him, for a time, an atheist. He was at pains to understand why Christianity was the one "true" religion while others, such as the Norse, were untrue, even though they elicited this unique religious response.

One of the most important experiences which helped bring Lewis back to Christianity after a period of serious doubt was his reading of George MacDonald's *Phantastes*, the book which "baptized" his imagination. It is also with this experience that we see a bridge created between the natural and supernatural, the two realms now being interdependent rather than mutually exclusive. Lewis felt that *Phantastes* gave him a unique experience of holiness, where what was encountered transformed the way reality was perceived. He states, "never had the wind of joy blowing through any story been less separable from the story itself" (*Surprised by Joy: The Shape of My Early Life* 180). Whereas before, his visions of joy had reminded him of another world, a world distinct

Three. "Further Up and Further In"

from this one, now he realized that the experience of reading *Phantastes* helped bring the worlds together. The reading aided in "transforming all common things and yet itself unchanged. Or, more accurately, I saw the common things drawn into the bright shadow" (*Surprised by Joy: The Shape of My Early Life* 181).

In summation, there are three important considerations to bear in mind concerning the present discussion. The first is that Lewis's concept of joy is analogous to Otto's concept of the numinous; these are both sensations or experiences which are awe-inspiring and indescribable. Secondly, unlike the first two authors, Lewis locates the source of the numinous as "outer" rather than "inner." When Lewis later converts to Christianity, he still experiences joy, but these experiences are not as important. Lewis argues that these experiences are only "signposts" to a realm utterly beyond this world, a Heaven which is only reached upon death. This is where Lewis diverges from mainstream Romantic ideology. Even though "joy" is an aesthetic experience comparable to Coleridge's "joy" or Wordsworth's "spots of time," the fundamental difference is that, for Lewis, joy points to a world which is external and beyond. It can be argued that if nothing in this world satisfies the desire experienced with joy, then it must be outside the world; in a Christian sense, Heaven must be the ultimate satisfier of the desire.

The third consideration to be kept in mind is perhaps the most important for the present argument: although the numinous experience is somehow external, it still has the ability to revise the way ordinary reality is perceived. Lewis believed that his imaginative works were vehicles through which the numinous could be experienced. As Honda argues, Lewis's fictions are ways of participating in an "Absolute Reality"; they give readers a foretaste of that reality. For Lewis, the mythopoeic fairy landscape was the appropriate means both to convey the experience of the numinous as well as to allow that experience to lift the "veil of familiarity" for complete access to the sacramental vision:

> It would be truer to say that fairy land arouses a longing for he knows not what. It stirs and troubles him (to his life-long enrichment) with the dim sense of something beyond his reach and, far from dulling or emptying the actual world, gives it a new dimension of depth. He does not despise real woods because he has read of enchanted woods: the reading makes all real woods a little enchanted. This is a special kind of longing [Lewis *On Stories and Other Essays on Literature* 38].

At the conclusion of the last chapter, Keith Wilson referred to George MacDonald as an "apocalyptic writer" due to the fact that texts like *Phantastes* attempt to discover God by an "unveiling" of illusion to perceive God's true nature. In the present study, as a sub-theme, I have broadened the argument by viewing all four authors as apocalyptic in differing contexts. In order to perceive the numinous, and to revision "right" relationships with the natural environment, the "veil of familiarity" to which Tolkien and Lewis specifically refer, must be lifted; the old must give way to the new. The unique religious response which the numinous experience allows for is the defining element of mythopoeic fantasy. In fact, it is the extent to which the numinous is present in a particular work which makes one author mythopoeic and another not.

Discussing the theme of the apocalypse in fantasy literature, Eric Rabkin says that "the goal of world destruction is world creation" (xv). It is no wonder, he argues, that writers provide us with images of the end of the world because we fear what our technologies can achieve. There is no doubt that technology has provided us with beneficial advances; however, what speculative authors contemplate are the negative effects which are the result of these same technologies. This is especially the case with environmental issues such as global warming, population explosions, pollution, and mass extinction. As discussed in the introduction, one possible starting place for engaging in the environmental debate is to involve not just the field of science, but also the humanities. By looking at literature which exposes our predominant views about ourselves and our relationship to the environment, the possibility exists for us to create new metaphors for these relationships and, as a consequence, change or revise our attitudes toward nature. This is the specific function of mythopoeic art. In a similar manner, the apocalyptic visions of the end of the world supply us with metaphors for the destruction of the world in order for us to contemplate a more sacred reality. As Rabkin states, "the world we see is the world we were raised to see; to have a world of our own we must destroy the world we inherit and project ourselves onto chaos" (x). This basic assumption underlies Ecocriticism as well. The proposal of ecocritics to offer an "alternative view of existence," in their case by analyzing literary texts, is precisely the function of the mythopoeic author.

The apocalyptic theme within mythopoeic fantasy helps in the revisioning of the relationship to the world; it offers new metaphors by destroying old ones and allows for fresh perspectives. The unique characteristic of mythopoeic fantasy is that, unlike myth which posits its stories as "true" for a particular culture, mythopoeic fantasy transfers the same sense of the numinous as myth but in a symbolic truth. Therefore, apocalyptic visions are not necessarily literal visions of the end, but speculations encapsulated in metaphors to help us think about certain issues. Apocalyptic visions are ways of thinking which help us "break free from a mental cage" (Rabkin x).

In terms of ecological discourse, the apocalyptic emphasis of these authors aids in contemplating a shift from Campbell's mythic dissociation to mythic association. As Campbell argues, the underlying ideology of religions such as Judaism, Christianity and Islam, is a separation between God, humans, and nature. Campbell's reading of Genesis emphasizes this separation where man is created by God and given "dominion" over the earth. This same line of argument is pursued by Lynn White who, as mentioned in the introduction, believes Christianity "bears a huge burden of guilt" for environmental problems. However, what is of importance in the present argument is that the mythopoeic writers, Coleridge, MacDonald, Lewis, and Tolkien are Christian, and at the same time they are challenging our ideas of a total separation between God, humans, and nature through their secondary worlds. Although Lewis and Tolkien locate the numinous as somehow "outer," and "beyond," they still present us with the possibility that experiencing the numinous can help us to revise our way of perceiving reality here and now. Thus what happens frequently in apocalyptic texts is that what is transcendent (i.e., beyond human limits) is made immanent or interiorized. As Robert Galbreath argues in his article "Ambiguous Apocalypse," "Thus immanentized or internalized, the transcendental is within nature, yet still beyond the known, still other (if not quite wholly), fully capable of eliciting awe, wonder, terror, but not truly a source of religious faith or an object of worship" (54). Galbreath concludes that this transcendence can be achieved through gnosis or visionary experiences, and the apocalyptic theme is a means by which mythopoeic authors can convey the experience of the transcendent.

Galbreath further states that "speculative fictions of eschatological transcendence may combine the end of the world or the species with internal awakening" (69). This comment validates Rabkin's contention that these texts help free us from mental cages in order for a revisioning of our relationship to the natural world. In mythopoeic fantasy, the perception of God as separate from humans and nature (mythic dissociation) moves more to a contemplation of mythic association, where the numinous consciousness is viewed as permeating the entire world. This challenging of normal modes of perception is the unique, subversive characteristic of mythopoeic fantasy. Viewing apocalyptic visions as symbolic ways of thinking about environmental problems enables us to participate in a hypothetical dialogue with our most basic cultural assumptions. In this sense, mythopoeic fantasy is a "game" in W.R. Irwin's definition, a way of changing anti-fact into fact in order to rearrange, rethink, and ultimately revise our ways of thinking (Irwin).

The efficacy of C.S. Lewis's strategy in producing a fantastic world and importing the experience of the numinous is apparent in the amount of criticism devoted to *The Chronicles of Narnia*, especially the first book, *The Lion, the Witch, and the Wardrobe*. It is a commonplace that the character of Aslan is an allegorical representation of Christ and that the whole story is a recreation of the death and resurrection of this religious figure. However, criticism has failed to take into account the highly religious didacticism in the other six books of the series. If Lewis's goal in the Narnia stories was to convey the numinous experience in fantastic texts, how might the religious dimension, specifically the apocalyptic theme, relate to the present thesis?

Although there are many religious elements in the Narnia stories, Lewis concentrated most of his imaginative efforts in the first and last books of *The Chronicles of Narnia*. For Lewis, there had to exist powerful structures allowing entrance into the fantastic world, as well as equally powerful exits. In a religious context, Lewis can be said to have dealt with "first" and "last" things in *The Lion, the Witch, and the Wardrobe* (1950), and *The Last Battle* (1956), respectively (for the most part, scholarly attention to *The Last Battle* has been lacking). Because his treatment of the end-time in particular unfolds the full vision of his religious thought, especially as reflected through his attitude towards the natural world, this chapter will turn to *The Last Battle*. In the text of *The Last Battle*, what Lewis offers the reader is a carefully constructed apocalyptic vision based on the book of Revelation, but he employs his own mythopoeic constructions of such themes as false prophets, final judgment, the destruction of the world, and the creation of a paradisal new world. It is within this apocalyptic structure that Lewis conveys, in a symbolic manner, a means of breaking our "mental cage" in order for us to view the sacramental vision. Lewis achieves this through a careful employment of the Platonic notion of our world as an "illusion," a world which must only be a foretaste of a deeper, more sacred reality. This is the "veil of familiarity" which must be lifted (or reality "unveiled" in apocalyptic discourse) for a more numinous revisioning of the world, one in which nature is fully appreciated.

From the Greek *apokalypsis*, apocalypse means "to reveal or uncover," and what is revealed is a vision of the end of the world. In showing this end, apocalyptic texts conform to certain identifiable characteristics which have been discussed with particular attention for obvious reasons by biblical scholars. These characteristics have led scholars such as John Collins, in his book *The Apocalyptic Imagination*, to define an apocalypse as "revelatory literature with a narrative framework, in which a revelation is mediated by an otherworldly being to a human recipient, disclosing a transcendent reality which is both temporal, in so far as it envisions eschatological salvation, and spatial in so far as it involves another, supernatural world" (*The Apocalyptic Imagination: An Introduction to Jewish Apocalyptic Literature* 5).

For purposes of Lewis's construction, this definition is useful. Identifying apocalyptic literature in terms of its generic characteristics allows these characteristics to be transferred and identified within other profane or non-sacred texts. Collins himself acknowledges the blurring of boundaries between religious mythology and imaginative fiction when he states that "the composition of highly symbolic literature involves a vivid use of the imagination, which may be difficult to distinguish from visionary experiences in any case" (*The Apocalyptic Imagination: An Introduction to Jewish Apocalyptic Literature* 40). Applying Collins's generic definition of apocalypse to Lewis's theories of fantasy, as experiences of the numinous contained within fantastic imagery, helps readers understand Lewis's mythopoeic construction in *The Last Battle* as a unique vision of an apocalyptic end.

The apocalyptic series of events in *The Last Battle* is initiated by an ape named Shift. Finding a lion's skin floating downstream, Shift constructs an elaborate plan whereby he can take complete control of Narnia: he fits the lion's skin onto his innocent companion Puzzle, a donkey, and convinces all the Narnian creatures that Aslan has come back. Using the false Aslan as his mouthpiece, Shift is able to destroy much of the Narnian landscape, as well as plant seeds for a false religion (he tries to convince Narnians that the god Tash and Aslan are one—"Tashlan") which he thinks will destroy confidence in the real Aslan. When the original kings and queens of Narnia arrive to help, they find the fake Aslan in a stable on Stable Hill, where the Narnians enter to communicate with Aslan. However, once the children (the original kings and queens of Narnia) enter the stable, they discover that it is actually the real Aslan's country. Within it, they find Aslan himself and, upon the other creatures' entry into the stable, a judgment occurs; based on their merits in life, the creatures are either accepted into Aslan's paradisal country or are never seen or heard of again. Once the judgment has occurred, the inhabitants of the stable are able to peer through the stable door to witness the destruction of the old Narnia. After the destruction, they are taken "further up and further in," realizing that inside the stable is the true Narnia, whereas the old had been a mere copy or shadow.

In terms of Collins's definition, *The Last Battle* fulfills all the characteristics of apocalyptic literature: it provides a narrative framework; it is revelatory in that it reveals an end (the destruction of the old Narnia); it is mediated by an otherworldly being (Aslan) to a human recipient (in this case those who are within the stable); and, it discloses a transcendent reality which is both temporal (the eschatological end of the old Narnia) and spatial (the supernatural world of the new Narnia, which is "more real" than the old). Not only does the text fulfill these generic characteristics of apocalyptic literature, it also has, not coincidentally, close parallels with the biblical text Revelation.

One of the signs of the apocalypse in the book of Revelation is the coming of false prophets. In chapter twelve of Revelation, there appears a great Dragon who is revealed as Satan or the Devil. In this chapter, the Dragon attempts to destroy a child waiting to be born of the Heavenly Mother. After a failed attempt, the child is rescued by God, and a battle ensues whereby Michael defeats the Dragon and throws him down to the surface of the earth. Revelation 12:17 states that after the Dragon reached earth, it "went to make war on the rest of her children." According to Adela Collins, this Dragon represents the negative force in the world which opposes justice and order; it is the primal sea monster which is the embodiment of chaos itself, and it is continually threatening the rule of the divine king (84).

Three. "Further Up and Further In"

The two beasts in chapter thirteen of Revelation reflect a similar symbolism. They are both Anti-Christ figures and are further echoes of the threat of chaos and sterility towards the order of the world. For Collins, more specifically, the beast from the sea "applies to the perennial desire of human beings to dominate one another," while the beast of the earth "applies to any situation in which false power demands total allegiance" (92, 98). Collins further identifies the beasts in this chapter with what she terms a "counterfeit cult" or "counterfeit power," where self-centered motivations oppose any consideration of the beneficent power in the world.

The dragon and the two beasts in Revelation clearly have parallels in Lewis's *The Last Battle*. In fact, in a letter to a child inquiring about the nature of the symbolism in the text, Lewis states "And of course the Ape and Puzzle, just before the Last Judgment (in *The Last Battle*) are like the coming of Anti-Christ before the end of our world" (Hooper 110). In the text, by disguising his donkey/servant in the lion's skin to deceive the Narnians into thinking it is Aslan himself, the ape Shift is engaged in a "counterfeit power," the self-centered power which allows him to construct methods for the takeover and destruction of the Narnian land. For example, by a decree from the false Aslan, Shift has the Narnian forests destroyed; he also enslaves the free creatures of Narnia into working to his advantage.

In having the forests destroyed, Shift symbolically represents the forces of chaos and sterility which, both in *The Last Battle* and Revelation, are equated with evil. In a similar manner, the nature of the evil act is specifically directed at environmental destruction, and it is here where our interests lie. In a revealing episode early in the book, King Tirian and his companion, Jewel the unicorn, are discussing the supposed return of Aslan to Narnia. Of course, this information turns out to be second-hand and, upon the arrival of Roonwit the Centaur, turns out to be false. As a reader of the stars, Roonwit tries to convince Tirian that the coming of Aslan is not in the stars; on the contrary, the ominous configurations of the stars predict a time of evil and deceit. Taking these signs from the sky, Roonwit concludes that the predictions concerning the coming of Aslan must be a lie.

As they are debating the true nature of the signs, they are interrupted by the voice of a Dryad, a mythical creature who is likened both to a woman and a tree. Upon her arrival, she exclaims, "Woe for my brothers and sisters! Woe for the holy trees! The woods are laid waste. The axe is loosed against us. We are being felled. Great trees are falling, falling, falling" (Lewis *The Last Battle* 16). Before the king can ascertain who is the culprit behind these murderous acts, the Dryad gasps in pain, falls on her side, and dies. Upon her vanishing, they realize that the tree in which she dwelled had been cut down. The crime against her is made more horrific in that she was no mere tree, but one of the surviving talking trees of Narnia.

As with Tolkien's imaginative creation of the Ents in *The Lord of the Rings*, Lewis's imagination drew upon the mythic equivalent of a creature who represents the fusion of the human with nature: the Dryad. By portraying the death of the Dryad, ultimately the result of Shift's "counterfeit power," Lewis connects pure evil with a blatant disregard for the natural environment. It is the symbolic power of Shift, which is revealed to be the apocalyptic equivalent to Satan, which must be overcome in order for a revisioning of a "right" relationship to the natural world. In *The Last Battle,* Shift represents the power of both beasts in Revelation, but is particularly close to the beast of the earth who, in Revelation 13:14, "deceives the inhabitants of the earth" and forces them to worship an image of the first beast. In this context, Shift represents the dominating influence of a self-centered power, which in Narnia becomes a threat to the natural world as well as the continued stability and freedom of the Narnian creatures.

However, the differences between the two texts are interesting as well. Puzzle, the donkey who is actually disguised as Aslan, is also the subject of Shift's dominating power. Puzzle never willingly accepts his role as a deceiver and, at the end of the text, he is actually redeemed by the real Aslan. So, although the symbolism of the two beasts is present in *The Last Battle*, it is not separated into two distinct beasts; instead, the power of the beasts is amalgamated into one figure, Shift, who embodies the qualities of both Satanic figures.

In the background of Shift's deceits is also a figure who parallels the Satanic dragon in Revelation. Tash, a name given to a false god in Narnia, is described as having a man's body with a bird's head, as well as four arms with sharp claws. At first glance, the god seems like a vast shadow, a smoky presence smelling of death itself. Tash "floats" on the earth and in his wake "the grass seemed to wither beneath it" (Lewis *The Last Battle* 82). The death imagery surrounding Tash clearly conflicts with the springtime beauty associated with the land of Narnia. In a mythopoeic context, this quality echoes the connection between the Dragon of Revelation and the negative powers of chaos and sterility which Collins points out in her text. In a symbolic manner, Lewis connects ultimate evil with a sterility which threatens nature itself. Tash also serves Shift's deceptive plan in that Shift tries to make the Narnians believe that Tash and Aslan are really one god, Tashlan. By trying to incorporate the two gods into one power, Shift is acting in the role of the false prophet, trying to introduce confusion and chaos into the Narnian world.

Apocalyptic literature is eschatological in that it envisions an end to the world, usually portrayed as the destruction of the cosmos. In Revelation, there are many poetic images of this end and, as Collins suggests, each of these visions are separate repetitions of the same theme of cosmic destruction. One of the most poetic versions of the destruction occurs in Revelation 6:12 with the opening of the sixth seal. It describes a great earthquake, followed by a blackening of the sun and the moon turning blood-red. In Revelation 6:14, the stars fall from the sky and the sky vanishes "like a scroll rolling itself up." Although this destruction of the world affects all of the inhabitants of the earth, Collins argues that certain people are singled out, specifically those who are strong, and this destruction is a form of judgment which "expresses the conviction that wealth and power carry heavy responsibility, that those who abuse them are held accountable" (49).

In *The Last Battle*, a similar destruction is envisioned for the Narnian world, and this destruction is the result of the gradual corruption of the land under the deception instigated by Shift. Once the inhabitants of Narnia enter the stable door, they meet the true Aslan and, from a position within the "new" Narnia (paradise), are able to peer through the door to witness the destruction of the "old" Narnia. This is the culminating moment in terms of the sacramental vision, for it is here that the old way of viewing Narnia gives way to the new. What the inhabitants of Narnia mistook for reality was really an illusion. The "true" Narnia is the deeper, numinous reality which the "veil of familiarity" has hidden. In a symbolic way, the inhabitants have here gained a new way of perception which pierces illusory nature for reality. As readers, we too experience this new form of perception and are freed from the "mental cage." We see the "true" reality of the world as an expression of the numinous consciousness.

As Rabkin states in his introduction to *The End of the World*, apocalyptic visions help one break free from a mental cage. In *The Last Battle*, one could argue that Lewis felt this same way, especially in his treatment of the dwarfs once they enter the Stable; what is of key importance is the difference in perception between King Tirian and his friends, on the one hand, and the dwarfs on the other. It is this episode which clearly demonstrates the sacramental vision. When Tirian and the others enter the stable, they are aware of a bright sky overhead, with groves of trees supporting the most exquisite fruits, "such as no one has seen in our world" (Lewis *The Last Battle* 136). The dwarfs, although they are in the same stable, perceive things quite differently. When Lucy asks if one of them can see the sky, the trees, or the flowers, the dwarf replies, "How in the name of all Humbug can I see what ain't there? And how can I see you any more than you can see me in this pitch darkness?" (Lewis *The Last Battle* 144). Not only is the vision of the dwarfs affected, but also their sense of smell. When Lucy holds up violets to one of the dwarfs to test his ability to perceive smell, the dwarf Diggle says, "What do you mean by shoving a lot of filthy stable-litter in my face?" (Lewis *The Last Battle* 145).

The reason for the dwarfs' inability to perceive the sacramental vision of the "true" Narnia is related to their unwillingness to accept Aslan or his paradisal country. The repeated phrase, "the Dwarfs are for the Dwarfs" echoes the same obsession with "self" which was analyzed in the previous chapters on Coleridge and MacDonald. The sacramental vision is only offered to those who are willing to experience a higher reality, one which transcends any concern with the finite self; it is a willingness to perceive the eternal through the temporal. This involves a realization that the boundaries between "self" and "other" are not static but fluid, and it is this realization which ecocritics posit as the fundamental paradigm shift which must be undertaken in order for our present cultural constructs to be replaced.

Lewis portrayed this vision effectively with the difference between what characters in the stable perceive. When Aslan appears within the stable, he comments upon the dwarfs' lack of perception:

> They have chosen cunning instead of belief. Their prison is only in their minds, yet they are in that prison; and so afraid of being taken in that they can not be taken out [Lewis *The Last Battle* 148].

Three. "Further Up and Further In"

The fact that the prison is only in the dwarfs' minds shows us that the dwarfs, by being overly self-reliant, are blind to the true nature of the numinous as it is experienced in the "new" Narnia. For the others, who have accepted Aslan, the "veil" has been lifted and they are about to witness the final destruction of the old Narnia.

What the inhabitants see within the stable bears a striking resemblance to that destruction envisioned in Revelation. Father Time, who upon waking is now called Eternity, blows his horn to signal the end of the world. Stars begin falling to the ground, but in Narnia the stars resemble angelic beings "with long hair like burning silver and spears like white hot metal" (Lewis *The Last Battle* 151). This angelic imagery of the stars is reminiscent of such Biblical passages as Daniel 8:10 where, according to John Collins' *Daniel* commentary "the host of heaven connotes both the stars and the heavenly beings, either gods or angels" (*Daniel [a Hermeneia Commentary]* 331). After these stars fall in Narnia, the whole world is blackened, and great dragons and lizards are loosed upon the world to destroy it. The text states that "minute by minute the forests disappeared. The whole country became bare and you could see all sorts of things about its shape—all the little humps and hollows—which you had never noticed before. The grass died" (Lewis *The Last Battle* 155). Further echoing Revelation, the sun and the moon draw into each other and take on a blood-red hue; Aslan commands, "Now make an end," and Father Time squeezes the combined sun and moon in his finger "as you would an orange" and the world is blackened forever (Lewis *The Last Battle* 157).

Before the world is completely destroyed in *The Last Battle*, however, there is a final judgment where Aslan determines the fates of the Narnian creatures. As they enter the stable door during the destruction, they must face Aslan himself. When some of the creatures look him in the face, their expression is one of fear and hatred, and "the creatures who looked at Aslan in that way swerved to their right, his left, and disappeared into his huge black shadow, which (as you have heard) streamed away to the left of the doorway" (Lewis *The Last Battle* 154). What happens to these creatures is never told; the narrator admits that they were never seen or heard from again. This unwillingness of Lewis to specify a place for those who hate and fear Aslan, an eternal place of punishment for instance, might result from the fact that Lewis was aware of his audience. Although Lewis disagreed with the distinction between children's literature and adult literature, he must have known that the primary fascination of his stories would be relegated to children; thus his imagery is less graphic than that found in Revelation.

For those who look into Aslan's face with an expression of love, they swerve to his right and join the other inhabitants within the stable which is, in fact, a new, paradisal version of the old Narnia. As these figures enter into the stable, what is noticed is that some of the creatures who were presumed dead are now brought back to life within the new Narnia. This idea of the dead coming back to life is central in the Biblical vision of the end.

Revelation 20:13 also envisions a final judgment where "the dead were judged according to their deeds as recorded in the books" and "all were judged according to what they had done." These books, according to Collins, are records of the deeds done by humans, and they are to be interpreted as an "image for the conviction that each deed is of ultimate significance and must be accounted for" (142).

Although *The Last Battle* does not employ the use of books as symbolic records of deeds which determine one's fate, there is a parallel in Lewis's use of the "expression" of each creature which determines its fate. If a creature fears Aslan, the expression betrays the evil actions that creature has performed in life; if a creature's expression bears love, this expression conveys a life led in accordance with Aslan's dictates. Thus these creatures are invited to participate in the new Narnia. So, although the metaphors are different, both the book of Revelation and Lewis's *The Last Battle* share a common theological premise: in the end, every action performed in life will have a determining role in the fate of the individual.

Throughout the sections of the destruction and judgment in *The Last Battle*, the imagery of darkness, death, and dissolution prevails. Whether it is the dark clouds which surround the god Tash or the stable door as a threshold upon which the creatures witness the "death" of the old Narnia, such imagery prepares the reader for the final end of the world. Peter Schakel, in *Reading with the Heart: The Way into Narnia*, equates these images with Northrop Frye's modal analysis of literary structures based upon their associations with seasons. Schakel argues that, for most of *The Last Battle*, the ironic phase is present. This is the mode which is associated with winter, and it implies either the death or absence of the hero, and the subsequent death of the land itself. However, what Schakel further notes is that the ironic mode is replaced by the romantic mode at the end of the text. The seasonal association which controls the romantic mode is the summer; the hero is victorious, and the land is transformed or healed. In terms of the present thesis, this shift in Frye's modal analysis from the ironic to the romantic reflects a "death" to old ways of perceiving the world (in the sense of Campbell's mythic dissociation where there is a total separation of the numinous and the world), to a new revisioning of the world via the numinous, where the world is a reflection of the sacred. Thus, in *The Last Battle*, a simple symbol such as the stable door, where the inhabitants of Narnia enter to be judged, represents, on the one hand, a death. When the creatures go through the door they experience a different way of perception than previously. However, that is not the end. The door is further an entry into a new paradise, a new beginning. By the end of the text, "The story of winter, of dissolution, has given way to a story of summer, of triumph, of entry into paradise, and of the ideal, wish-fulfillment of romance" (Schakel 126). The apocalyptic structure, which typically portrays a cosmic destruction followed by a renewal, reflects this literary shift in the story from ironic to romantic.

This new triumph of the romantic mode is envisioned as a new Narnia. As the creatures enter into this new paradise, referred to as Aslan's Country, it is "more real" than the old Narnia. To convey this new experience, Lewis uses the metaphor of the mirror: looking at a landscape in a mirror is, in some sense, like looking at the real thing; however, at the same time, it is somehow different in a central way. It is "deeper, more wonderful, more like places in a story: in a story you have never heard but very much want to know" (Lewis *The Last Battle* 170). This reference to the mirror connects *The Last Battle* to Lewis's theories of the imagination as being a vehicle to allow readers to revision the world in a more sacred way. In terms of the ecological debate, Lewis reminds us, "If you are tired of the real landscape, look at it in the mirror" (*On Stories and Other Essays on Literature* 90). By rethinking our cultural assumptions about nature, specifically the separation of the numinous from the world, we may begin to form new relationships to the world around us. Through its subversiveness, mythopoeic fantasy can aid us in this endeavor.

What Lewis also conveys in this metaphor of the mirror is central to his view of the world as expressed in the new Narnia: it is an inverted world, an exact replica of the old Narnia, but it is a world which is more real: "The new one was a deeper country: every rock and flower and blade of grass looked as if it meant more. I can't describe it any better than that: if you ever get there, you will know what I mean" (Lewis *The Last Battle* 171). Thus the revisioning of the world via the numinous means that every object in it, whether it is a rock, flower, or blade of grass, is seen as sacred. The only means to achieve this sacramental vision is to destroy old ways of relating to the world so that a new vision is created.

The underlying ideology of this new Narnia is specifically Platonic, revealing Lewis's belief in the validity of forms. For Plato, the world in which we live, or to relate it directly to Lewis, the world that we imagine, is a mere image of a more true world which exists elsewhere. In *The Last Battle*, Lewis transfers this Platonic philosophy to Narnia to suggest "The physical world is only the realm of appearances rather than solid reality—illusory, transitory" (Sammons 11). What the inhabitants of Narnia find when they travel "further up and further in" is that this new Narnia existing within the stable is the perfected image of what they thought was a reality.

To use Lewis's terminology, this world is a shadow land, a copy of a more stable reality to be found only after death. However, even though the focus here is on what we have analyzed as an "outwardly" directed numinous experience, glimpses of the numinous can be seen here in this world. As Elaine Tixier has already pointed out, the longing for the "true" land must co-exist with seeing the "footprints of the divine" right here in this world. As with Lewis's experiences of "joy," these "signposts" can lead us to revision our relationships to the natural world; they can allow us to see the numinous in all things.

The concept of the "heavenly" form of an earthly image is also present in the book of Revelation with the New Jerusalem. In Revelation 21:11, the New Jerusalem comes down out of heaven from God; it is a holy city which has "a radiance like a very rare jewel, like jasper, clear as crystal." Adorning the walls and gates of this city are various jewels, and the city is depicted as pure gold and as clear as glass. In this new city, according to Revelation 21:27, death and crying cease and "nothing unclean will enter it, nor anyone who practices abomination or falsehood, but only those who are written in the Lamb's book of life." To complete the beauty of this heavenly city, the waters of life flow forth from the throne of God, and the Tree of Life is present.

Three. "Further Up and Further In"

In a mythopoeic context, this imagery is represented in the new Narnia as well. Although most of the children experience the idealized Platonic Narnia in this new world, there are additions to it. For example, after the inhabitants swim up a waterfall they are led to a green hill with trees "Whose leaves looked like silver and their fruit gold" (Lewis *The Last Battle* 176). They notice twelve golden gates leading to Aslan's palace, and they are greeted outside the gates by past figures of Narnia thought to have been long dead. Thus the new Narnia, like the New Jerusalem, is a natural paradise where death, pain, and suffering do not exist. Metaphorically this place is, for Lewis, the heavenly goal for which all humans strive; it is the end result of a longing which is satisfied only at the end of time. Unicorn describes the end result of this longing quite succinctly: "I have come home at last! This is my real country! I belong here. This is the land I have been looking for all my life, though I never knew it till now" (Lewis *The Last Battle* 171).

This "longing" for a true home embodied in the German Romantic term *Sehnsucht* was at the center of Lewis's entire life; he also imported this idea in his creation of the Narnian world. Influenced by the Romantic tradition, Lewis believed that the imagination contained a true path to God, and this longing for a heavenly place is "a call for a home we cannot remember, the desire to return to the country we belong" (Trixier 146). In Lewis's own life, this desire was the literal longing for heaven, a world Lewis really believed existed at the end; however, Lewis's belief that "all things, in their way, reflect heavenly truth, the imagination not least," allowed him to reflect these same truths in his mythopoeic construction of Narnia (*Surprised by Joy: The Shape of My Early Life* 167). As a vehicle to experience the numinous dimension of the world, Lewis's mythopoeic constructions help us see the natural world anew.

Charles A. Hutter has described *The Chronicles of Narnia* as "a sort of Bible for a Bibleless age" (123). His position is that the seven books in the series form a coherent literary structure which is both linear and directional: they point to the stages of the world from its beginning to its end. This unification of materials is not unlike the structure of the Bible, a text written over a long period of time by various authors but containing what Jonathan Edwards called "The Grand Design of God." In Hutter's argument, the Narnian books can be taken as a distinct genre which he terms "scripture." In this sense, the Narnian books contain religious messages which are valid, and the question of whether a place called Narnia really exists or is a fictive construction becomes irrelevant. At the center of any religious construction, whether it is mythic, as in Revelation, or mythopoeic, as in *The Last Battle*, is the root word "myth," a word which denotes "story." What Lewis adds to myth in *The Last Battle* is that "mythic quality" of the numinous which allows for the sacramental vision.

This text is deserving of serious critical attention, for in many ways it embodies deep religious beliefs Lewis held for a good portion of his life, and its apocalyptic structure gives us a unique insight into the author's full theology as expressed in his mythopoeic art. When reading his autobiographical *Surprised by Joy*, one is struck by the many references to "joy" which occurred throughout his life. This "joy" is finally fulfilled in *The Last Battle* after the false prophet's reign, the destruction of the world, the final judgment, and the creation of the new Narnia in which grass, water, trees and the natural world as a whole can finally be truly known. By using fundamental apocalyptic themes and clothing them in the mythopoeic symbols of his own imagination, Lewis was able to illustrate his prophetic vision: "This world will come to an end; it was never meant to be our real home—that lies elsewhere; we do not know, we cannot possibly know, when the end will come; and the end will come, not from within, but without" (Hooper 125).

CHAPTER FOUR

The Fading of the World
Tolkien's Ecology and Loss in The Lord of the Rings

> "To mortal fields say Farewell,
> Middle-earth forsaking!
> In Elvenhome a clear bell
> In the tower is shaking
> Here grass fades and leaves fall,
> And sun and moon wither,
> And we have heard the far call
> That bids us journey thither."
> —Tolkien, "The Last Ship," [250]

C.S. Lewis once described the effect that the first volume of *The Lord of the Rings* had upon him; it was "like lightning from a clear sky" (*On Stories and Other Essays on Literature* 83). Lightning is an interesting word to use in praise of Tolkien (1892–1973), especially given its associations in many mythologies with that which represents the highest power (e.g. both Zeus and Indra's weapon of choice was the lightning bolt). Clearly this book had a profound effect on Lewis, who goes on to state that the book "does something to us," and "we are not quite the same men" when we finish reading it (*On Stories and Other Essays on Literature* 90). What exactly is it that *The Lord of the Rings does* to us? How are we *changed* upon our reading of it, so that we are not the same people when we first encounter it? Certainly it cannot be denied that this book has remained one of the top choices for readers around the world, so much so that Tom Shippey's recent work *J.R.R. Tolkien: Author of the Century* discusses various polls, including a 1996 Waterstone's poll and a BBC 4 poll, which show that *The Lord of the Rings* continues to be in the top tier of the most influential books of the 20th century.

Shippey backs up this claim by showing Tolkien's continued influence on three separate levels: the democratic, in which polls seem to show Tolkien to be the author of the century; the generic, since Tolkien created the epic fantasy genre which now is a major commercial market; and, the qualitative, because it is a worthy text for literary critics and has established itself as a modern classic (Shippey xxvi).

Understanding the religious dimension of Tolkien's work is especially problematic due to an apparent paradox pointed out by Shippey: "It was written, we know, by a devout and believing Christian, and has been seen by many as a deeply religious work. Yet it contains almost no direct religious reference at all" (xxxii). Certainly if one reads the created mythology which is the backdrop of Middle-earth, texts such as *The Silmarillion* or *The Book of Lost Tales*, one may find more obvious references to religion, but *The Lord of the Rings* itself contains almost no explicit religious images at all. What is this religious quality that readers instinctively perceive in the work which is not there explicitly? One possibility is the connection to the numinous which gives one the *experience* of the holy without relying on traditional religious motifs.

In his foreword to *The Idea of the Holy*, Otto states that his book will attempt an analysis of "the feeling which remains where the concept fails" (Foreword). What Otto means by this statement is that beneath "rational" concepts of religious discourse, there exists a core religious feeling which informs the entire religious framework; this core of religion Otto describes as a "hidden depth" which is "inaccessible to our conceptual thought" (58). The concept itself "fails" because it is merely a human attempt to clothe the numinous response in conceptual terms, when the non-rational experience cannot be conceptually known at all. However, Otto does not argue that concepts are totally faulty in attempting to capture the numinous. On the contrary, one may experience the sense of joy or awe without knowing an objective reference, but there must always be one present. These objective references of the feeling-orienting religious response may only be symbolically represented by what Otto terms "ideograms," attempts to conceptualize that which cannot be conceptualized.

Within the context of mythopoeic fantasy, and specifically within Tolkien's discourse on fairy-stories, one can see the similarities to Otto's ideas concerning the numinous. By its subversiveness, the fairy-story allows readers access to dimensions or orders of experience not available

Four. The Fading of the World

in the primary world. Critics often refer to this experience as that of wonder, and it is this experience which aids in the challenging of our normative perceptions of the natural world and helps us understand the mystery of which we and our world are a part. For Tolkien, fairy-stories contained this dimension of the numinous; in fact, as Otto argues, one of the earliest manifestations of the numinous is within the fairy-story itself: "the fairy-story proper only comes into being with the element of the 'wonderful,' with miracle and miraculous events and consequences, i.e. by means of an infusion of the numinous" (122).

The most comprehensive discussion of Tolkien's theory of fantasy is his often cited essay "On Fairy-Stories" published in 1947. Although most of the ideas have been thoroughly discussed by critics, it is worth considering those points which relate directly to the present thesis that fantasy can reflect the numinous as well as aid in a revisioning of our normative perceptions of the natural world. In the introduction, it was pointed out that, for Otto, the numinous consciousness is non-rational in the sense that it is a "feeling-oriented" response which defies language's ability to fully express it; Otto states "like every absolutely primary and elementary datum, while it admits of being discussed, it cannot be strictly defined" (7). This quality is frequently referred to in the field of fantasy criticism as the sense of "wonder" which is evoked through the fantastic images; it is that "extraliterary" dimension of fantasy to which Brian Attebery refers (155).

In a similar manner, Tolkien discusses this indescribable quality of fantasy, a quality which makes it a "higher" form of art. After an attempt at deconstructing the origins of the word "fairy-story," showing the problems of associating the fairy-stories with the "folk" of fairy (and such faulty characteristics of them as diminutive in size and their supernatural aspects), Tolkien turns his attention to "Faerie." Referring to the poet Gower, Tolkien notices that one particular reference before 1450 states that a young gallant was "*of* Faerie." Tolkien asserts that the true nature of fairy is within the realm itself; indeed, for Tolkien it is the "Perilous Realm," filled with both wonders and dangers, both of which have the unique ability to engender a "peculiar mood." This experience of the realm of fairy is difficult to describe; "its very richness and strangeness tie the tongue of a traveler who would report them" ("On Fairy-Stories" 33). It is the indescribable nature of the realm of faerie as well as its association with a particular experience or mood that allows for a connection between the unique religious response which Otto argues is the core of religious thought, and the appeal of *The Lord of the Rings* as a text which implicitly evokes a religious response without presenting a structured theology.

Many critics have pointed out the similarities between Tolkien's theories and Romantic thought, especially as mediated by Coleridge. It is worth considering some of these points. Tolkien agrees with Coleridge's definition of the imagination as that faculty which is engaged in "image making." However, for Tolkien, the grasping of the implications and perceptions of the image is a difference of degree, not kind. The imagination's ability to alter reality (fantasy's subversive function) makes this type of art a form of "sub-creation" whereby the artist imitates God's original act of creation. For Tolkien, the product of this sub-creative art is a secondary world which, although not to be taken as a literal world, still retains an aspect of believability.

Concerning himself with any "truth" value a fairy-story may have, Tolkien refers specifically to children when they are presented with a secondary world and their questioning of its truth value (it must be noted, however, that Tolkien disliked the association of children and fairy-stories; in fact, Tolkien argues that the love of fairy-stories increases, not decreases, with age). When children ask if a particular story is true, they really only want to know what type of literature they are reading so they can respond appropriately. For Tolkien, any "belief" one has upon reading a story, and subsequently any enjoyment of a story, depends on how it is told, not how much it imitates the real world. Challenging Coleridge's views directly, Tolkien states that any child may have a "willing suspension of disbelief," but that is not really what happens in the reading of a fantasy text. What happens, Tolkien argues, is that the sub-creative art produces a secondary world which you believe while you are inside it; once disbelief arises, you are out of the secondary world, and any experience provided by the text dissipates. Tolkien believed that to "will" yourself to "suspend disbelief" was too simplistic; it was similar to a child who has to play pretend. Tolkien states, "suspension of disbelief is a substitute for the genuine thing, a subterfuge we use when condescending to games of make-believe, or when trying (more or less willingly) to find what virtue we can in the work of art that has for us failed" ("On Fairy-Stories" 61).

Far from an effort of will which allows a reader to participate in a

Four. The Fading of the World

particular work of art, Tolkien believed that a true piece of art produced a form of "enchantment"; if a reader is under the spell of the secondary world, it commands a secondary belief. This secondary belief makes the fantastic world "real" during the reading of the book. In a strange comparison, Tolkien likens this state of enchantment to a game of cricket. The real cricket enthusiast, Tolkien asserts, is one who can fully participate in the game; there is nothing outside the sheer excitement of the game which holds the spectator there. This is what happens in a successful piece of fantasy. Enchantment takes over, and there is no questioning of the motivation for the work. One who is not an enthusiast for the game, Tolkien argues, has to be held by some other motivation for being there. Tolkien believed that, unfortunately, this is what happens for most adults when they read fantasy; since they cannot be enchanted by the particular work, they must be held by an outside motivation, such as a memory of childhood. Thus, this adult reader performs a "willing suspension of disbelief," one which can only produce a "let's pretend" mentality that, for Tolkien, ruins the true intention of the work. The differences, then, between the aesthetic theories of Tolkien and Coleridge are greater than one would expect.

However, in "Tolkien's Revisioning of the Romantic Tradition," Chris Seeman argues that the sub-creative art is not as central to Tolkien's theories as is his restriction of fantasy to the narrative mode. This emphasis is what really sets Tolkien apart from Romantic thought. For Tolkien, fantasy is naturally hostile to drama both because of drama's reliance on the visual as well as its anthropocentricity, which places the human in the center. As Seeman states, "these two aspects of Tolkien's aesthetic (the non-anthropocentric and the non-visual) ultimately join forces to lay the foundation for his vision of fantasy as a narrative of alterity—of otherness, of transcendence" (79). In Seeman's view, Tolkien is not necessarily ruling out Coleridgean applications to certain aesthetic experiences; rather, he is diverging from Romantic thought by privileging fantasy as a "higher" mode of art. Tolkien elaborates on this point in his essay "On Fairy-Stories" by stating that "Fantasy is a thing best left to words" ("On Fairy-Stories" 70). In this sense, fantasy differs from drama, especially when drama is presented as it should be, as that which is *visibly and audibly acted*. For Tolkien, this is drama's flaw: it presents a substitute magic through stage effects and costumery, neither of which allow for the imagination's ability to create images not experienced in the primary world. As Tolkien states, "for this reason—that the characters, and even the scenes, are in Drama not imagined but actually beheld—Drama is, even though it uses similar material (words, verse, plot), an art fundamentally different from narrative art" ("On Fairy-Stories" 70).

In viewing fantasy as a "narrative of alterity," Seeman allows us to see Tolkien in respect to environmental concerns. As argued in the introduction, many ecocritics envision the need for a paradigm shift, a learning of a new language which places the non-human in a central position as part of the whole; this paradigm shift would replace anthropocentric worldviews with ecocentric worldviews, where the environment is treated with respect. With Tolkien's aesthetic, the focus on the non-visual, that is the imagination's function as creating forms which are not in the primary world, becomes central to this debate. In contrast to successful fantasy, once we are presented with "images" which are not our own (through the *visible* and *audible* stage effects of drama), we are subject to imaginative passivity, and any attempt to revise normative modes of perception are mute; we are, in essence, seeing through another's eyes, not our own. In a similar manner, the anthropocentricity of other forms of art fails to allow for "otherness" or "transcendence," both of which are central to our present thesis. Fantasy's subversiveness is what allows for a shift from the human to the non-human and allows readers to experience what is not covered by our rational modes of knowledge. In this way, fantasy is a "higher" form of art because it allows the participation of both the author and the reader. Of course, any type of literary experience involves a participation of both the author and the reader, but fantasy is unique because of its presentation of images not present in the primary world; through its departures from reality, fantasy permits other modes of experience, in the present case experiences of transcendence. Thus if it is the author's role to provide images of "otherness" which reflect "transcendence," then it is the reader's role to grasp the implications of the images within his or her own experiential field. In contrast to drama, where the *visible* form of the play is the result of "stage magic," fantasy allows the reader's active participation in the contemplation of imaginary forms not present within a stage production; fantasy similarly differs from the more mimetic works of literature which attempt to reproduce "reality." It is precisely the departures from reality which initiate the active participation of the reader's imagination.

Four. The Fading of the World

Tolkien's greatest contributions to the field of Ecocriticism are his theories of recovery, escape and consolation, all of which are interrelated. As argued in the introduction, recovery is perhaps the most important theory because what we are recovering is the sense of "awe" which is Otto's core of religious thought. As Tolkien defines it, "recovery (which includes return and renewal of health) is a regaining—regaining a clear view" ("On Fairy-Stories" 77). What Tolkien means is that we appropriate our world through language acquisition and familiarity, and we lose a sense of total participation in the natural world. Fantasy, by its subversiveness, allows us to view the world in a new and unfamiliar sacramental manner, as a reflection of the numinous. As Tolkien states, it allows us to view the world "freed from the drab blur of triteness or familiarity—from possessiveness" ("On Fairy-Stories" 77). It is a way of respecting the environment and seeing things as apart from ourselves, to see difference but to realize that difference is also a manifestation of that which is holy. Viewing the world in this manner allows us to see the simple, most fundamental things in our world with a renewed vision. For Tolkien, fairy-stories had this ability to recapture the sacramental vision. As he states, "it was in fairy-stories that I first divined the potency of worlds, and the wonder of the things, such as stone, and wood, and iron; tree and grass; house and fire; bread and wine" ("On Fairy-Stories" 78).

With Tolkien's tripartite construction of recovery, escape and consolation, one may benefit from a comparison between Tolkien's aesthetic and that of Romantic thought. Although my intent is not to comprehensively examine mythopoeic fantasy within the framework of Romantic thought, there is an important connection between what is recovered in Tolkien's theory and that of the "natural sublime" within Romanticism. In his article "The Fantastic Sublime," David Sandner states, "in the sublime moment, the contemplation of a natural object leads to an aesthetic rapture, which produces a corresponding overflow of feeling, revealing the transcendent" (83). He summarizes three key phases of the sublime moment from Thomas Weiskel, all of which are applicable to Tolkien's aesthetics: (1) The habitual relationship between subject and object; (2) The overflow of feeling which necessitates a breakdown of the habitual and a subsequent indeterminacy between subject and object; and (3) The renewed relationship to the transcendent in which a balance is achieved between the subject and the object.

Nature and the Numinous in Mythopoeic Fantasy Literature

This Romantic framework helps in understanding how the sacramental vision is achieved. Within the second phase of the sublime moment, there occurs a breakdown of normative modes of perception, and, as argued in the introduction, the subversive nature of fantasy facilitates this process. It must be remembered, however, that this breakdown is not a change in the object itself but a change in perception, in the mind, which then evokes an experience of the transcendent. This requires, as argued in the earlier chapters on Coleridge and MacDonald, a loss or death of the self. Fantasy's ability to facilitate this sense of loss through departures from consensus reality makes it a form of art which is experiential by nature. It allows for a perception of other modes of being, modes that are beyond the rational. As Sandner states, "In fairy-stories, as in the natural sublime, the breakdown of the imagination becomes less a failure than a method for the self to loosen itself, through crisis, from the constraints of reason, consciousness, society—whatever is known, defined, explained" (6).

For Lewis and Tolkien, the experience of the sublime moment involves not so much the inner dimension of the self, but the outer dimension of the world; thus, their works are on an epic scale, where the whole world, not just the self, must be transcended for the experience of the numinous. Tolkien's concept of recovery, then, is an extension of the natural sublime in that it asks its readers to depart from consensus reality to properly transform normative modes of perception into the sacramental vision. As Tolkien argues, it is seeing the world not as it *is* but as it was *meant* to be seen. What this involves is a perception of the eternal working through the temporal, a lifting or tearing of the veil between worlds. Discussing Tolkien's concept of recovery as an extension of the natural sublime, Sandner states, "recovery is the tearing of the veil between worlds, an apprehension of the otherness of things, the movement into the second phase of the sublime" (6).

For some critics, the second phase of the sublime moment, the breakdown of the habitual, becomes a reason for viewing fantasy with derogation, criticizing it for its "escapism." Tolkien addresses this issue in his essay, arguing that people often misunderstand the meaning of escape as it applies to fantasy; escapism must be seen in its positive, not negative, sense. For example, Tolkien discusses the position of a prisoner who is confined to a small cell. Just because the prisoner thinks of more than the trivialities of cell life, contemplating the outside world, does not mean he is "escaping" the world. As Tolkien states, "the world outside has not become less real because the prisoner cannot see it" ("On Fairy-Stories" 79). For Tolkien, many people confuse what he terms the "escape of the prisoner," the positive sense of escape as contemplating a better world, with the "flight of the deserter," the negative sense of disengaging with the world entirely.

In fantasy, the escape allows one to perceive the sacramental vision. This relates, specifically for Tolkien, to the perception of those things of the natural world. Fantasy is directed at the recovery of the natural world, so any criticism concerning fantasy as escapism fails to understand the proper function of the art. When critics discuss escapism as disengaging from what is "real," Tolkien questions their most basic assumptions. Using the analogy of the motor-car, Tolkien says that to view a motor-car as "more real" than a Centaur is curious; viewing motor-cars as "more real" than horses is absurd. Thus Tolkien's point has clear connections with ecocriticism. Deeming the products of industrial society as "real" and failing to appreciate the wonder of the natural world causes a misdirected view of the world. In fact, Tolkien argues, what is considered "real" is always that which is natural: "how real, how startlingly alive, is a factory chimney compared with an elm tree: poor obsolete thing, insubstantial dream of an escapist" ("On Fairy-Stories" 81).

The positive sense of escapism for Tolkien is thus related to his theory of recovery, one that helps in understanding how one may perceive the sacramental vision. It is further reminiscent of Lewis's contention in that by reading fantasy, "we do not retreat from reality: we rediscover it" (*On Stories and Other Essays on Literature* 90). This is the main characteristic of mythopoeic fantasy. As Lewis argues, what we really escape in this type of literature is the illusion of ordinary life; through mythopoeic fantasy, we rediscover the world around us. In this sense, we see the world more clearly and with renewed wonder. Using the analogy of a child's use of imagination when eating meat, Lewis discusses the potency of mythic forms:

> The child enjoys his cold meat (otherwise dull to him) by pretending it is a buffalo, just killed with his bow and arrow. And the child is wise. The real meat comes back to him more savory for having been dipped in story; you might say that only then is it real meat [*On Stories and Other Essays on Literature* 90].

Escape from the world is positive in that it equates with the second phase of the sublime moment, where habitual or normative modes of perception break down. However, mythopoeic fantasy also offers a transition to the third phase of the sublime moment, the renewed relationship to the transcendent. The world is revised or recovered in a sacramental manner. Fantasy offers certain consolations, which is the third area of concern for Tolkien. One of the highest forms of consolation comes in the form of eucatastrophe, a word Tolkien coined which means "good catastrophe." It is a "sudden joyous turn" which occurs even in the face of ultimate defeat. This sense of joy is the most important element in a fairy story which offers "a sudden glimpse of the underlying reality or truth" ("On Fairy-Stories" 88). All true fairy stories must have eucatastrophe and Tolkien, as a devout Christian, believed that the most powerful fairy story of all, that of the Christian, was the eucatastrophe which actually occurred in the primary world. Apparently, some fairy tales do come true.

What is most interesting about Tolkien's discussion of consolation is his inclusion of various levels of consolation. For example, there are "lower" forms such as the desire one has to fly or swim, and "higher" forms such as the desire to converse with living things. It is with this latter desire that Tolkien's theories intersect with environmental concerns (this desire is reminiscent of Jonathan Bate's argument that the ecopoet has as his motivation the desire to engage with the non-human). Tolkien argues that the root of this desire to converse with living things arises from the sense of separation from the natural world, that "a strange fate and a guilt lies on us" ("On Fairy-Stories" 84). This sense of separation was discussed in the introduction as "mythic dissociation," Joseph Campbell's term for Western ideologies which locate the holy as apart from the world and from us. Echoing this sentiment, Tolkien says, "other creatures are like other realms with which man has broken off relations, and sees now only from the outside at a distance, being at war with them, or on the terms of an uneasy armistice" ("On Fairy-Stories" 84).

The sense of wonder at the world Tolkien describes as enchantment, and this enchantment can help us revise our ways of viewing the world around us. As Patrick Curry states in his article "Magic vs. Enchantment," we are in a condition of dis-enchantment, where the "drab blur of triteness or familiarity" has blocked our view of that which is most holy. He states, "enchantment has become uniquely precious and important as a resource for resistance, and for the realization of better alternatives" ("Magic Vs. Enchantment" 7). What is needed is a new language, one which engages the non-human, and mythopoeic fantasy, through its subversiveness, offers a plausible alternative. It offers one the experience of enchantment, which Tolkien believed was at the heart of Faerie. Concerning enchantment, Patrick Curry states, "enchantment must indispensably include an experience of wonder as a reality that, so far as the person(s) involved are concerned, could otherwise or hitherto only ever have been imagined" ("Magic Vs. Enchantment" 6).

Mythopoeic fantasy's ability to offer "better alternatives" for the revisioning of the environment is due to its subversive function which allows a shift from an anthropocentric paradigm to an ecocentric or biocentric paradigm, a shift which is evidenced in Tolkien's *The Lord of the Rings*. As Lucas Niiler points out in "Green Reading: Tolkien, Leopold, and the Land Ethic," "*The Lord of the Rings* showcases fantasy writing as an apt vehicle for representing, discussing, and resolving problems related to the relationship between nature and culture" (276). Fantasy has the unique ability to subvert normal categories of thought, such as those between "human" and "non-human," in order for a fusion of new possibilities which are not available in mimetic works. Subverting normative categories permits what Tolkien terms a "recovery" of the world, a renewed relationship to the earth which acknowledges its numinous essence. This renewed relationship with the natural world seeks to view nature as a part of a community, not a commodity. For Niiler, it is the relationship formulated by Leopold in his desire for a new "land ethic," one which replaces the "conquer" metaphor for a metaphor of interrelatedness. The difference between the two metaphors has been discussed previously as Campbell's "mythic dissociation," where God, humans, and nature are separate, and "mythic association," where the three are interrelated.

The new language which ecocritics call for must involve a change in perception, in how we view the world. It will also involve an awareness of how political, religious, and cultural forms play a part in how we think about the world around us. Discussing this new perception, particularly in Leopold's land ethic, Niiler states, "Leopold urges that public perception of land be transformed from a doctrine of Abrahamic appropriation to a sensibility of husbandry and a recognition of human membership in a biotic community" (281). Tolkien's theories of recovery, escape, and consolation urge this transformation through the vehicle of fantasy, and the textual embodiment of this transformation is in *The Lord of the Rings*.

What is so striking in *The Lord of the Rings*, notes Patrick Curry, is its "profound feeling for the natural world" ("Less Noise and More Green" 130). It has been argued in earlier chapters that this feeling-oriented response has its expression in the non-rational experience of the numinous as outlined by Rudolf Otto in *The Idea of the Holy*, which helps in understanding the paradox pointed out by Shippey, that *The Lord of the Rings* is a work written by a devout Christian with nothing really Christian in it. Why do people feel it is a religious work? Precisely because it is infused with the emotive, non-rational dimension which is the core of religious thought. Furthermore, it aids in what Curry states is a "resacralization of life," a new ethic which values basic necessities such as a good earth and clean water. Concerning *The Lord of the Rings*, Curry states, "It is in fact a work in which a deeply sensual appreciation of this world is interfused with an equally powerful sense of its ineffability" ("Less Noise and More Green" 133).

My concern involves a consideration of the religious dimension of the numinous and how it relates to some of the characters and settings in Tolkien's *The Lord of the Rings*: Tom Bombadil, Lothlorien, Treebeard, and the Shire. However, discussing these images towards nature should not blind us to the hint of despair attached to Tolkien's world. As with Lewis, there is in Tolkien's work a sense of a fading or disappearing of this relationship towards nature; it is, in essence, an apocalyptic story. Thus in *The Lord of the Rings*, although life is affirmed in its most holy sense, much is lost.

Tom Bombadil

One of the most perplexing aspects of *The Lord of the Rings* is the character of Tom Bombadil. Critics have wondered why he is included in the book at all, being a minor character who has no direct tie to the plot. Many of the critics, however, try to point to Bombadil's "applicability" as some sort of nature spirit or God. The difficulty in placing Bombadil is, in part, understandable, especially given Tolkien's own admission in a letter written to Naomi Mitchison (1954) that Tom was

Four. The Fading of the World

an intentional enigma. As he further states, although Tom is not an important character in the story, he does serve as a "comment." What sort of "comment" does Tom serve? Perhaps the best answer is given in the same letter: "He represents something that I feel very important, though I would not be prepared to analyze the feeling precisely" (Tolkien *The Letters of J.R.R. Tolkien* 178). Tolkien's comments are reminiscent of the non-rational, emotive core of the numinous. The applicability to Tom of "the feeling which remains where the concept fails," is obvious. For Tolkien, Tom represents the experience of the numinous which defies language's ability to express it; furthermore, Tom reflects Tolkien's own views of nature, views which are consonant with his theory of recovery.

The fact that Tom symbolizes nature is fairly obvious, and critics have covered the map in their variety of nature connections. Don Elgin claims that Tom represents an "elemental life force"; Slethaug argues that Tom is a sort of "genius Loci"; Hargrove contends that Tom is a Vala (angelic beings sent into Ea to fulfill Iluvatar's vision of creation); and even Herbert argues that Tom is akin to a "moss-gathering Socrates" (Don Elgin, *The Comedy of the Fantastic: Ecological Perspectives on the Fantasy Novel* [Westport, CT: Greenwood Press, 1985]; Gordon E. Slethaug, "Tolkien, Tom Bombadil and the Creative Imagination. *English Studies in Canada* 4 [1978]: 341–350; Gene Hargrove, "Who Is Tom Bombadil?" *Mythlore* 13.1 [1986]: 20–24; G.B. Herbert, "Tolkien's Tom Bombadil and the Platonic Ring of Gyges," *Extrapolation* 26.2 [1985]: 152–159). It is easy to interpret Tom as a symbol of nature due to Tolkien's own admission to Stanley Unwin, his publisher, that Tom represented "the spirit of the (vanishing) Oxford and Berkshire countryside" (*The Letters of J.R.R. Tolkien* 26). While any interpretation leads one to Tolkien's own warning not to take Tom too seriously, the connections with nature which directly relate to Tolkien's theory of recovery, and the experience of wonder which is at the core of mythopoeic fantasy, is Tom's representation of the attitude of non-appropriation.

In the previous discussion of Tolkien's theories, I pointed out that recovery means a regaining of a clear view of things without our appropriations. When we claim to "know" something through familiarity or language abstraction, we lose the sense of wonder at the natural world; as Tolkien says, we possess a thing and then cease to look at it. It loses its sense of holiness. Tom's association with this sense of seeing the world without appropriations is seen in *The Lord of the Rings* when, after the hobbits are rescued from Old Man Willow by Tom, they come to Tom's house. Frodo asks Goldberry who Tom Bombadil actually is, to which she states mysteriously, "He is" (Tolkien *The Fellowship of the Rings* 160). This statement has caused many critics and readers to speculate on Tom's connections with nature, and an even higher association, with God. In a draft to Peter Hastings, Tolkien denies that Tom is God; rather, Goldberry's statement calls into question the propriety of naming beings that represent the "other." Tolkien's view of the God-man relationship was personal, in which no proper "names" are required. Just as in man's relationship with God, Goldberry has no concept of explaining "who" Tom Bombadil is, he just "is." Tolkien says that Tom is "a particular embodying of pure (real) natural science: the spirit that desires knowledge of other things, their history and nature, because they are 'other' and wholly independent of the inquiring mind..." (*The Letters of J.R.R. Tolkien* 192). Tolkien's statement corresponds to Goldberry's answer to Frodo's question as to whether the land "belongs" to Tom: "the trees and the grasses and all things growing or living in the land belong each to themselves. Tom Bombadil is the Master" (Tolkien *The Fellowship of the Rings* 161). There is a similar passage which shows the theme of non-appropriation of nature when the hobbits are confined to Tom's house during the rain. To pass the time, Tom tells tales to the hobbits relating to things in the natural world and "as they listened, they began to understand the lives of the Forest, apart from themselves, indeed to feel themselves as the strangers where all other things were at home" (Tolkien *The Fellowship of the Rings* 167).

From the above passages, it can be seen that Lucas Niiler is correct in his contention that "Bombadil, in sum, serves as a lens through which the hobbits 'recover' a clear view of their relationship with the environment, and 'escape' middle-earth's dynamic of war, at least for a time" (284). The relationship towards nature which Tom embodies corresponds with Leopold's "land ethic" which strives to go beyond the appropriation of nature to recognizing one's role in a wider, biotic community. The foundation for this relationship is not to view nature as a commodity to be used but, instead, to appreciate the wonder of the created world as a representation of that which is "other." Thus, as Niiler argues, Tom's role is that he represents a paradigm for a certain attitude towards nature.

However, what is to be remembered is the hint of despair which

Four. The Fading of the World

underlies all of Middle-earth. The despair connects Tolkien's view with the Christian apocalyptic tradition shared with Lewis, a view which holds that final glory is not to be found within the confines of this world, be it fantastic or otherwise. So, while it is true that Tom is associated with the recovery of nature and the wonder of "otherness" which is the result of the numinous consciousness, ultimately Tom does not involve himself with the world. This is most clearly evident during the council of Elrond, when the debate focuses on whether Tom can help with the destruction of the Ring. Gandalf states:

> No, I should not put it so ... say, rather that the Ring has no power over him. He is his own Master. But he cannot alter the Ring itself, nor break its power over others. And now he is withdrawn into a little land, within bounds that he has set, though none can see them, waiting perhaps for a change of days, and he will not step beyond them [Tolkien *The Fellowship of the Rings* 318].

The hint of despair, that Tom will not leave his circumscribed area, is related to Tolkien's theme of power and corruption. In the same letter to Naomi Mitchison, Tolkien says that there are always two sides, good and evil, and each of them desires control in some form or another. However, he states further, "if you have, as it were, taken a 'vow of poverty,' renounced control, and take your delight in things for themselves without reference to yourself, watching, observing, and to some extent knowing, then the question of the rights and wrongs of power and control might become utterly meaningless to you, and the means of power quite valueless" (*The Letters of J.R.R. Tolkien* 179). Although Tom embodies the sense of nature without appropriation, he also distances himself from involvement in the world. It is a shame that, as Tolkien once speculated, Tom could not be made into the hero of a story, because he does represent an important aspect of Tolkien's land ethic; however, the fact that Tom was not entirely removed from the text shows that he is, indeed, an important "comment."

Lothlorien

As Patrick Curry suggests, *The Lord of the Rings* is exceptional due to its expression of a "profound feeling for the natural world" ("Less Noise and More Green" 130). It is this feeling which is the core of the religious expression of the numinous consciousness discussed by Otto in *The Idea of the Holy*. However, as I have argued, this profound feeling for nature comes about by a perception of nature as "other," a perception which is non-appropriative and is the basis for Tolkien's concept of recovery. What must occur with recovery, Tolkien suggests, is "to clean our windows" from our perception of the world as a commodity, as something which is "possessed" or "known" by us ("On Fairy-Stories" 77). When we clean our windows, we see the world in its original sacredness, as a wonder to be appreciated. The fact that nature can be viewed as "other," is similar to Niiler's argument that Tolkien's land ethic is comparable to "land autonomy," which is the argument that nature has the ability to care or fend for itself and that it should be respected as that which is "other." This is especially the case in Niiler's cited example of the Ents' destruction of Isengard which he states "depicts an angry nature responding violently to cultural intrusion and abuse" (280).

The sense of a profound feeling for nature is clearly seen in certain episodes in *The Lord of the Rings*, the most memorable being the chapter on Lothlorien. When the company enters Lothlorien for the first time, it is interesting to note that they must be blindfolded. This is due to the fact that Lothlorien's location must be protected, but the connection with Tolkien's views of recovery is also suggested. When the company is led to Cerin Amroth, they are able to uncover their eyes, and the world of Lothlorien is revealed, reflecting the sense of newness Tolkien suggests with cleaning our windows. When they open their eyes they see the circles of trees, the outer of which have bark of brilliant white, and the inner, the Mallorn trees of golden hue. The green grass is studded with flowers of vibrant colors: gold, white, and green. Up above, the sky is clear blue and the sun illuminates the beauty of the whole scene. When Frodo opens his eyes, his experience reflects Otto's numinous:

> Frodo stood awhile still lost in wonder. It seemed to him that he stepped through a high window that looked on a vanished world. A light was upon it for which his language had no name. All that he saw was shapely, but the shapes seemed at once clear cut, as if they had been first conceived and drawn at the uncovering of his eyes, and ancient as if they had endured for ever. He saw no colour but those he knew, gold and white and blue and green, but they were fresh and poignant, as if he had at that moment first perceived them and made for them names new and wonderful. In winter here no heart could mourn for summer or for spring. No blemish of sickness or deformity could be seen in anything that grew upon the earth. In the land of Lorien there was no stain [Tolkien *The Fellowship of the Rings* 414-15].

Four. The Fading of the World

The fact that Frodo looks on the scene with "wonder" suggests the connection with fantasy critics' defining element of "wonder" as the core of the genre, that feeling-oriented experience which is also undefinable. This is why Frodo's "language" cannot account for what he sees as the beauty of Lothlorien. It relates to Tolkien's ideas of recovery in that although Frodo sees the same colors from the primary world, golds, greens, and whites, they are "fresh" and "poignant," as if he beheld the world for the first time. As Tolkien suggests, it is the world not as it *is*, but as it was *meant* to be seen; it is a recovery of the sacramental vision. The same indefiniteness of this experience of the beauty of Lothlorien is later echoed by Sam when he tries to explain his experiences of Lothlorien: "If there's any magic about, it is right down deep, where I can't lay my hands on it, in a manner of speaking" (Tolkien *The Fellowship of the Rings* 426).

This indescribable quality of a felt experience is exactly that of the numinous consciousness. The reason why it is difficult to explain this experience is its positioning of two realities interfused with the landscape, one sacred, the other profane. In this sense it is also apocalyptic because what is "unveiled" is a transcendent reality which is reflected in the temporal world. It is similar to the animistic thinking of oral cultures where, as Marta García de la Puerta states, "a specific object acquires worth and, in this way becomes real, because it takes part, in one way or another, in a reality that transcends it" (24).

Perceiving this sacred dimension of Middle-earth is life-affirming and involves what Curry views as a sensual appreciation for *this* world. In this respect, Lewis and Tolkien are similar: both authors desire to recover a sense of the sacredness of this world through the vehicle of fantasy, and they achieve this through a consideration of a renewed perception of the world, whether it is Narnia or Middle-earth. Both works involve the second phase of the sublime moment, where the relationship to the habitual breaks down; this is reminiscent of Rosemary Jackson's view that fantasy is subversive. However, in the authors' visions, the transition to the third phase always follows, and it is this phase where a renewed relationship with the natural world may occur. As Tolkien states in his essay "On Fairy-Stories," "in fantasy he may actually assist in the effoliation and multiple enrichment of creation" ("On Fairy-Stories" 89).

Such an appreciation for nature is a view of nature as part of a community, not as a commodity. This involves an appreciation of nature as it is, not for how it can be used. Tolkien had this in mind in many of his scenes involving nature. In the chapter on Lothlorien, again, Frodo climbs up a tree to a flet with Haldir. Frodo's experience of the feel of the tree is described thus: "never before had he been so suddenly and so keenly aware of the feel and texture of a Tree's skin and of the life within it. He felt a delight in wood and the touch of it, neither as a forester nor as carpenter; it was the delight of the living Tree itself" (Tolkien *The Fellowship of the Rings* 415). The chapter on Lothlorien is, perhaps, the most moving chapter in relation to the love of the earth itself; in fact, it was the chapter that moved Tolkien the most, and he felt that the chapter had been written by someone else.

One of the most powerful qualities of the Lothlorien chapter is in its presentation of "Timelessness," a quality which connects it to myth. This is most clearly seen after the company has left Lothlorien and are at a loss to account for the time spent there. Frodo tells Sam: "In that land, maybe, we were in a time that has elsewhere long gone by" (Tolkien *The Fellowship of the Rings* 457). Clearly Lothlorien is meant to symbolize an earthly paradise where time is entirely different from the rest of Middle-earth. This earthly paradise is similar to other images of perfection which Tolkien drew on for his work. Shippey points out that *The Lord of the Rings* is a "mediation" between Christian belief and a pre-Christian world, and Christian belief and the post-Christian world of Tolkien. Concerning the former, Tolkien's image of earthly paradise is similar to the poem "Pearl," a poem which had a particular appeal for Tolkien. In the poem, a father falls asleep on a mound, mourning for his dead daughter Margaret. As he dreams, he is given a vision of her across the river; he is, in effect, in an earthly paradise, where he experiences what Shippey terms "liminal uncertainty," an awareness of the literal world, but also a consequent awareness of a deeper reality underlying the literal world, which is mythic in import. Tolkien is at his best with chapters such as Lothlorien because they show the natural world viewed from the sacramental vision. It is a vision which appreciates nature as it is, beautiful because it is "other." Commenting on this point, Tolkien states in the *Daily Telegraph*, "Lothlorien is beautiful because there the trees were loved" (*The Letters of J.R.R. Tolkien* 419).

However, even in this earthly paradise there exists Tolkien's hint of despair. Most of the characters and settings in *The Lord of the Rings* face what Shippey calls "universal final defeat": the changed Shire, the Doom

Four. The Fading of the World

of the Ents, and the dwindling of the Elves. One is reminded of the fading of the beauties of Middle-earth through the character of Galadriel. She is the character who reminds the company of the inevitability of loss. When Galadriel allows Frodo a glance into her mirror, she explains to him what his coming means to Lothlorien:

> Do you not see now wherefore your coming is to us as the footstep of Doom? For if you fail, then we are laid bare to the enemy. Yet if you succeed, then our power is diminished, and Lothlorien will fade, and the tides of time will sweep it away. We must depart into the West, or dwindle to a rustic folk of dell and cave, slowly to forget and to be forgotten" [Tolkien *The Fellowship of the Rings* 431].

This same sense of loss is seen when Galadriel gives her gift of earth to Sam for him to use for his garden if he ever makes it back to the Shire. She hopes that when he uses the earth for planting he will remember Lothlorien, even though he has only seen it in winter. She says, "For our spring and our summer are gone by, and they will never be seen on earth again save in memory" (Tolkien *The Fellowship of the Rings* 443).

Passages such as these serve to point out that although Lothlorien is an earthly paradise, it too is subject to loss and final defeat, and Galadriel is one of the representations of this loss. This sense of loss is always in the background of *The Lord of the Rings*. Universal final defeat is what most of the characters must face in one form or another, and the Third Age, that Age which gives readers beautiful glimpses of nature as seen through the sacramental vision, must give way to the Fourth Age, the Dominion of Men. In this way, *The Lord of the Rings* acts as a "mediation" between Tolkien's Christian belief and the post–Christian world in which he was living. Symbolically the mediation is represented by two characters, one who symbolizes the wonder inherent in the natural world, the other its destruction by means of technological advance: Treebeard and Saruman.

Treebeard and Saruman

Tolkien once stated in the *Daily Telegraph*, "In all my works I take the part of trees as against all their enemies" (*The Letters of J.R.R. Tolkien* 419). Certainly Tolkien's "tree-love" (as one critic describes it) is one of the most vividly expressed sentiments in *The Lord of the Rings*, especially in the character of Treebeard and the Ents. As with all of Tolkien's forest scenes, however, one must be on the constant alert. Tolkien never romanticizes nature, and this point is related to his expression of the numinous. It has been stated that, for Otto, the numinous is a sense of "holiness" in the original meaning of the word as that which inspires awe but is beyond such moral categories as "good" or "evil"; this is why, in fact, it is referred to as that which is non-rational. It is interesting that Treebeard never claims to be on the "side" of anybody. Pippen and Merry seem consumed by this point, constantly trying to figure out if Treebeard is willing to help in the quest. However, concerning such future events, Treebeard states, "I do not know about the future. I am not altogether on anybody's side, if you understand me: nobody cares for the woods as I care for them, not even Elves nowadays" (Tolkien *The Two Towers* 75).

The fact that Treebeard does not care for "sides" shows that, like Tom Bombadil, he symbolizes something which is beyond the rational, beyond the mere duality of "good" or "evil." This unaligned quality has its origin in the numinous, that sense of awe which is feeling-oriented rather than part of a rational, dualistic universe. Furthermore, the encounter with the Ents is similar to the sections on Tom Bombadil and Lothlorien due to the emphasis on indescribability, a quality which has been argued as foundational both for a consideration of the numinous as well as the quality of wonder to which fantasy critics refer. Upon meeting Treebeard for the first time, Pippen is at pains to describe his encounter with the Ent:

> I don't know, but it felt as if something that grew in the ground—asleep, you might say, or just feeling itself as something between root-tip and leaf-tip, between deep earth and sky had suddenly waked up, and was considering you with the same slow care that it had given its own inside affairs for endless years [Tolkien *The Two Towers* 66].

The indescribable quality which Pippen and Merry "feel" when they meet Treebeard is related to the awakening of the Ents, a process which was started with the Elves who first started talking to trees but which was hindered by the "Great Darkness," after which some of the trees began to get "sleepy." It is an important environmental message which is at the center of the conflict between nature as wonderful and nature as utilitarian. This view of nature as utilitarian is revealed by the enemy, Saruman.

Four. The Fading of the World

As Shippey points out, the etymology of the word Saruman traces its meaning to something similar to "cunning man," and what he stands for is "a kind of mechanical ingenuity, smithcraft developed into engineering skills" (170). He is the voice of modernity, a "restless ingenuity, skill without purpose, bulldozing for the sake of change" (Shippey 171). Saruman's orcs aid him in his quest for ultimate power, and this quest for power Tolkien equates with a destruction of the environment. The orcs fell trees, often just for the sake of felling trees, and Saruman is referred to by the Ents as "tree-killer." As Treebeard says of Saruman, "he has a mind of metal and wheels; and he does not care for growing things, except as far as they serve him for the moment" (Tolkien *The Two Towers* 76).

This type of attitude is what leads to an appropriation of nature, a utilitarian mindset in which nature is viewed as property without an intrinsic value in and of itself. The Ents' battle against this attitude of Saruman and his minions is an important environmental message. The attitude of "environmental owning" is precisely what keeps one from acquiring the sacramental vision. We cannot experience the sense of awe to which Otto refers unless we divorce ourselves from a possessive, utilitarian worldview. Saruman is typical of Tolkien's appropriative view of nature. As Shippey states, "the Sarumans of the real world rule by deluding their followers with images of a technological paradise in the future, a modernist utopia; but what one often gets ... are the blasted landscapes of Eastern Europe, stripmined, polluted, and even radioactive" (171).

Today, forests cover less than 6 percent of the earth's surface; whereas, they used to cover 60 percent. Treebeard represents that final struggle for nature against what Tolkien called the "machine-loving enemy" (*The Letters of J.R.R. Tolkien* 420). What is validated in Tolkien's *The Lord of the Rings* is the survival of nature itself, in contradistinction to the appropriative, utilitarian attitude of Sauron and Saruman. This is similar to Elgin's argument that the comic mode, which values the survival of the system, is more important in Tolkien's vision than the domination of one technocrat. Tolkien's book is a validation of life itself, a validation of the survival of nature. Treebeard represents this survival of nature. Indeed, one may applaud Treebeard and the Ents' battle for survival, especially due to the fact that they are successful at destroying Isengard and imprisoning Saruman in his own tower. However, even in the face of the survival of the system, there is the ever-present hint of despair. Despite their victory, the Ents are also a part of the fading of Middle-earth.

The hint of despair associated with Treebeard and the Ents is that, as Treebeard states, there are very few Ents left in Middle-earth. Although the true Ents were awakened by the Elves in the distant past, there is reference to the "Great Darkness" which came, and the Elves "made songs about days that would never come again" (Tolkien *The Two Towers* 70). Treebeard laments this same loss when he tells Pippen, "some of us are true Ents, and lively enough in our own fashion, but many are growing sleepy, going tree-ish, as you might say" (Tolkien *The Two Towers* 69). So, despite the fact that the remaining Ents are awakened and have considerable success in their battle with Isengard and Saruman, one is reminded that the Third Age is drawing to a close and that the Ents will slowly diminish, as is the fate of so many of the characters in *The Lord of the Rings*. The recovery of nature cannot last; the sacramental vision must fade. Answering Aragorn's wish that the forests will eventually grow again in peace, Treebeard laments "forests may grow ... woods may spread. But no Ents. There are no Entings" (Tolkien *The Return of the King* 280).

Of course, the fading of the Ents is related to the loss of the Entwives, which is recounted to Merry and Pippen during their stay with Treebeard. Although in a time past the Ents and the Entwives existed together, eventually the two were sundered, and the Ents are unable to discover the whereabouts of the Entwives. As Treebeard relates the story to Merry and Pippen, he tells them about what he believes is their fate:

> We believe that we may meet again in a time to come, and perhaps we shall find somewhere a land where we can live together and both be content. But it is foreboded that that will only be when we both have lost all that we now have. And it may well be that that time is drawing near at last. For if Sauron of old destroyed the gardens, the Enemy today seems likely to wither all the woods [Tolkien *The Two Towers* 80].

Thus the fate of the Ents seems bleak, and although these characters are Tolkien's closest embodiment of the necessity of recovering a new relationship with nature through the sacramental vision, the message seems to be that, with the dominion of Men, all will be lost. As Treebeard states, "for the world is changing: I feel it in the water, I feel it in the earth, and

I smell it in the air" (Tolkien *The Return of the King* 281). The sacramental vision must give way to the "machine-loving enemy."

The Shire

As many critics have pointed out, the Shire represents Tolkien's recreation of the pastoral and the longing for some sort of "idealized land." As Tolkien was well aware in his time, and as we are more so in our own time, the industrialization of our world divorces us from an experience of the sacramental vision, and there is more of a need to experience it within literary forms. Douglas A. Burger says in his article "The Shire: A Tolkien Version of Pastoral," that "the pastoral is marked by a yearning for a simpler, more natural, more meaningful way of life" (149). Critics have pointed out that many of the images of the pastoral are presented at the beginning of *The Lord of the Rings*: the Shire is a peaceful place, the occupations are largely agricultural, the dwellings of the hobbits are within the earth (note that their short stature and bare feet connect them to the earth), and the Shire is largely unaffected by the outside world. Thus at the beginning of the novel, Tolkien immediately evokes a sense of home, and as the novel progresses, the Shire will embody a sense of nostalgia for this home.

The Shire acts as a "foil" for other images of home in *The Lord of the Rings*. Burger further argues that we feel the wonder of such places as Fangorn forest or Lothlorien precisely because we have been introduced to the pastoralism of the Shire first. It is the first image of home which is recreated in fantastic forms over and over again: "its appeal is to the deep-rooted human desire for a more natural way of life, a simpler society, and a recovery of a sense of home" (Burger 153). In terms of the ecological arguments presented in this thesis, the Shire represents a closeness to nature, and the hobbits' attitude is one of community, not of commodity.

However, as with all such images in Tolkien's world, the Shire must also undergo change. As Don Elgin points out, even though nature is a powerful image in Tolkien's Middle-earth, it cannot beat the abstraction of evil: "Nature is not enough: it can be destroyed by those who through carelessness or actual intent try to bend it to their own will" (40). The powers of evil, those of Sauron and Saruman, represent this threat to the natural world, and one feels this loss most poignantly in the chapter "The Scouring of the Shire." It is the chapter which contains much of Tolkien's own childhood experience, where the idealized landscape of his youth was transformed by the advance of industry.

The first real awareness of the scouring in the text is when the hobbits reach Bywater, their own country, and are confronted with the destruction of their land:

> The pleasant row of old hobbit-holes in the bank on the north side of the Pool were deserted, and their little gardens that used to run down bright to the water's edge were rank with weeds. Worse, there was a whole line of the ugly new houses all along Pool Side, where the Hobbiton Road ran close to the bank. An avenue of trees had stood there. They were all gone. And looking with dismay up the road towards Bag End they saw a chimney of brick in the distance. It was pouring out black smoke into the evening air [Tolkien *The Return of the King* 307].

The hobbits continue to be amazed at the destruction of their environment. Not only that, but they are at pains to understand the gates, guards, and the laws which have challenged the sense of simplicity which the Shire represents.

Eventually they come to discover that all the destruction started with Pimple. Farmer Cotton says of this character that it "seems he wanted to own everything himself, and then order the folk about" (Tolkien *The Return of the King* 316). This echoes the idea of the appropriation of nature which Tolkien's theories of fantasy counter; it represents nature as something to be used. Before long, Pimple's attitude leads to a felling of trees, a building of houses and sheds, and a looting among the people. However, even though Pimple is responsible for beginning the scouring of the Shire, it eventually becomes clear that Sharkey, an appellation for Saruman, is to blame; thus, the tree-slayer is again responsible for the destruction of nature:

> They're always a-hammering and a-letting out a smoke and a stench, and there isn't no peace even at night in Hobbiton. And they pour out filth a purpose; they've fouled all the lower water, and its getting down into the Brandywine. If they want to make the Shire into a desert, they're going the right way about it. I don't believe that fool of a Pimple's behind all this. It's Sharkey, I say [Tolkien *The Return of the King* 318].

Thus the threat to the Shire which Sharkey or Saruman represents is the same threat he represents to the Ents; it is a threat of appropriation, a

Four. The Fading of the World

sense of ownership or possession of nature, and it is that which dissociates one from a recovery of nature.

The scouring of the Shire represents the effects of industrialization and the problem is quite bleak. It is true, however, that Tolkien validates the pastoral in the form of the Shire, and he similarly validates the role of Sam. Sam's main concern, other than Frodo, is with the Shire, and it must be remembered that the last images in *The Lord of the Rings* are Sam, his wife Rosie, and their daughter Elanor. The tragic figures, such as Aragorn, are important, but they are all subject to fading. Of course, as readers we know that the hobbits will eventually retreat as well, but we also know that the hobbits represent Tolkien's final validation of nature, of the survival of life itself: "Hobbits know from the start of the novel about the relationship between themselves and nature, and they cannot rule over, dominate, or change it" (Elgin 51).

In the end, however, what must be remembered is that most of the characters do confront universal final defeat. We know that the end of an age has come and that the world of Middle-earth will never be the same. Thus what images such as Tom Bombadil, Lothlorien, Treebeard, and the Shire represent is the nostalgia for a recovery of the sacramental vision; Tolkien's fantasy is a way for images associated with nature to come to life, and for readers to participate in the sacramental vision, for however brief the duration. I have argued that fantasy's subversion is what allows for nature to become real and for us to contemplate our relationship to nature in a new, more imaginative manner. As with Lewis's *The Last Battle*, *The Lord of the Rings* provides readers with this relationship on the epic scale. The numinous, that which lies behind the sacramental vision, is to be seen in the outer landscape of the created world. Readers sense the numinous in *The Lord of the Rings*, and this is the reason the text can be religious without containing any direct religious reference. Even though the sacramental vision in *The Lord of the Rings* is an embodiment of Tolkien's own theory of recovery, we also know that the age has come where these images of the close relationship to nature must give way to the Dominion of Man in the Fourth Age. This final hint of despair is presented when Aragorn, the king returned, is overlooking his own city with Gandalf by his side. Gandalf reminds him of the inevitability of change:

> This is your realm, and the heart of the greater realm that shall be. The Third Age of the world is ended, and the new age is begun; and it is your task to

order its beginning and to preserve what may be preserved. For though much has been saved, much must now pass away; and the power of the Three Rings also is ended. And all the lands that you see, and those that lie round about them, shall be dwellings of Men. For the time comes of the Dominion of Men, and the Elder Kindred shall fade or depart [Tolkien *The Return of the King* 269].

CHAPTER FIVE

Affirming the World That Swerves

The Alter-Tales in Algernon Blackwood's The Centaur *and Ursula Le Guin's* Buffalo Gals and Other Animal Presences

So far, the discussion of fantasy's potential to subvert normative views of the world in favor of a more sacramental vision of nature has resulted in an examination of authors who have been male, who are now deceased, and who have Christianity as their dominant worldview. We have analyzed how some environmental critics are quick to blame the Christian mythos for the separation between humans and nature, but that these Christian fantasists are using the Christian mythos in exactly the opposite way: they are subverting ways of looking at the world in order to engage with it. However, is the Christian worldview the only accessible vehicle for fantasy authors? Are there authors who have the same mythopoeic message in their fiction but are drawing perhaps a bit more widely from the mythological well? Are any of them still alive? Are any of them female? The answer to these questions is, of course, yes. The purpose of this transitional chapter is to set up two authors in particular who, through their fiction, want their readers to participate in the sense of the numinous as well as subvert their views of nature so that it is seen in a new way.

The question may be asked, "For what reason?" Since authors such as Lewis and Tolkien (and Coleridge and MacDonald), are often lumped together, it seems only logical to end the discussion here; it makes sense to discuss these authors, you may ask, so why are you bringing in Algernon Blackwood and Ursula Le Guin? However, what we face in a post-modern, posthumanist world, is the question of meaning. What about those authors or readers who don't subscribe to the Christian mythos but who still sense the numinous in nature? What about those for whom fantasy is now their primary means of encountering something of the spiritual but who can't find it in the postmodern world? What about those of us for whom life is disenchanted?

One approach to these issues is to draw on the form of "enchanted materialism" as offered by Jane Bennett in her work *The Enchantment of Modern Life: Attachments, Crossings and Ethics*. The problem with the modern world, Bennett argues, is that our Western emphasis on rationalism and skepticism has led to a sense of meaninglessness, that anything which is nonhuman (the rocks, the wind, the earth), is merely "inert matter"; nature, as well as the whole world, becomes disenchanted.

What is at the heart of this disenchantment tale that we so often tell ourselves? Bennett argues that the tale takes many forms. Our modern, highly rational world is in direct contrast to more holistic ways of perceiving the world. Yes, we have mastery over the world, but we pay a price for it, mainly in that we feel a sense of meaninglessness. We miss the point that "progress" entails both hope and despair; and, that our only safety valves for these forms are the "recalcitrant fugitives" of the erotic and the mystical. What I am arguing is that fantasy as we have been defining it, is one of those recalcitrant fugitives that offers an alter-tale or a different way to counter the disenchantment tale.

Throughout the course of her book, Bennett argues that Eden is always at the back of the disenchantment tale. According to Bennett, in retelling the disenchantment tale through the writings of Max Weber, Hans Blumenberg, and Simon Critchley, religion is partly to blame because science has robbed the world of the gods so that the focus has shifted not to this world but to the otherworld where salvation can be found. The dismissal of this world de-sanctifies it and leads to seeing the world as disenchanted.

The alternative to the disenchantment tale, the alter-tale that Bennett offers, is a world filled with enchantment. Bennett defines enchantment as follows:

> Enchantment entails a state of wonder, and one of the distinctions of this state is the temporary suspension of chronological time and bodily movement. To be enchanted, then, is to participate in a momentary immobilizing encounter; it is to be transfixed, spellbound [Bennett 5].

Five. Affirming the World That Swerves

And further:

> To be enchanted is to be both charmed and disturbed: Charmed by a fascinating repetition of sounds or images, disturbed to find that, although your sense-perception has become intensified, your background sense of order has flown out the door [Bennett 34].

Bennett argues that enchantment implies both a pleasurable and disruptive mood; it is a surprise that comes in the form of the unexpected. Otto's definition of the numinous also implies that which is disturbing. Otto refers to the numinous as that feeling of holiness that is devoid of any moral implications. In fact, the numinous in religion actually started off as a feeling of dread and only later evolved into more complex forms. It seems, then, that Bennett would be in agreement with our thesis: fantasy, defined broadly as any departure from consensus reality, evokes a sense of wonder at the natural world precisely because it subverts (and disturbs) our normative views of the world only to replace them with a profound sense of the numinous.

Bennett calls her enchanted materialism a neo- or quasi-pagan model that goes against a Western tradition that posits a divine creator behind the world. Throughout history, many thinkers (such as Paracelsus) were determined to find divine signs in nature, thus being influenced by Christian cosmology. Bennett asks us to consider alternatives. Can we find enchantment in a world without *telos* or intrinsic purpose? Are there any options other than the Christian for a life of enchantment? For Bennett, such enchantment can be found in various sites, including the literary, the machinic, and the electronic. Bennett's discussion covers a wide variety of sites of enchantment including Kafka, Thoreau, nanotechnology, bureaucracy, and even the 1998 Gap ad "Khakis Swing." Instead of looking to some purposive element behind all of this, enchanted materialism looks to a world where literary characters morph, nanotechnology can transform food into razor blades, khakis can dance, and nature can speak. For Bennett, surely that world is enchanted. How is it? Because enchanted materialism does not proclaim that the human is the only source of agency. In enchanted materialism, agency is distributed more widely, to include sites of enchantment that disrupt the human as center.

Drawing upon Epicurus and Lucretius, Bennett discusses the fact that the world is not disenchanted. For Epicurus, matter is wondrous and there need not be a divine creator behind anything. Atoms or *primordia* fall through the universe, but they do it with a twist, or a swerve, so that things are repeated but never in the same way. This swerve is what makes the world vibrant and filled with life; it is that sense of quirkiness of matter that makes all things mobile.

Bennett takes issue with ecospiritualists, those who feel that nature is dull and lifeless and their need to re-enchant nature; nature was never disenchanted for Bennett. Our forms of enchantment have just shifted. If we look, not to the heavens for the numinous, but in the unique specificity of the things of nature, there we will find our enchantment. For Bennett, "Enchantment is a feeling of being connected in an affirmative way to existence; it is to be under the momentary impression that the natural and cultural worlds *offer gifts* and, in doing so, remind us that it is good to be alive" (Bennett 156). Two such authors who offer us literary gifts are Algernon Blackwood and Ursula Le Guin. It is these authors who offer non-teleological fantasies which engage our sense of the numinous and wake us up to the marvelous specificity of nature.

CHAPTER SIX

"A daisy is nearer heaven than an airship"
The Utopian Vision in Algernon Blackwood's The Centaur

"He read the book of Nature all about him, yes, but read it singing."—Algernon Blackwood, *The Centaur* [217]

"Few hear the Pipes of Pan as you do. Few care to listen. To-day the world is full of other sounds that drown it."—Algernon Blackwood, *The Centaur* [241]

"You ... come ... with ... us?"

These words of invitation are offered to Terence O'Malley, the central character of Algernon Blackwood's novel *The Centaur*, by a mysterious and massive Russian man whom O'Malley meets aboard a ship bound for the Caucasus. What O'Malley doesn't realize is this is an invitation from an *Urwelt,* a German word Blackwood interestingly leaves un-translated, but which comes to mean something like "primeval man"; the *Urwelt* will take O'Malley (and the reader) on a journey literally through the Caucasus and figuratively to a mystical experience of nature. It is a journey that will require an expansion of consciousness and a revisioning of the sacramental nature of the world

It is unfortunate that Blackwood (1869–1951), who was such a mystic and a powerful writer, should be largely ignored by critics. In fact, S.T. Joshi, the leading scholar of the weird tale, refers to Blackwood as a "cypher" in the world of academia and popular literature, and an author who is just waiting to be discovered. What makes Blackwood relevant as an author is his attempt to, through his writings, introduce readers to an extra-sensory experience of the world where the mundane is perceived in a new, more sacramental manner. Through his fiction, Blackwood is trying to revise our perceptions of the world in a radical way.

Since Blackwood is frequently referred to as a "weird writer," one must address exactly what this term means. Unfortunately, this is impossible, especially given the blurring of lines between genres such as fantasy, horror, and science-fiction. Further confusion results from the fact that many of the authors now known as writers of the weird (Arthur Machen, M.R. James, Lord Dunsany) never considered themselves to be writing anything other than mainstream fiction. H.P. Lovecraft was the only writer who consciously identified himself as an author of the weird. Therefore, it's only retrospectively that we can call them "weird." What is clear is that these authors all had as their aim the creation of an atmosphere or a mood that resulted from some unknown force(s), and that this mood could aid in what Joshi defines as the key element of all weird fiction—the refashioning of the readers' view of the world (118). This refashioning or revision of perceptions has been pointed out clearly in Joshi's critical work, *The Weird Tale*. In his introduction, Joshi admits that the weird tale is impossible to define but can loosely be seen as an umbrella term for the related fields of fantasy, supernatural horror, non-supernatural horror, or quasi-science-fiction. A refashioning of the world, or a revision of the world as we have been describing it in other chapters, is at the heart of the weird tale. Joshi says that it should not be seen as a genre in and of itself but as "a consequence of a worldview" and that these authors create their tales to help readers revise, restructure or rethink their views of nature and their relation to it. This makes the weird tale a highly philosophical art form, a form of art that helps readers question fundamental attitudes towards the world, our place in the universe, and our purpose.

Since most of Blackwood's work is highly autobiographical, it is helpful to delve into his interests. At various times, he wanted to be a poet, a violinist, a mountaineer, and even a holy man. Being raised in a religious household, there was an ever-present fear of hell and damnation. To counter this fear, Blackwood learned early on the importance of the inner self as the source of what was, to him, the only *real* religion. Early in his life, he became a member of the Society for Psychical Research (SPR), investigating paranormal activities residing in "haunted houses." Later in life, his interest in theories of karma and reincarnation drew him to learn hypnotism and meditation, at one point even declaring

Six. "A daisy is nearer heaven than an airship"

himself a Buddhist. Through these Eastern influences he found out about the Theosophical Society, and although he never became a member, he was immersed in reading all the materials he could get his hands on, materials that synthesized religions, philosophies, and sciences and which taught a "Universal Brotherhood" for all. He actually did become a member of the Hermetic Order of the Golden Dawn, whose most famous members were William Butler Yeats and Aleister Crowley. The purpose of the Golden Dawn was to explore the Hebrew mysticism present in the Kabbalah and to understand one's relationship with deity.

The mystical aspects of Blackwood both in his writing and in his personal life are what connects him with the numinous and his desire for his readers to view the world sacramentally. In Blackwood's autobiography, *Episodes Before Thirty*, he indicates that his interest in mysticism and the occult was largely the result of his upbringing in a strict religious home. His father was a revivalist and part of the evangelical movement during his time, and he describes both of his parents as unshakable in their faith. Although Blackwood disagreed with the strict upbringing, he was aware that his father instilled in him a passion for all things religious. Two key elements shaped Blackwood's religious sensibilities during this time. The first was his stay at a Moravian Brotherhood school in the Black Forest. A young Blackwood realized that he was deeply affected by the natural surroundings of the Black Forest, and he says, "It left upon me an impression of grandeur, of loftiness, or real religion ... and of a deity not specifically active on Sundays only" (Blackwood *Episodes before Thirty* 26). This awareness of the beauty in nature continued through his younger years, so much so that Blackwood would feel himself to have a much different temperament than most. One of his favorite pastimes was to walk out to a pond near his house at night while everyone was asleep. Contemplating the beauty of his natural surroundings, Blackwood wondered how anyone could remain asleep to these beauties; such people seemed, to him at least, to be from a different race.

The importance of nature in Blackwood cannot be overemphasized. Although he experienced a closeness with nature at a early age, this increased throughout his life and became the dominant influence in all his writings. Nature always offered companionship, joy, and a sense of the numinous that no other relationship in his life could offer. The most often cited passage from *Episodes Before Thirty* clearly points out Blackwood's attitude towards nature:

> By far the strongest influence in my life, however, was Nature; it betrayed itself early, growing in intensity with every year. Bringing comfort, companionship, inspiration, joy, the spell of Nature has remained dominant, a truly magical spell. Always immense and potent, the years have strengthened it. The early feeling that everything was alive, a dim sense that some kind of consciousness struggled through every form, even that a sort of inarticulate communication with this 'other life' was possible, could I but discover the way—these moods coloured its opening wonder. Nature, at any rate, produced effects in me that only something living could produce [Blackwood *Episodes before Thirty* 32-33].

The second experience that shaped Blackwood's religious sensibility was his discovery of Eastern religions. The story goes that one of the Blackwood family friends was staying with the family and writing a pamphlet on the dangers of Eastern religious thought. When he left, he accidently left one of the books he was researching for his pamphlet: *Yoga Aphorisms* by Patanjali. Blackwood devoured this book and said that "a deeper feeling than I had yet known woke in me" (Blackwood *Episodes before Thirty* 28). Blackwood continued to read books on Eastern religious thought, especially books such as the Upanishads and The Bhagavad-Gita, which he believed were the most profound books he had ever read.

What Blackwood sensed from these books is of interest because Blackwood was reforming his religious views of the world. Instead of a deity "active on Sundays only," which he witnessed from his Christian upbringing, he sensed a deeper reality, a unity, and one-ness of all things. In *Episodes Before Thirty*, Blackwood is clear in pointing out that this awareness of the unity of life was not something that was discovered but recovered. Furthermore, this truth was something that he *knew*, a conclusion he grasped intuitively through his readings rather than through the intellect.

This awareness of the unity of all life, which Blackwood "recovered," is what leads critics and readers alike to refer to Blackwood as a "mystic." This term is not to be taken lightly. When critics such as S.T. Joshi, Peter Penzoldt, or Stuart Gilbert use the word "mystic" as applied to Blackwood, they mean it in the most technical way. Mysticism is a form of consciousness that, while akin to religion, is actually quite different. Mysticism is free of dogma, and the mystics' experience is one of a direct revelation of a higher power. It is beyond the purview of the intellect and can only be experienced in an intuitive manner. It is often indescribable, but the mystic is absolutely convinced of the truth of the expe-

Six. "A daisy is nearer heaven than an airship"

rience. This is interesting when applied to the above statement from Blackwood; he always refers to the experience as being somehow "known."

Mysticism is what leads one to an experience of the numinous. Mysticism is the root of all religions, often being referred to as the *perennial philosophy* because the same experiences are perceived regardless of their particular religion. According to F.C. Happold's book *Mysticism*, there are a number of assertions of mysticism; so, before we show their applicability to Blackwood's work, we must identify these assertions:

1. We only see reality from a partial perspective. This is the result of having made a "primary act of intellectual faith" where one way of viewing reality is chosen over another. We often assume that this is the only way of viewing reality when it is not. Part of the problem is our Western European tradition that values logic and reason as the only means to understand reality. Mystics assert that there is a deeper reality, sometimes referred to as the "Ground of Being," which we can experience.

2. We can know or experience this "Ground of Being" through insight, intuition, or imagination and *not* through reason. In fact, reason, by its very nature, is antithetical to the mystical experience.

3. Usually what prevents one from having a mystical experience is the exclusionary dominance of what we refer to as our "ego" or "self." We fail to recognize that we have a dual nature, and that only the foreground of consciousness is the ego. The background, the "Ground of Being" is the eternal "Self" which is often equated with "God."

4. It is our chief concern to realize or experience this eternal Self or Ground.

There are many different types of mystical experiences, so much so that the term mysticism is impossible to define. Some of the most prevalent forms, however, can be characterized as Soul-Mysticism, God-Mysticism, and Nature-Mysticism. This last form, obviously, is the one that closely relates to Blackwood and his fiction. Nature-Mysticism involves a belief that there is a divine energy that is immanent in nature, meaning that it is "inner" rather than "outer." As with other forms of mysticism, the way to access this divine energy is through what critics call a "purgation of the self." Once the self or ego has been "purged" or "renounced," a widening of perception occurs where all of nature is seen as the manifestation of "God." What happens is "a continuous cleansing of the perceptions and a scouring of the windows of the soul, so that the light of a new reality may stream in and completely illuminate and transform it" (Happold 58). The reference to "the scouring of the windows" is reminiscent of Tolkien's view of the function of fantasy to clean our windows. This quote from Happold precisely sums up mythopoeic fantasy is a subversive act which helps readers re-envision our relationship to nature and allows us to experience the numinous.

What is perhaps most interesting in Happold's book on mysticism is that the mystical experience is always one of an extension or expansion of consciousness that widens the perception of the mystic. In relation to the fourth assertion—that the goal is to experience this deeper self—Happold interestingly refers to the process of evolution. If evolution is a movement from the simple to the complex, might it not be possible that mystics are on the forefront of a totally revolutionary way of relating to the world, a way for us to realize our connection with all things? If our consciousness is used in a different way, would we see reality differently? Blackwood seems to have "known" this truth from an early age. It was spending time in the Black Forest in Germany, and reading Eastern religions, then, that made Blackwood a true mystic. What is even more interesting, however, is that Blackwood used his fiction to promote this mystical outlook.

Blackwood was known to his audience as the "Ghost Man" due to his prolific output of supernatural stories. It is interesting to note, however, that he takes issue with this association. In his *Preface* to *Tales of Terror and the Unknown*, Blackwood believes that the association is a derogatory one, and that his only interest in writing tales of the supernatural is to engage in what he calls the extension or expansion of the human faculty. He again refers to this extension of consciousness in his essay "The Genesis of Ideas." He admits that when he was younger, he felt a strange thrill at anything supernatural, but that when he got older, he became more interested in what made someone actually see a ghost or anything other-worldly. In short, what he wanted to know was what *enabled* one to see a ghost. Blackwood states, "My interest lay then in the extension of human faculty, and in the possibility that the mind has powers which only manifest themselves occasionally" (Blackwood "The Genesis of Ideas" 37).

For Blackwood, stories always have to begin with a strong, deep emotion. He says that this can be caused by anything, the beauty of

Six. "A daisy is nearer heaven than an airship"

nature, music, wonder, or even supernatural horror. What is of most importance for Blackwood though, is always the emotion. As an example, Blackwood points to the genesis of the novel *The Centaur*. He refers to the "stupendous grandeur" of the Caucasus when he traveled there and that they made such a profound effect on him that he couldn't find the words to write about the experience. He says, "bewildered and confused with so much wonder and 'awful loveliness' the mind seemed literally speechless" (Blackwood "The Genesis of Ideas" 36). This emphasis on emotion that Blackwood favors is exactly that experience of the numinous which I have been describing through the theories of Rudolf Otto. The "wonder" and "awful loveliness" Blackwood refers to is the thrill one gets in the presence of something greater than oneself, an experience or an emotion which goes beyond mere description but which is powerfully felt. It is an experience for which, Blackwood admits, reason must abdicate. So, when Blackwood takes offense at the term "Ghost Man," he doesn't mean that he is a mere writer of stories that involve a ghost, but tales that give readers that sense of awe leftover from primitive times. We all have it, Blackwood asserts, and the successful writer is the one who can invoke this feeling and embody it in a story. This feeling of the ghostly, that which inspires awe, is what connects him with the ideas of the numinous. It is also, for many of Blackwood's critics, a function of what the present study is identifying as mythopoeic writing, writing which engages the reader with the feeling of the numinous.

This mode of writing is very different from other supernatural works before Blackwood. For example, any cursory reading of such Gothic classics as Walpole's *The Castle of Otranto*, or Radcliffe's *The Mysteries of Udolpho* will notice the artificial or mechanistic way in which the material is treated; it is as if the writer's are trying their hand at this new medium, and trying to get as much entertainment value as they can. Not that there is anything wrong with what they are doing. It's just that Blackwood has a much broader goal in mind. He focused all his energy on writing that has the ability to expand the human consciousness. Blackwood would more than likely agree with critic Stuart Gilbert's assessment of the function of art in today's world: "Surely the function of art to-day, in whatever medium, is the opening of windows, the letting in of light into that house of bondage, the mind of modern man, slave of his vaunted emancipation" and that artists who have a "recognition of the miraculous," perhaps something that is lacking in modern man, "may well be the beginning of wisdom, and to revive our sense of wonder is, perhaps, the highest function of imaginative art" (Gilbert 90–91).

Reviving the readers' sense of "wonder" (or the numinous as we have been calling it in our discussion) is what occurs in much of Blackwood's work, but especially in the novel *The Centaur* (1911). It is in this work that readers get the full expression of Blackwood's mystical outlook, and in fact, *The Centaur* is the work that Blackwood believed was the closest to his own views. There are problems with the book to be sure. As critic S.T. Joshi clearly points out, the novel fails as a novel. There is just not much of a plot to consider, and one can tell that Blackwood himself is not so much concerned with plot as he is in getting across his views about the horrors of civilization. It's more Blackwood's philosophy given novel form than anything else.

The Centaur is interesting also because it contains within it what I would argue is not only a fictional account of an experience of the numinous, but a subtext which promotes Blackwood's own rallying for a paradigm shift: one where "modern" man goes back to the "primitive." This subtext which Blackwood supplies is what makes the novel fit into mythopoeic art, not only "awakening" the numinous for the reader but also revising reality (Hume) and, as a subversive act, challenging the reader's perception of reality (Jackson).

The evidence for this subtext is seen in various passages through *Episodes Before Thirty,* Blackwood's autobiography of the early years of his life. As has been mentioned previously, the biggest influence on Blackwood's life was nature. It was here where he felt most at home, and it was in nature where he experienced the unity of all things and felt a divine connection. However, there was something else which nature offered Blackwood: an almost religious calling to help humanity in some form or another. In *Episodes*, Blackwood states:

> Nature drew me, perhaps, away from life, while a the same time there glowed in my heart strange unrealizable desires to help life, to assist at her utopian development, to work myself to the bone for the improvement of humanity [Blackwood *Episodes before Thirty* 218].

And further:

> The intense longing to lose my self in some utopian cause was as strong as the other longing to be lost in the heart of some unstained and splendid wilderness of natural beauty [Blackwood *Episodes before Thirty* 218].

Six. "A daisy is nearer heaven than an airship"

What is this "utopian" vision that Blackwood seems to have desired in his life? Did he ever realize it? What did it entail? By looking at passages in *The Centaur*, we can argue that the character O'Malley is the mouthpiece of Blackwood, and the utopian vision that is presented is Blackwood's attempt at mythopoeic art that helps to revise our perceptions of nature to allow readers an experience of the numinous. What is different with Blackwood, however, is that he is presenting his worldview primarily through the influence of Eastern religions such as Hinduism and Buddhism, and secondarily through religious metaphors from the West. This is in direct contrast to the previous authors (Coleridge, MacDonald, Lewis, and Tolkien) who have attempted the same revision of the natural world but who *only* did it under the influence of the Judeo-Christian worldview. So it would be safe to say that their outcomes are the same but their means of achieving it differ.

In the introduction, it was mentioned that another way to orient oneself with the world is not through mythic dissociation, which is characteristic of Western thought, but through mythic association, where the oneness of all things is experienced in a numinous manner. There is no separation between "God," humans, or nature due to the inherent oneness of these things. This is also characteristic of the mystical view of which Blackwood's vision is a part. In *The Centaur*, mythic association is central to Blackwood's subtext of viewing the world in a sacramental manner. This worldview is influenced heavily by the philosophy of Gustav Theodor Fechner, a German experimental psychologist who believed that the universe was consciously alive, that just as humans could project or expand their personalities, so to could the Earth. In fact, the projections of the Earth have survived from the past in the form of gods, monsters, and other mythical beings. The Russian, who is a central figure in *The Centaur*, is actually a survival of one of these projections of the past and thus part of Earth herself. This is evident in the novel when the doctor explains to the narrator some of Fechner's ideas; he uses the analogy of the ocean and tree, saying that humans are mere wavelets on the ocean, or that humans grow from the earth as leaves on a tree. Some, the Doctor explains, have a "cosmic consciousness" and are aware of the unity of all things, but not many; most, in fact, are only aware of separateness, of a mythic dissociation where all things are divided. The Doctor says that the problem lies in our own egoistic, selfish desires; we cling to our own individuality without seeing a connection among all things. This is the same way humans tend to view nature: "Men to-day prided themselves upon their superiority to Nature and beings separate and apart" (Blackwood *The Centaur* 15).

This mythic dissociation is part of the way Blackwood himself sees the present state of the world, and part of the reason why in his novel he sets up the dichotomy between civilization and nature, wanting the reader to question how to see the world and to consider a new way of perceiving it. Here, Blackwood's prose is at its most eloquent. Addressing the narrator about how O'Malley seemed not to be of this century, he says, "why, it's not even my world! And I loathe, *loathe* the spirit of to-day with its cheap jack inventions, and smother of sham universal culture, its murderous superfluities and sordid vulgarity, without enough real sense of beauty left to see that a daisy is nearer heaven than an airship" (Blackwood *The Centaur* 40). Further into the novel, when O'Malley is reflecting on his closeness to nature, he states, "I asked myself how the opinions of men could ever have spun themselves away from life as to deem the earth only a dry clod, and to seek for angels above it or about it in the emptiness of the sky—only to find them nowhere" (Blackwood *The Centaur* 103).

What is noticed with these two quotes is that civilization tends to look "outer" for the numinous and never "inner" to the source of it all. To seek the numinous in the daisy or to see the angels in the dry clod and not without is the result of a new way of seeing the world, a revisioning of our perceptions of it. In fictional terms, this idea is presented in the form of the Russian, who is seen as a projection of the Earth herself. When referring to the Russian, Blackwood retains the German *Urmenschen* to help in his understanding. Doctor Stahl tells O'Malley about the word not referring to a "primitive being" but a "Cosmic Being," a survival from the past of a mythological power, a fragment of the Earth herself, which calls to O'Malley.

What this involves is a shift in perception, one that sees the world in a child-like way. Again, the fictional embodiment of Blackwood's ideals is in the Russian himself. When seeing him for the first time, O'Malley uses the analogy of the child and states that his age was indeterminable, that he seemed to pre-date time itself. He was a powerful and terrific being and "the presence of this stranger took him at a single gulp, as it were, straight into Nature—a Nature that was alive" (Blackwood *The Centaur* 36) and that "he made the inanimate world—sea, stars, wind, woods, and mountains—seem all alive. The entire blessed universe was conscious—and he came straight out of it to get me" (Blackwood *The Centaur* 39).

Perception

Two of the more common tropes that one sees in both mystical literature and religious texts are the child-like and the Garden, both of which are employed by Blackwood to further his subtext of revisioning the world in a sacramental manner. The first, that of seeing the world through the child, appears in many religions, in particular Christianity and Daoism. The child trope goes far beyond a mere experience of the world as "innocent." Though innocence in children is debatable, using the metaphor of the child implies that their seeing the world is non-dual and, in this sense, mystical. As metaphors, children are unaware of differences between themselves and nature, themselves and "God," or even distinctions between male and female. They are also in a constant state of wonder. This idea mirrors Tolkien's claim earlier that to "clean our windows" means that we are to see the world without our appropriations made through language. Again, mythopoeic fantasy has the unique ability to bring nature to life by its own subversive means: anthropomorphizing the tree brings it to life in a new way. Not being aware of distinctions allows children to see the oneness of things.

This child-like perception creates the bridge to the numinous and the ability to view the world sacramentally. The most common reference to the child-like may be seen in Jesus's teachings in Matthew 18:3 where he tells his disciples that unless they become like little children, they will not enter the kingdom of heaven. Similarly, in Daoism, the same message is present. Chapter 10 of the Dao De Jing asks the reader a series of questions, one of which is: "attending fully and becoming supple, can you be as a newborn babe?" It is interesting that this question follows a preceding one which asks if one can avoid separation and see the oneness of the Dao. It seems as if these two religions/philosophies are drawing upon one of the central tenants of Happold's characteristics of mysticism, which is to view the "Ground of Being" that allows one to transcend dualistic thought. This, indeed, is the perennial philosophy.

In *The Centaur*, Blackwood frequently refers to this child-like state to back his subtext of trying to aid the world by giving readers an alternate vision. As mentioned earlier, his most powerful prose is evident when O'Malley is making the distinction between Civilization and Nature. Civilization, for Blackwood, is the place of "cheap-jack inventions" and a place where life seems meaningless and trivial. As Blackwood's mouthpiece, O'Malley "aches" for an experience of beauty in the world, a state that can only be found before civilization has ruined it with strife and clamor. This idea also clearly connects Blackwood with Happold's theories of the mystical experience and to Otto's sense of the numinous. For example, Happold's second characteristic states that the mystical can be found through insight and intuition and not through the intellect. Blackwood would seem to agree with this statement, and it becomes fictionalized in *The Centaur*. Thus the equation Blackwood sets up is: Civilization = intellect = duality = God only operative on Sundays. What he seems to ask of readers is the opposite: Nature = intuition = nonduality = numinous. Early on the text, when the Narrator is discussing his conversation with O'Malley, he mentions that O'Malley said that the greatest teacher (Jesus) didn't need the intellect to find God (which for O'Malley and Blackwood himself, was the only thing worth finding out). What one needs is to be like a child, "a child that feels and never reasons things—one that shall enter the Kingdom." O'Malley then makes his point clear by asking, "Where will the giant intellects be before the Great White Throne when a simple man with the heart of a child will top the lot of 'em?" (Blackwood *The Centaur* 14).

The other tropes that occur frequently in *The Centaur* are the references to the Garden or the Golden Age. Again, it must be emphasized that even though in the Introduction it was mentioned that Joseph Campbell's ideas of mythic association were characteristic of Eastern religions such as Buddhism, Daoism, and Hinduism, and that White's "burden of Guilt" for environmental destruction was largely due to the story of Adam and Eve, Blackwood here seems to be arguing that this mythical association is in all religions, whether it be Buddhism, Christianity or even the paganism of the Greeks. On the one hand, the Garden image can be a destructive one if it is interpreted as a separation between man/woman/nature/God. It can be further destructive if two angels guard it with flaming swords. What Blackwood offers, through his fictional character O'Malley, is the possibility of getting past the flaming swords and getting back in to the Garden. When O'Malley is in his cabin with the Russian, he hears the gates of ivory and horn swing open, and he longs for a vision of the Garden itself. As a literary image, the Garden can function as a non-dual state before the Fall in the Garden of Eden. It is interesting here that Blackwood uses the classical reference in conjunction with the biblical to show the similarities of both. In classical literature, the gate of horn is connected to occurrences (usually dreams) that are deemed true. In contrast, the gate of ivory is associated with those occurrences that deceive. So why does Blackwood mention that O'Malley hears both doors swing open with a vision of the Garden? Because for the mystic, the flaming swords that guard the Garden are the same doors of true and false, both dualities which must be transcended in order for the oneness of life to be experienced. This is exactly what the Garden represents.

In Blackwood's novel, O'Malley also refers to it as the Golden Age, possibly derived from Hesiod's "Ages of Man" which describes a Golden race created by Zeus and a mythical time where there was no strife in the world. So O'Malley says whether one calls it the call of the wild, the Garden, paradise, or the Golden Age, it is the foundation of all religions, and it is what people strive for. He states, "For it is possible and open to all, to every heart, that is, not blinded by the cloaking horror of materialism which blocks the doorways of escape and imprisons self behind the drab illusion that the outer form is the reality and not the inner thought..." (Blackwood *The Centaur* 100).

Expansion of Consciousness

As S.T. Joshi points out in his book *The Weird Tale*, the key to understanding Blackwood's work is the expansion or extension of consciousness, which brings the main characters (and by extension the readers), outside of their normal perceptions of reality and allows them to recover a sacramental vision in order to revise their perceptions of the natural world. Nature, argues Joshi, acts as an ersatz religion for Blackwood, and one can't help feeling when reading the majority of his work, that Blackwood means what he says, and that he is genuine in his mystical temperament. Works such as *The Centaur* are not heavily plot-oriented because, as a weird writer, Blackwood is more concerned with the emotive rather than rational aspects of art. This may be one of the reasons why some critics believe *The Centaur* is a flawed masterpiece. In a personal e-mail to Mike Ashley, the respected critic and author of *Algernon Blackwood: An Extraordinary Life*, Ashley states that it would not be beneficial to read other people's views of *The Centaur*: "It is such a personal novel that its impact on any individual reader will be different, and I think the strength is in seeing what your interpretation of the work is" (Ashley).

What is interesting for the purposes of this work are the similarities Blackwood shares with our previous authors. For example, Coleridge's view was that in order to revise one's perception of reality, one needed to break from the "lethargy of custom," and as argued in chapter one, the Mariner accomplishes this only after viewing the sea creatures as part of God's universe and as a part of himself, not as something separate. MacDonald also believed that the best thing you can do for your fellow (and the fundamental role of art) is to "wake a meaning" rather than intellectualize it. In a similar manner, when Lewis and Tolkien refer to a longing for fairy land or a cleaning of our windows, the messages are the same: in order to experience that which is numinous, one must get beyond the rational ego and enter into a new realm of the mystical.

Blackwood, perhaps the most mystical of all the writers presented here, would have agreed with the sentiments of these fantasists, but his work betrays an influence not exclusively based on Judeo-Christian ideologies but, as stated earlier, based on many characteristics of the perennial philosophy whether it be references to Paganism, Christian, or Eastern influences such a Hinduism or Buddhism. In his fiction, Blackwood follows Happold's assertions of mysticism: we only normally see partial reality; we can know a "Divine Ground" only through emotions and not intellect; what prevents us from seeing this divine ground is the ego; and, most importantly, it is our chief concern to realize this ground. This, I would argue, is the subtext of *The Centaur*, even though it is a flawed masterpiece in that the plot doesn't succeed in sustaining the readers through that many pages. It is Blackwood's autobiographical call to his readers to perceive nature in a more sacramental way; and the most fundamental trope he uses in *The Centaur* is the constant reference to the expansion of consciousness.

This expansion of consciousness occurs early in the novel when O'Malley refers to the Russian (whose name we never know) as having an unusual bigness, or massiveness, which rather than smothering, is actually "revealed." Throughout the novel, Blackwood frequently refers to the Russian (and later his son) with terms such as "exultation" or "evocation," and when O'Malley tells the narrator about the Russian, he equates his seeing of him as a "possession." Clearly these religious words were deliberate on Blackwood's part, and early on in the novel, he wants his readers to pay close attention to what this massiveness might signify. In an interesting episode, after O'Malley has a conversation with Stahl, he sees the Russian staring at him and he was immediately filled with alarm and wonder. O'Malley states that "he was no longer caged and manacled within the prison of a puny individuality," and that people around the Russian seemed like puny dolls or puppets.

The emphasis on being caged in a prison of individuality has interesting parallels with Eastern religious traditions such as Buddhism that Blackwood clearly embraced. In traditional Buddhism, for instance, the cause of suffering in the world is due to an over-reliance on the ego or self, which for Buddhists is an illusion. In fact, the term *Maya* in Buddhism, which is translated usually as "illusion," refers to a kind of magic trick. When one watches a magician, it is not as if he or she is performing some kind of miracle, but that the wool has been pulled over one's eyes: if one could only know what was behind the trick, it could be performed by anyone. Similarly, in Buddhism, the universe plays a trick on everyone due to the tendency of people to experience the world in dualities. In the Christian worldview, people feel they are separate, unique individuals with a permanent soul that will be rewarded or punished for eternity. In contrast, Buddhists believe that the sense of individuality is what causes one to feel separate from everything. Nirvana, that ultimate goal in Buddhism, is the realization of the fundamental unity of all things, and this is achievable by anybody; in fact, for Buddhists, it is one's chief concern.

As the novel progresses, the massiveness of the Russian and his son translates into O'Malley's own inner expansion of consciousness which is what allows him to achieve a mystical state where he perceives the world anew. When O'Malley is in the cabin with the Russian and the son, for example, just the proximity to the two of them makes him dread to see his own reflection in the mirror, lest he see his own expansion, which, he says, corresponds to his "interior expansion." It is interesting that Blackwood uses the word "dread" to refer to O'Malley's reaction to his expansion, but it makes sense in the context of our present argument.

When Rudolf Otto describes the experiences of the numinous, there is a dual sense of "awe" and "dread" for the subject, and that a degree of humility must be present in the face of the numinous in order for there to be a transcendence of the small self. This is eloquently stated in a later episode when O'Malley watches as the Russian turns his head toward him in welcome, and O'Malley states that the head was big, "like a fragment of the night and sky" and that "the whole presentment of the man was impressive beyond any words he could find. Massive, yet charged with a swift and alert vitality, he reared there through the night, his inner self now toweringly manifested" (Blackwood *The Centaur* 125). It is also this expansion that O'Malley is feeling within himself.

In terms of the experience of the numinous, what O'Malley is undergoing is a sort of death to the self in order for a widening of the perceptions of the natural world to occur. In *Mysticism*, Happold identifies one of the characteristic states of the mystic as an awareness that the phenomenal ego (or small self) is not the real self, that there is a higher form of consciousness which presents itself. Interestingly enough, once there has been a renunciation of this phenomenal ego, there is a completely new way of viewing the world in a sacramental manner. Blackwood also knew of this distinction between the small self and the real self and the need to identify with the higher self. In *Episodes Before Thirty*, Blackwood gradually becomes aware that the "I" (or phenomenal self) is that day-to-day self that experiences the world but that can lead to displeasure and suffering. There is, however, a deeper self, which is more real and that is beyond pleasure and pain, a "royal spectator" Blackwood calls it. He states further "into this eternal Self was gathered the fruit and essence of each and every experience the lower 'I' passed through; the secret of living was to identify oneself with this exalted and untroubled royalty..." (Blackwood *Episodes Before Thirty* 258).

Although Otto argues that the core of all religions is an experience of the numinous, and Happold argues that the perennial philosophy is the common mystical experience, there are still some differences in the way they are approached by these authors. In the introduction, it was argued that some environmentalists see the problem of environmental destruction as that based on the Western mythological ideology (which Campbell refers to as *mythical dissociation*). If humans are meant to have "dominion" over nature, and if God is transcendent (outer) rather than immanent (inner), then there is a hierarchical relationship that has, as its core, separation. As I have argued, this is particularly evident in scholars such as Lynn White who stated that religions like Christianity bear the blame for environmental destruction, or Neil Evernden who argued that the "Western" stress on the ego (as separate from the self) denies the recovery of the numinous. Interestingly enough, the same point is also argued in Happold's text. He says that when we choose one way of perceiving reality over another, we are making a "primary act of intellectual faith." In our Western European tradition, Happold argues, there is an over-emphasis on logical reasoning which we tend to think of as our only response to reality. We do not realize that we can choose another path, one that relies on intuition, insight, and imagination. In fact, Happold even stresses that these ways of responding to the world are actually more powerful than logical reasoning.

The connections to Blackwood's *The Centaur* should be now quite clear. As a true mystic, Blackwood was well aware of the core of all religions—the numinous. This is why, in *The Centaur*, Blackwood can easily shift from the pagan imagery of the centaurs and the Golden Age, to the Judeo-Christian imagery of Jesus and the Garden. However, in contrast to the mythic dissociation that the environmental critics of Western ideology argue, what Blackwood is most interested in is the "Eastern" ideology of seeing totality instead of separateness. Being a highly autobiographical author, his characters often embody Blackwood's own beliefs. O'Malley is no exception. Just as Blackwood himself felt the need to improve humanity through his utopian cause, so too does O'Malley. And how did Blackwood believe this could happen? Through his readers' identification with O'Malley. And what did O'Malley experience? A mystical experience with the Russian and his son that gave him a glimpse of an expanded consciousness, which was possible only through the identification of the totality of all things, including all of nature. This involves a death of the smaller ego or self, and a revisioning of the world in a more sacramental manner. So, in contrast to authors such as Coleridge, MacDonald, Lewis, and Tolkien, Blackwood is drawing on mystical traditions, and his own experience with Eastern religions such as Buddhism and Hinduism, which led him to accept the totality of all things and to easily see the phenomenal ego as the pure illusion that he believes it to be.

Revelation: The Centaurs

Due to the philosophical nature of *The Centaur* (and its lack of a normative plot), it is difficult to discuss the work in a chronological manner. Themes show up throughout the work, but any attempt to plot out the events in the book proves futile. Thus, the strategy I've opted for is to present larger thematic concerns which thread through the work and highlight Blackwood's central concerns. When these themes are pursued, it doesn't seem that there is much of a "fantasy" element in the text (as we have been defining it). However, what makes the work powerful is its subtlety in presenting the fantastic way that Blackwood offers his readers the experience of nature as sacramental. The most fantastic element in the work is the vision of the centaurs. Why would Blackwood use the image of the centaur to convince his readers of the truth of his message? S.T. Joshi points to a story Blackwood was working on when he was having difficulty completing *The Centaur,* a story called "Imagination" in his *Ten Minute Stories*. When the narrator is contemplating what creature to use that could bring the ancient mythological values into modern life, he thinks of the centaur. In a way, it is the perfect symbol for what Blackwood is trying to achieve: the lower half of the centaur, that of the horse, keeps the animal grounded in the earth and thus comes to represent the instinct; the upper half of the creature, that of the human, represents the upright nature of humans and the desire to move towards deity. This fantastic creature fulfills our definition of the mythopoeic because the centaur does "depart from consensus reality" (Hume), and does subvert normative categories of being by fusing the horse and the human (Jackson). Further, it is the culmination of Blackwood's subtext of perceiving the world anew: Blackwood seems to be saying through the imagery of the centaur that civilization has focused merely on the human and the intellect at the terrible expense of the instinctual part of ourselves. As Joshi argues, the optimum state of consciousness for Blackwood is not that we go back to primitivism, but that a balance be restored in order for the world to be seen sacramentally.

This point is made quite clear with the vision of the centaurs. As O'Malley and the Russian are walking through fields of giant rhododendrons, creating magnificent colors of mauve, pink and purple, the narrator remarks that O'Malley felt the "inner change of being" as they traveled outward; the landscape became their feelings. O'Malley is on the verge of *seeing* something which will change his life forever. He feels himself a worshipper, one who must go to the inner self where the heart knows that these mythological being are real. Again, Blackwood draws upon the Garden imagery to make his point. As the sun sets, O'Malley lies down outside the Garden, the image of mythic separation. As he lies down, he hears the pipes of Pan blowing gently in the wind.

As dawn comes (in literature, many times a symbol for awakening), O'Malley realizes he has been asleep. Or has he? He doesn't quite know and instead prefers to call the state a "transition-blank" stating "whatever that may mean" (Blackwood *The Centaur* 206). With the wind blowing, he suddenly hears a trampling noise and realizes that what he thought was the wind blowing the rhododendrons was "the splendor of ten hundred velvet flanks in movement" and these glorious bodies "dazed the sight" (Blackwood *The Centaur* 207). O'Malley knows now that he has passed through the gates of ivory and horn and entered into the Garden into a great at-one-ment. The consciousness of the earth included him, and he was one with everything. He experiences the centaurs as an "early form she had projected—some of the living prototypes of legend, myth, and fable—embodiments of her first manifestations of consciousness, and eternal, accessible to every heart that holds a true and passionate worship" (Blackwood *The Centaur* 208). O'Malley realizes that he has had a complete revelation and, as a consequence, he literally transforms into a centaur to run and feel the consciousness of the earth; all the while the pipes of Pan are blowing.

Indescribability

Again, *The Centaur* was the work that Blackwood believed was closest to his heart. It was his masterpiece but, as mentioned earlier, it is not without its flaws. Joshi points to the lack of sustainable plot as the major flaw in the work, but there is another: what Blackwood is trying to describe in the novel is that which is beyond description. This fact is evidenced in Blackwood's personal life. He had traveled to the Caucasus, and his experiences there were so extraordinary that when he returned home, he was at a loss to write about his experiences. He knew he needed to somehow write about these experiences, but he was also aware that it was beyond his ability as a writer to convey exactly what he felt. In fact, it wasn't until 1910, when he was staying with a friend, Stephen Graham, and he heard the sound of a penny whistle that he began to try to write his experiences down.

The notion of indescribability is also one of the key characteristics of the mystic. In *Mysticism*, Happold cites the number one characteristic of a mystical state is ineffability—the experience cannot be put into words due to the fact that the experience is more feeling-oriented rather than intellect-oriented. The emphasis on feeling leads us back to Otto's concept of the numinous as "feeling-oriented" or experiential and that while it can be discussed, it cannot be defined. In fact, the primary attraction for many authors and critics of mythopoeic fantasy is in its indescribability. As Tolkien says of the perilous realm of Faerie, "I will not attempt to define that, nor to describe it directly. It cannot be done" (Tolkien 39).

It should come as no surprise then that Blackwood's novel *The Centaur* is filled with references to the ineffable. Most of the episodes that refer to indescribability are O'Malley's encounters with the Russian and his son. O'Malley constantly refers to a feeling or connection between him and the Russian as that which transcends all language. Language is referred to as "impossible," "fatal," "limiting," and "destructive." When O'Malley is staying in the cabin with the Russian, he hears him singing from the bed and is immediately struck by the awe and wonder of the song. He reflects that the singing reminds him of a primitive utterance, a time before language was formed, and when the power of the emotions was so strong that "little modern words" were inadequate. O'Malley believes that he and the Russian are survivors from a world where language was not yet created.

This connects to the sacramental vision in that the mystical, numinous encounter may only be indirectly experienced through symbols or metaphors that are a pale reflection of the true reality. When one is struck by awe, there is no way to convey this sacramental vision by mere words. As one can see when George MacDonald, for example, discusses the fairytale, or sonata, of a gathering storm: "Do you begin at once to wrestle with it and ask whence its power over you, whither it is carrying you?" (MacDonald 319). For Blackwood—and probably for all of our authors—they answer would be a resounding "no."

When O'Malley is describing his visions to the narrator, he says that is was not so much the splendor of the events but really the "sublime

Six. "A daisy is nearer heaven than an airship"

simplicity of it all." He says there is no language simple enough to convey it, and that it is as difficult to recover as a dream, the ecstasy of religion, or even the revelation of John. It is, as he says to the narrator, simply divine. The problem for O'Malley, and for Blackwood himself, relates to his utopian dreams of helping humanity. It may be recalled that Blackwood had an intense desire in his own life to "improve" humanity, to help people experience the sacramental vision that revised perceptions of nature, and to deplore civilization with its terror and desolation. He wanted people to enjoy the simple life, the call of childhood, the Golden Age, the Promised Land that doesn't see the earth as a simple dry-clod with no meaning, but as a projection of the divine itself. The conflict that bothered Blackwood so deeply is the same conflict that O'Malley faces. Now that he has seen the extraordinary vision of the centaurs, and now that he knows Nature is alive in the deepest sense, how does he convince others of his truth? This is evidenced when O'Malley is on the ship and sees both peasants and others such as an engineer and an over-dressed woman. O'Malley feels closer to the peasants. Referring to the others, he wonders "how in the world could he ever explain a single syllable of his message to these latter, or waken in them the faintest echo of desire to know and listen?" (Blackwood *The Centaur* 242).

It is a good question, but in the book, as well as Blackwood's life, it is not resolved in any expected way. When O'Malley is sick and on his deathbed, the narrator has his last conversation with him. O'Malley has been recently talking about a Mr. Pan and how he will take care of everything once O'Malley goes away. The narrator asks where O'Malley is going, and he says, "into myself, my real and deeper self, and so beyond it into her—the Earth" (Blackwood *The Centaur* 277). O'Malley's great realization, then, is that the Garden is everywhere. That one does not need to travel to the Caucasus to realize this. One need merely go deep into oneself, to that greater, deeper self, which is the divine source of all, and once this is achieved, the world is seen in a sacramental way, and nature reveals all her beauties. It is to this place that O'Malley goes, and the last the Narrator sees of him, he is walking away with a beggar playing a penny whistle, who is, obviously, Pan in disguise.

Blackwood achieved his utopian dream through his fictional world. Whether it's *The Centaur*, or Blackwood's other fiction, his writing reveals his intense passion for nature; it is literally in the beauty of his words. Blackwood wanted his readers to look to nature for solace and to understand that the deeper life of all of us is connected to the divine ground. As with our previous authors, Blackwood never considered himself an ecologist. As scholar Mike Ashley points out, Blackwood had no qualms with hunting or felling trees; however, he did feel that an expansion of consciousness could help one sense a wider, more divine world. So even though Blackwood was not an ecologist, his message is still relevant today. According to Ashley, "his ideas and stories thus fit straight down the middle of the ecological and New Age beliefs of this generation" (Ashley 4699).

CHAPTER SEVEN

"Yes. You can keep your eye"
Ursula Le Guin's Buffalo Gals and Other Animal Presences

> "It is true that all creatures talk to one another, if only one listens."—Ursula Le Guin, *Buffalo Gals and Other Animal Presences* [12]
>
> "Coyote walks through all our minds."—Ursula Le Guin, *Conversations with Ursula K. Le Guin* [103]

What should be noticed at the outset of this chapter is that, thus far, the study has focused on authors who have been male, white, and Christian. In a certain sense, this has helped with the argument of the numinous in mythopoeic fantasy. Many of the thematic concerns are the same because each author has been profoundly influenced by Christian ideology. However, this narrow focus obviously leaves out works that can take readers outside Christian ideology. One such author—who challenges Christian beliefs, and whose works contain that "extra-literary" quality of "wonder" is Ursula Le Guin (1929–). By examining one of her most mythopoeic works, *Buffalo Gals and Other Animal Presences*, readers can see how much Le Guin has to offer within the context of the numinous.

In fact, Le Guin addresses the issue of what happens when an author (and by extension the reader) caters to the "in group" in her essay "Unquestioned Assumptions." She points to five basic assumptions that writers make—we are all men, white, straight, Christian, and young. This leads to a kind of exclusionary thinking. Those included in these categories have something important to say, while others, those on the outside, simply don't matter. But they do matter. If a scholar such as Lynn White can make the argument that Christianity "bears a huge burden of guilt for environmental destruction," then what may we learn from a Buddhist or a Daoist, or any other religion that is not part of the Judeo-Christian tradition? Through her work, Le Guin shows the impact of environmental problems from a distinctly American Indian background. This comes as no surprise as Le Guin's early life was filled with encounters with American Indians. Her father, Alfred Kroeber, was the first person to earn a Ph.D. in anthropology at Columbia, and he founded the second America Department of Anthropology at Berkeley. Thus Le Guin's early years, especially those summers in the Napa Valley, were shared with many of what she calls her "Indian Uncles." American Indian ideology was a direct influence on Le Guin, but readers must be careful not to assume that the views of the American Indians are exactly her own. In a personal letter written to the author, when asked about her "beliefs" she stated, "I don't have a clear picture of my thinking, either. Really, I think through story. I don't have ideas or beliefs, I just have stories" (Le Guin).

The Challenge to the West

In Le Guin's essay "A Left-Handed Commencement Address," she discusses the idea that our true home is in the dark places, and the earth is our country. Further in the essay, she makes this statement: "Why did we look up for blessing—instead of around and down?" (Le Guin 117). With this statement, Le Guin is criticizing a particular worldview that posits the sacred as transcendent rather than immanent. As discussed in the introduction, this particular view of the world is fundamental to Judeo-Christian religions. Le Guin is challenging the West's indebtedness to Christian dualism and exclusivism, which draw a hard line in the sand between what is considered "human" and what is considered "nonhuman." For Le Guin, the nonhuman is essential, and fantasy is the only genre that displaces the anthropocentric bias of the West and puts in its place the importance of the connectedness between all of nature. This connection, Le Guin asserts, comes from hunter-gatherer societies that had a spiritual kinship with animals. As Le Guin says, "we knew we were different but we knew also that we belonged" (Cheek 445). We were "among" nature, not "above." In contrast, the tribes of Judea saw it quite differently. Instead of the kinship to nature, the stress was on nature as a kingdom to be ruled. "The animal was set entirely apart from the human and the divine: and mankind was to dominate everything else by divine mandate" (Cheek 458). This is what I have referred to as mythic dissociation.

What Le Guin offers in *Buffalo Gals* is a conversation between the human and the nonhuman. As Mike Cadden points out in his essay "Le Guin's Continuum of Anthropomorphism," Le Guin wants dialogue, and she uses the anthropomorphism of the animal tale to show the limits of the dialectic or the binary. Cadden argues for a shift from the vertical, hierarchical relationships between human and nonhuman to the horizontal connections among lines of a continuum. What he shows through his essay is that Le Guin offers the reader a different way to mediate along the lines of animal sentience. Cadden uses this ability to shift perspectives as the ability to be "conscious." He says that to be conscious is to "define yourself not strictly in opposition to but in concert with other conscious beings, both close to and distinct from yourself in a variety of ways" (19).

The Sacred

Le Guin's particular form of mythopoeic fantasy is to employ myth, which she believes tells more truth than fiction, to dismantle these Western hierarchical and hegemonic systems. She offers her readers a new world to live in. What she wants is to tell a different story. To do this, Le Guin uses mythopoeic fantasy because she feels that to be an artist is to listen to a "sacred call," which opens up our world and cleanses our perception. In referring to fantasy as sacred, Le Guin follows in the tradition of Otto in calling attention to the numinous aspects of this form of literature. Referring to this sense of sacredness in literature, Le Guin states, "we don't hold anything sacred except for what religion declares to be so" (White 93). In contrast to religion, art, and more specifically mythopoeic fantasy, offers us a "nonintellectual mode of apprehension"; it is not anti-rational but para-rational and it employs both the emotions and the body. In fact, echoing connections both George MacDonald and Rudolf Otto make, as I discussed in earlier chapters, mythopoeic fantasy is similar to music. As Le Guin points out, we will never be able to convey what a particular song means to us because the language of the intellect can't fully express what we feel through our emotions and our bodies.

One of the benefits of Le Guin's particular form of mythopoeic fantasy is that she believes that fantasy is subversive. It is an artist's most flexible tool because it allows for a remaking of reality, a retelling of events, and an imagining of alternatives to our world. This idea of fantasy as subversion is exactly what I have suggested Rosemary Jackson has in mind.

The Postmodern

"The interrogation of foundational assumptions" is, according to ecocritic Patrick Murphy, the greatest contribution postmodernism gives to writers who allow nature to speak for herself. Challenging and disrupting such boundaries as self/other, nature/civilization, male/female, or sacred/profane, the postmodern praxis flies directly in the face of what the West has inherited since the Enlightenment. In fact, with the emphasis on the rational, patriarchal, and Judeo-Christian, the Enlightenment has produced a hyper sense of human alienation as its basic "onto-theology," and therefore regards all of nature as an object. In contrast to the focus of the absolute alienation of the human subject, and the resulting placement of everything else as "other," to be viewed as an "object," postmodernism allows for the freedom to question these assumptions and to discover new ways of relating to the natural world. According to Murphy, certain questions must be asked. What if we use *relation* as a key term in the human/nature discussion rather than *alienation*? What if we work from *relational difference* or *anotherness* rather than otherness? This proposal has interesting connections with Cadden's idea of dialogue that occurs horizontally rather than vertically. The ability of the human and the nonhuman to be in dialogue, and to mutually change and develop each other, requires a process of *interanimation*, where agency is not relegated to the human alone but is spread out to that which is viewed as "another"; the human and nonhuman are in equal dialogue with each other.

For Murphy, Le Guin offers a unique version of nature writing. It is unique due to its author's participation in nature, as a conversation with nature, instead of an observation of nature that has been characteristic of such writers as Thoreau or even Dillard, who follow the same imitative self/author, passive/listener role. Defined slightly differently, fiction, or in the context of our argument mythopoeic fantasy, can been seen as a form of nature writing.

Seven. *"Yes. You can keep your eye"*

The Stories

"Buffalo Gals, Won't You Come Out Tonight"

In terms of a shift in perspective, the title story highlights insights gained through a look into the mythical past, the time of the First People. Myra, the story's main character, has survived a plane crash on the way to see her father, only to realize that she has landed in a mythical time, a sort of aboriginal "Dreamtime," where the distinctions between "animal" and "human" are blurred. She is helped through this world by Coyote, a familiar trickster figure in American Indian mythology, but one that Le Guin also makes her own. Typical tricksters such as Prometheus, Loki, or Anansi, often exhibit familiar traits: they are mischievous, self-serving, shape-shifters, half-human, half-animal and, interestingly enough, usually male. Le Guin makes the Coyote female, and her identity is never static. While Coyote does function in the story as a mother figure to Myra, she is not a typical mother. Throughout the story, Coyote pisses everywhere, cusses, has random sex, and even talks to her turds (who, interestingly, talk back).

Readers are alerted to Le Guin's perspective shifts when Myra learns that upon her crash she has lost an eye. In this mythical place, however, losing an eye is not that painful, and she is able do get a new one with the help of Bluejay, who acts as a healer and performs a ceremony where Myra's new eye is made of pine pitch. As a protector of Myra, Coyote distrusts Jay, and even comments harshly on his work when the eye is completed: "Boy, that is one ugly eye. Why didn't you ask Rabbit for a rabbit dropping? That eye looks like shit" (29). Acting in her role as a comforter and savior, Coyote then takes care of Myra's eyes. The description evokes the maternal aspects of Coyote: "She put her lean face closer, till the child thought she was going to kiss her; instead, the thin, firm tongue once more licked accurate across the pain, cooling, clearing. When the child opened both eyes again the world looked pretty good" (29).

As Myra begins to get used to seeing this new world with her new eye, she begins to question Coyote about her world. Why is it, for instance, that Coyote sometimes appears to her as a real coyote, and at other times she appears as a woman? Coyote explains to her that "resemblance is in the eye," and that "it all depends on how you look at things" (31-32).

> "There are only two kinds of people," Coyote explains.
> "Humans and animals?"
> "No. The kind of people who say, 'There are two kinds of people' and the kind of people who don't" [32].

Although Coyote laughs this statement off as a joke, the implication is important. By employing mythopoeic fantasy, Le Guin is able to have Myra experience this world not only by being there, but also by "seeing" the world with her new eye; and, what she learns is a new perspective. In Coyote's world, all things are interconnected, so much so that there is not even a distinction between human and animal.

Coyote becomes, then, literally and figuratively, what Karla Armbruster calls "an openness to interconnection" (110). Literally, coyotes are able to thrive under harsh conditions due to their adaptability; figuratively, the coyote represents the postmodern challenge to ideas of identity. Rather than looking at the world monolithically, with a static view of identity, Coyote challenges the readers to blur boundaries, to question distinctions, and to forge new ways of viewing the relationship between human and nonhuman. As Le Guin has said, "Coyote is an anarchist. She can confuse all civilized ideas simply by trotting through" (White 103).

And confuse civilized ideas she does. This occurs in many episodes when Myra, or Gal, confronts an alternative reality where civilized rules might mean something a little different. Many examples prove this point. When Coyote is carelessly crossing the river to get to her home, Myra remembers that "wet shoes make wet feet" (19); or further, when Coyote pisses on the fire and exclaims "Ah, Steam between the legs," Myra gets embarrassed and refuses to follow suit (21); or, the last thing that Myra thinks about before she goes to sleep in Chipmunk's house is "I didn't brush my teeth" (25). These seemingly irrelevant asides are paramount to understanding Le Guin's art. She is having Myra adapt to the world of the First People, a world of relationship between all things, where the perspectival axis is horizontal, and not, as in Western Civilization, vertical.

The critique of this Western, hierarchical, hegemonic civilization that relegates the nonhuman to an inferior position (as that which is "other") can hardly be any harsher in *Buffalo Gals*. When Myra asks

Horse if he has ever visited the place where the "New People" live, he asks if she means the glass and metal places, the places where all the walls are. And, once Horse takes her closer to the land of the New People, she sees a car which is described as moving too fast, at terrible speed, a "fiery burning chariot, the smell of acid, iron, death" (41). Later, when Coyote takes Myra to the place of the New People, they sense in the air increased pressure, like time was pressing on them, pounding on them and telling them to hurry, like there was no time left: "things turned, flashed, roared, stank, vanished" (46). Eventually, hunters see them, and they can't believe that Coyote is so bold to be right out in the open, like one of the hunters' wife's ass. They open fire on Coyote and Myra, who barely escape to a nearby draw in the hills. Myra wants to get away from her people, and Coyote asks her why. "But they're your folks ... all yours. Your kith and kin and cousins and kind. Bang! Pow! There's coyote! Bang! There's my wife's ass! Pow! There's anything—BOOOOM! Blow it away, man! BOOOOOOM!" (47).

Although there is tragic humor in these episodes, the narrative point is quite clear: The world of the New People, or the "civilized culture," is a place of mythic separation where things are competitive, violent, and hierarchical. So, what is Le Guin's answer to the problem of Western Judeo-Christian civilization? Just where is the place that Coyote made? As Le Guin states, it is not to be found in going back to a mythic or Edenic time or place, as in Coyote's world, but in coming back to this world with a vision transformed. This point is explicitly made at the end of the story when Myra asks Grandmother if she can keep her new eye, the one she acquired with the help of Bluejay, when she returns back to her time. Grandmother, or Spider, represents the Weaver of the Web of Life, another one of Le Guin's complex symbols. Spiders do literally weave webs, and Spider herself says to Myra to look for her in her dreams, her ideas, and "in the dark corners of the basement," but more importantly Spider represents the new vision of the world that Myra has acquired. It is a vision of blurred boundaries, a radical de-centering of the human as the only source of agency, and an awareness of the sacredness of all things. "Yes," says Grandmother, "you can keep your eye" (51). Thus Myra comes back to the world transformed (as does the reader), with one eye firmly grounded in the reality of a dualistic and Western hierarchical world, and with the other eye—the eye of subversiveness—that can now view the world sacramentally.

"Mazes" and "The Wife's Story"

In introducing these two stories, Le Guin tells readers that the stories are about betrayals—reversals of what is expected. What is reversed, in most cases, is the reader's perspective. We are asked to identify not with the human perspective but with the "other." In this way, Le Guin want us to question and revise how we treat the subject of "othering." She wished us to think about how our habitual ways of acquiring knowledge, especially as it is influenced by the Judeo-Christian Western tradition, may cloud the way readers look at the environment. If we can learn new ways of perception, by subverting these old habits, then nature can be seen sacramentally.

"Mazes" is a story that concerns a "narrator" and an "alien." While the story seems unequivocally about a scientist and a lab rat, Le Guin is quick to betray her readers. She points out that the story is not about rats, thus making us rethink what we think the story is about and leaving it open-ended. In the story, the first person narrator (the "I") is being tortured in a series of mazes by the alien. In the opening, the narrator is close to death and refers to the actions of the alien as "cruel" and "irrational." At first, when the narrator is put down in a maze, the narrator believes it is the alien's way of trying to achieve communication. It states, "we are both intelligent creatures, we are both maze-builders: surely it would be quite easy to learn to talk together!" (62). The reason that the narrator assumes this is an attempt at communication is that the narrator and the alien communicate in two different ways. Making its way through a maze is, for the narrator, a form of dance. It assumes the alien knows this, but he doesn't. The alien can only communicate with its mouth (orally), which seems strange to the narrator. There is a disconnect between ways of communicating. After the narrator wonders if the alien is trying to communicate by its mouth, it states "it seemed a limited and unhandy language for one so well provided with hands, feet, limbs, flexible spine, and all; but that would be like the creature's perversity" (64). Now, if we assume the alien is a human, then this would be the narrator's (and Le Guin's) criticism of the androcentric bias of our rational West. The narrator's way of communication is through all of its movements through the maze, and there are actual names for these movements such as the "Ungated Affirmation" or the "Maluvian Mode." The alien (human) is unable to make communication an art and can only use its mouth. This puzzles the narrator because it sees all the similarities between the two: they both have eyes, a mouth, four limbs and grasping hands, but for all that, they can't communicate. The narrator reflects that the alien must be a solitary creature and totally self-absorbed because its motions are always purposeful and cruel. It never seems to want to communicate at all, only torture the narrator with mazes and knobs for rewards, and greenbud leaves which were almost inedible due to their not being fresh.

At the conclusion of the story, the narrator would rather die than become objectified by the human. The narrator pays close attention to the movements of the alien (even though they seem the movements of an imbecile), and it notices a signification of angry sadness. The alien admits defeat with its movements, and the narrator dies knowing that communication is never possible between the two. The narrator dies in a dance of death, which it knows the human (alien) won't understand. So, this story shows readers what it is like to be the "other" and look at the human as the one who is "alien," incomprehensible, and cruel. It subverts the hierarchical God-Human-Nature and points to a relationship with the nonhuman on a vertical rather than horizontal line. As Mike Cadden reminds us, dialogue is a conversation of separate position in concert with each other; different voices are different points on a continuum, not to be greater than or less than. The space in between these points is the place of relationship, where the nonhuman other is not wholly the same but also not wholly different. This is the sacred ground that Le Guin refers to in her introduction to *Buffalo Gals*; we come into "Animal Presence" only when difference or otherness is asserted (in both love and cruelty) and where the space between the human and nonhuman is respected.

"I saw him ... turned into the hateful one," the narrator says towards the end of "The Wife's Story" (70). With this story, Le Guin is also dealing with the theme of transformation and of shifting the reader's perspective so that humans are seen as the other from the nonhuman perspective. Again, Le Guin is clever at betraying the reader because we assume that the story is about a man turning into a werewolf. The narrator describes the "he" as a good husband, a good father, and one who didn't grouch or whine when things didn't go his way. He would lead the singing during lodge meetings. His voice was beautiful, people looked up to him, and he was one full of wisdom.

But then things turn darker. It has to do with a "curse" and "something in the blood" when the moon is dark. Of course, the logical assumption on a first-time read is that this is going to be a werewolf tale and something bad is about to happen. But wait. The transformation into a werewolf usually happens when the moon is full, not when it is dark. This is the reader's clue that something is different here; Le Guin may be trying to betray us. So, what happens is the "awful thing." It starts when the youngest child, a baby, turns on her father. The baby notices something wrong with her father and wants it to go away. The wife plays the episode down (although she is sad that the father has to witness the distance of the child). He stays away the whole day, but when he comes back, the transformation begins: his feet become long fleshy and white, with no hair on them, "like his hair fried away in the sunlight" (70); his face flattens, his ears go, and his teeth flatten and become dull. He stands on two legs. She sees her husband now and he is referred to as the "hateful one." Now, the wife is scared because she knows that even though he has no gun ("like the ones from man places"), he will still try and kill her children. Before this happens, however, the wife's sister rushes towards the hateful one, and behind her, the whole pack joins in, and they are able to hunt down the human. When the wife finally arrives on the scene, her sister's teeth are in the human's throat and he is already dead. While she yearns to see him turn back into his original form, he does not. He remains only a dead man, white and bloody.

So what seems to be a story about the curse of turning from a human to a werewolf is really the curse of being human as seen from the perspective of the nonhuman. Not only does Le Guin use the words the "hateful one" to describe the human, but his transformation with its white, flabby, and dull skin makes the reader view the human body as repulsive and gross.

"The Direction of the Road"

In Le Guin's introduction to *Buffalo Gals and Other Animal Presences*, she states that the stories contained in the book are not all about animals. She says it's more of a Twenty Questions anthology: animal, vegetable, or mineral? Since animals are more "talkative" and more "active," they seem to have much more to say. Or do they? When the question of nonhuman agency arises in posthumanist discourse, does this include not only the animal but also the vegetable and the mineral? Le Guin says that our dependence on plant life is usually ignored in a lot of science fiction and more so in the modern world, where she says that the human-plant relationship "can be completely ignored by a modern city dweller whose actual experience of plants is limited to florists' daises and supermarket beans" (83). In addition, because of the immobility of plant life, references to the relationship between human and vegetable sentience, she says, is usually "terminally uninteresting." In Le Guin's story "The Direction of the Road," however, readers are granted yet another perspective shift, but this time the perspective is not from the nonhuman animal but the nonhuman tree, the oak.

And in this story the agency comes from the oak, and not the human. Humans are under the illusion of progress and think they are going somewhere, when in reality it is the oak (and the other trees) that grow and shrink as they approach humans. The humans are really going nowhere. The story is also a diatribe against modern life and progress. With the invention of the car, the relationship between human and plant gradually lessons until the sacramental vision of the tree is no longer relevant. As Kasi Jackson puts it in her article "Feminism, Animals and Science in Le Guin's Animal Stories," the perspective shift from human to tree allows readers to reflect on the negative consequences of progress. Jackson states, "in their hurry to get from place to place, humans no longer take the time to notice trees" (215).

It is perhaps relevant to notice that the perspective of the tree is reminiscent of Tolkien's love of trees and the example used in my thesis to refer to the subversiveness of mythopoeic fantasy. It should be recalled that many of the presented authors refer to seeing nature in a sacramental manner. Whether it is Tolkien's need to "clean our windows" or Coleridge's "lethargy of custom" or even MacDonald's "weary or sated regards" all refer to the need for mythopoeic fantasy to recover the vision of the sacredness of the natural world.

The story begins with a positive relationship between the humans and the trees. As the oak reflects on days past, it says that humans would often lie down with their backs on the oak. The oak states, "I was touched by the way they would entrust themselves to me, letting me lean against their little warm backs, and falling sound asleep there between my feet. I liked them" (85). The perspective shift is interesting in that the humans are not the ones with agency but the oak; it is the one who leans itself against the humans' back. The oak then goes on to state that back in those days, humans would use horses to travel, and with the exception of when the horses would gallop, the oak enjoyed it. "And they seemed not to have so many urgent needs, in those days," the oak remarks (85).

But urgent needs do come when the oak notices that the horse has been replaced by the car. Here the oak notices the ugliness of the car itself and how it had an "uncomfortable, bouncing, rolling, choking, jerking gait" and was so loud that the noise from it drowned out the songs of the sparrows (86). And, year after year, cars became more and more common until the dirt roads which the horses travelled on were replaced with paved roads ("remetalled" Le Guin calls them), that are nasty as a slug's tail and leave no room for flowers, rocks, pools, or shadows. The "wise" creatures now know to stay clear of the paved roads, but the "unwise" creatures run the risk of being squashed by the cars.

As cars become more the natural "Order of Things," the oak laments. The oak says that humans started to really believe that they were "going somewhere" when, in fact, they were going nowhere at all. It was the trees that would move toward the cars to give them the false illusion of progress. Additionally, the oak says that humans now would not even bother looking at the trees. The oak says, "they seemed, indeed, to not see anymore" (89). This statement has interesting parallels with my thesis of recovering the sacramental vision. In this story, Le Guin is showing readers in mythic language that our modern idea of progress has severely limited the way we perceive the natural world, so much so that we don't see trees or flowers, and creatures are merely there to be squashed by us as we make our way to where we think is somewhere.

Fittingly, the story ends with death. One rainy evening in March, one of the cars is in such an unusual hurry to "get somewhere" that the oak has no choice but to crash into the car, instantly killing the driver. What the oak regrets, however, is not that it killed the driver but that the driver "saw" the oak in its wholeness and confused the image with eternity. The oak will not accept that it is seen as eternity because it is a part of life; it is not death. The oak says that if humans want to see death, they should look into each others' eyes. Thus, in this story, Le Guin leaves the reader with associations of progress = not seeing nature sacramentally = death.

Seven. "Yes. You can keep your eye"

"Vaster Than Empires and More Slow"

After an attack has occurred on World 4470, one of the crew members jokingly speculates on the mysterious attacker. Ape-potato? Giant fanged spinach? Why does the thought of such creatures not inspire fear? In "Vaster Than Empires and More Slow," Le Guin seems to be speculating on the notion of agency. What if agency is just as prevalent in the vegetable world? What if an ape-potato or a giant, fanged spinach could evoke fear? How might we rethink our anthropomorphic biases?

Le Guin acknowledges that science fiction often ignores our "plant-dependence" and that plants' passive nature makes them uninteresting. However, with "Vaster than Empires," Le Guin deals with a specific fear, linked to panic, that is sometimes felt by those alone in the wilderness. Le Guin once experienced such a fear on an Oregon trail and she fictionalizes this feeling in her story bringing readers to question our very ideas of sentience.

The story concerns a survey crew searching for planets that are truly alien, ones that were not seeded by the Hainish. Among the ten crew members of the ship *Gum*, there is one who is an empath, Osden, whose bioempathic receptivity picks up on anything that feels. Some of the other crew members dislike Osden because he is so intolerant, not realizing that the hatred he has is only a projection of the hate that they feel towards him.

The story gets interesting when the crew finds World 4470, "a dark-green jewel" which has life, but not human life. It is a world of infinite plants, all living by photosynthesis. It is a world where nobody eats anyone else, a place of peace and the silence of a million years. When Harfex questions why "no men?" Osden answers, "you don't think Creation would have made the same hideous mistake twice?" (99). As Le Guin tells us here, it is the humans who are the misfits, the one's who don't belong. Readers might pause to consider the question of the "other." What do we mean by the "other?" Who exactly is the "other?" In "Vaster Than Empires," it seems as if readers are to take the perspective of the plant sentience of World 4470 and that Le Guin is suggesting that the "other" are the humans who are invading this peaceful planet.

And the planet starts to take notice. There is a report from Porlock, the hard scientist, that something is moving with a purpose in the forest and trying to attack him from behind. The other crew members are at a loss to understand this report as there is no animal life on the planet to attack. They begin to fear something although they are not quite sure what it is. Then, the crew finds Osden, who had been sent away from the ship to try and pick up any empathic response from the planet. They find him beaten and bloody lying on the ground. Having accepted that there is no animal life on the planet, the crew begins to speculate on plant sentience and vegetable monsters. This increases their sense of fear, and Osden confirms that there is "a sentience" on the planet.

What readers also see is the crew getting more and more anxious, and there are references to insanity and the losing of one's mind. It is eventually discovered that Porlock has been the one responsible for the attempt on Osden's life. This is related to Le Guin's own desire to write a story about a certain fear, panic, that overcomes one when alone in the wilderness. The etymology of the word panic shows a sense of loosing one's head and is derivative of the Greek *panikos* meaning "of Pan," the god of the wilderness who is the cause of mysterious sounds in the woods, frequently leading people to the fear of being in lonely spots.

The crews' speculation on the source of the fear leads them to think that there is an interconnectedness between the root nodes of the forest and the branches, and that just as it is impossible to locate the sources of human sentience or intelligence, it is impossible to locate the same in the plant world. As Osden states, it is "Nothing comprehensible to an animal mind. Presence without mind. Awareness of being, without object or subject. Nirvana" (118). In fact, this connectedness also extends to all parts of World 4470. When the crew decides to leave the spot where they felt fear and travel to another part of the world, they still feel the sense of fear; they cannot escape it. It is, as Osden states, "one big green thought" (122).

Osden finally realizes what the source of the fear is. It is not that the forest is isolated and that it is fearful because of the motility of the humans on the planet, but simply that the humans are "other," and from the planet's perspective, there has never been an "other." Osden reflects on the beauty of the idea of nature as being without enemies, a place of no invasion, and oneness with everything. Osden realizes that before there was fear, he sensed a serenity in the forest, and he is becoming more and more attracted to it.

Osden finally decides to give in to the planet (as the reader must). He has had enough of the humans and yearns for communion with something truly other, something vegetable. He leaves the ship and stays as a colonist on the planet. The crew members come back to try and find him and they leave him supplies just in case, but he had already learned to give himself to the fear: "He had learned the love of the Other, and thereby had been given his whole self" (127).

"The White Donkey" and "Horse Camp"

There seems to be a special bond between a child and an animal. This bond goes far deeper than the Disneyfied "cute and cuddly" and possibly into the realm of the numinous. As we have seen with most of the authors studied, as well as in many of the religious philosophies mentioned, the sense of the numinous is accessed through being a child or being child-like. Not that children are necessarily "innocent" or "pure" but because they are aware that all things are animate, all things are holy. They also are not as indoctrinated with separation, whether it be a separation between sacred/profane, God/humans, or child/nature. They have yet to be kicked out of the Garden, and therefore offer us a metaphor for getting past those flaming swords that keep us from re-entering Eden.

Le Guin explores this unique relationship in two of her stories: "The White Donkey" and "Horse Camp." The former was written at a writer's conference in Indiana where participants were to write a story of a "last encounter." (In science fiction, a "first encounter" is a frequently used trope. Here, Le Guin is trying something different by turning the trope on its head.) Sita is the main character in the story, a goatherd who one day while making an offering to the goddess, encounters what she believes to be a donkey. Upon a closer glance, however, Sita "thought then that the donkey was a god, because it had a third eye in the middle of its forehead like Shiva" (141). She then realizes that what she thought was an eye was really a horn. It is interesting that Sita never identifies the animal as the mythic unicorn but as something to be worshipped like the god Shiva. The references to Hinduism are what bring the story to life. Sita is the devoted wife of Rama, the hero in the epic the *Ramayana*; she represents the ideal woman and wife who is abducted by the ten headed demon Ravanna. Shiva is the god of destruction and one of the three forms (*Trimurti*) of the god. Destruction in Hinduism is viewed as something transformative—you can't have something new unless that which is old is destroyed.

Nature and the Numinous in Mythopoeic Fantasy Literature

Le Guin's use of ideas from Hinduism helps make sense of the story. Sita is known for her purity, dedication, and courage. Interestingly, she may have been named for an older Vedic deity named Sita who was connected with fertility. The reference to the third eye of Shiva is a reference to seeing reality from the chakra of knowledge. In Hindu symbolism, two eyes represent the vision of duality, the separateness of all things in the universe. The spiritual goal of opening the third eye is to see the sacramental vision where all things are one and all things are holy. Sita in this story realizes this and after some hesitation on the "donkey's" part, she provides offerings of flowers for the animal every day. The donkey comes to her every day, accepts her offering and keeps her company.

The "last contact" is rather a sad one. Sita is to be married off to Moti Lal from another village, and the price for the bride is a mere bullock and one hundred rupees cash. It's clear that Sita doesn't want this marriage. When Moti Lal first notices her, she does not want to look at him; and, when she realizes she has to stop seeing her donkey-god forever, and that her brother will take her place, she cries. Sita says a final goodbye to the donkey, and the donkey slowly walks off into the darkness.

As Mike Cadden points out in his essay of Le Guin's use of anthropomorphism, the story concerns a betrayal, where the gap between the human and nonhuman is unbridgeable. This betrayal is facilitated by the uncle who sells her off to Moti Lal. Sita must say goodbye to the unicorn that represents virginity and freedom when she marries Moti Lal. As Cadden notes, "her uncle ... betrays the relationship and mediation between the girl and the mythical beast. Separation is forced and the gap is made impassable" (5).

In "Horse Camp," Le Guin shows readers the same conflict between the bond created by the female child and the animal on the one hand, and the compromise of this bond in relation to a patriarchal system on the other hand. As with many of Le Guin's stories, the child is the one who has access to the sacramental vision due to an appreciation and understanding of otherness, an acceptance of pure wilderness. Norah is the main character in the story and she is learning the ins and outs of horse camp from her sister, Sal. Sal is described as "cool" and "a tower of ivory," a source of authority and wisdom for her little sister. As Sal discusses the camp, Norah remembers stories of the camp, and the main character in the stories is always Jim Meredith, or Meredy, the horse handler. "Meredy said, Meredy did, Meredy knew" (143). The campers get settled into their cabins, and the atmosphere is that of female innocence: styling mousse, t-shirts with "I love Teddy Bears," combs with hair left in them, and a paperback *The Black Colt of Pirate Island*. This female innocence is interrupted by a description of Meredy, a bow-legged man of fifty who had ridden horses since his teens. He walked behind the girls' cabin and "walked along the well-beaten path" with lips tightly closed and looking from side to side (144). So, exactly what is it that "Meredy knew?" What is the "well-beaten path?" What Meredy represents is the initiation of the girls into adolescence, a transition from the freedom of their childhoods to a new world of sexual maturity dominated by the male. This, then, is the well-beaten path that Meredy treads, a path that takes the girls symbolically from a horizontal line of relationship between human and nonhuman nature to the vertical line of authority coming from the male.

As readers start to sense this shift, Le Guin blurs the boundaries between humans and animals by describing the girls as horses. Meredy slaps the hip of Philly, one of the girls, and he shouts, "Nothing wrong with you. Get up!" (145). Norah goes along with Philly, and Norah notices a deep trembling inside her body; this trembling is symbolic both of her transformation into a horse and also the transformation to a new life of sexual maturity. What this new life represents is freedom. Le Guin makes this clear by her continual references to freedom: "Freedom, the freedom to run, freedom is to run" (145) and further in the story when Norah reflects on her return to horse camp, "This is what freedom is, what goes on, the sun in summer, the wild grass, coming back each year" (146). The sun, the summer, the wild grass, the return, are all metaphors for the transition to a new way of being in the world.

However, this initiation has a hint of despair to it. As the girls/horses are walking back from Stevens Mountain, always careful to be "in line," Norah sees her sister Sal just starting up the mountain and she is filled with despair. On Sal's back a man sits erect with one hand on his thigh and the other holding the reins to guide her. Norah shouts, "No, no, no, no," but Sal is unable to hear her and continues on her path. Norah goes back to the other girls/horses, but instead of getting back in line, she teases the others, and finally disruption occurs, and all the horses break free of the line and run wildly back to horse camp. Thus, the final note of the story is the freedom to refuse the vertical relationship with the patriarchal on top. Running back to horse camp free, the story opens up the possibility that there are other ways to engage with the world; sexual maturity does not have to be accepting the "well-beaten path" with the male on top and the female and nature on the bottom.

"Shrödinger's Cat" and "The Author of the Acacia Seeds"

Richard Erlich describes "Shrödinger's Cat" as an existentialist story of the comic-absurdist variety. It concerns a world that is in a state of entropy, a state of systematic disorder, where the increasing rapidity of life has caused the meltdown of the world. Couples literally break apart from the heat, stove-burners remain hot even when off, and a kiss is like a branding iron. The narrator, who has apparently found a cooler place to be, gives readers his thoughts about the world as the heat continues. He feels he is grieving for something; that something has been lost though he can't figure out what it is.

He is interrupted by a yellow cat that sits on his lap. He feels that the cat has been sent to help with what the narrator feels he has lost. As he is reflecting upon the silence of the cat, someone arrives at his door. Thinking it is the mailman, he opens the door, only to be surprised that his visitor is a small dog. Subsequently, he names the dog Rover. Rover enters with his knapsack and immediately recognizes the cat. It is Schrödinger's cat. Erwin Schrödinger was a physicist who conducted a thought-experiment to explain the impossibility of arriving at any kind of certainty in 1935. The experiment is known as Schrödinger's cat and has been described as a paradox. Imagine that a cat is in a soundproof box. At zero time, a photon will be emitted towards a half-silvered mirror. If the photon passes through the mirror, a trigger on a gun will be fired and the cat would die. If, on the other hand, the photon is deflected, the trigger on the gun will not fire and the cat will be alive. There is no way to know if the cat is dead or alive until the lid of the box is opened. Until then, the cat is neither dead nor alive, and one can only be certain when one opens the box.

Rover decides to conduct the experiment because he wants to be certain that "God does play dice with the world" and the only certainty you can achieve is what you create yourself (i.e., by opening the lid to

Seven. "Yes. You can keep your eye"

the box). To his surprise, both the cat and the box have disappeared. When the narrator reflects that maybe there needs to be larger boxes, the roof of the house lifts off, letting in the inordinate light of the stars. The story concludes with the narrator identifying the sound that he has heard. It is the A note, the note that drove the composer Schumann mad.

After reading the story a number of times, readers will understand Erlich's contention that the story is comic-absurdist. Absurd events do happen, there are puns throughout, and readers are left with the central question of what it is that the narrator has lost? What is it that the cat knew all along, and that it was sent to teach the narrator? The answer lies in both animal presence—and absence. As Le Guin says in her introduction to the story, the reason the story is an animal tale is that the cat in the story was a real historical cat by the name of Laurel who entered Le Guin's story as a real subject and not as a parable-cat as in Schrödinger's experiment. When animals are dealt with as subjects with "a sentient existence of the same order as the scientist's existence," then the nature of any experiment changes (157). And when animals are seen in this way (as in Cadden's horizontal line or continuum), then they are granted presence and agency. This is the key to the whole story. If God really does play dice with the world, and the only certainty we can create is what we choose to do, then the answer to what the narrator (and the whole world) has lost is what the cat always had—presence. Reflecting on the slowness of the cat, the narrator states "He hasn't the frenetic quality most creatures acquired—all they did was ZAP and gone. They lacked presence" (161).

What is language? What is art? Is there a connection between the two? These questions are raised in many of the stories and poems in *Buffalo Gals and Other Animal Presences*, but probably most directly in the story "The Author of the Acacia Seeds and Other Extracts from the *Journal of the Association of Therolinguistics*." Many critics in the field of animal studies criticize the gender bias and anthropocentrism present in Western philosophical discourse and seek new alternatives. They want us to think deeply about how our habitual knowledge systems "construct" the nonhuman other and deny agency to anything that is not human. In the three "extracts" from the *Journal of Therolinguistics*, Le Guin asks readers to question their most basic assumptions about art and to open up the possibility that art can be studied in the realm of the nonhuman as well.

The first extract deals with messages on acacia seeds found outside a tunnel and next to an ant hill. The translation of the seeds proves difficult as these messages seem to differ from other ant texts, which have been studied. For instance, there is no way to tell if the message is an autobiography or a manifesto. What is clear, however, is that the message is written by a "strange author ... in the solitude of her lonely tunnel" and that she is communicating blasphemies for the ant kingdom. For example, Seeds 14–22 end with the exclamatory phrase "Praise!" which is usually part of a customary salutation "Praise the Queen." The fact that the word for Queen has been omitted means that this author is rejecting the hierarchical system of domination and that perhaps the praise is for the freedom and affirmation of the world *sans* a queen. Similarly, with Seeds 30–31, the translation of "Eat the Eggs! Up with the Queen," is viewed as blasphemous from the ant perspective. It is in this translation that Le Guin has readers question habitual anthropocentric systems of interpreting language. From the human perspective, it would seem that "Up with the Queen" would be an affirmation of the queen's power. However, what does the direction "up" represent from the ant's point of view? It represents the burning sun, frozen nights, exile, and maybe even death. "Down," on the other hand, represents home, security, peace, and comfort. So, when the passage is translated from a human point of view, it really means: "Eat the Eggs! Down with the Queen!" It is clear that these messages are from a solitary, nonconformist ant that wishes to break free from the habitual ways of what ants usually do.

Could these blasphemies have any relation to a message Le Guin wants to impart to her readers? Richard Erlich provides some interesting speculations on this. For humans (particularly in the West), "up" has meant the realm of God (or other sky gods), a place of transcendence and immortality. It is, according to Erlich, the source of "all the ills those ideas have brought" (29). "Down," on the other hand, is the direction of Mother Earth, immanence and mortality. If this interpretation is accepted, it seems to support my thesis: that mythic dissociation, the Western worldview which separates humans from God, and humans from nature, and God from nature, needs to be revised or subverted into a mythic association, where sacredness and agency is found in all things.

The second extract is a request from D. Petri to join an expedition to Antarctica to study the language of penguins. Much headway has

Seven. "Yes. You can keep your eye"

been made in the study of penguin due to the use of an underwater motion camera and the tentative glossary of Penguin made by Professor Duby. With the camera, motion can be slowed down, and the close study of the penguins has revealed that their communication is kinetic. It is "a script written almost entirely in wings, neck, and air" and it is also an art form. When Professor Duby reminds the others that penguins are birds, and that they fly through the water (and not swim), the movements are re-examined as art.

It is interesting to note that the dialect of the emperor penguin is the most difficult to understand. As Professor Duby states, "the literature of the emperor penguin is as forbidding, as inaccessible, as the frozen heart of Antarctica itself. Its beauties may be unearthly, but they are not for us" (171). As with the previous extract, words like "emperor" or "queen" connote a hierarchical system of domination that, for Le Guin, must be subverted.

So, for D. Petri, the call is for an expedition to further study the kinetic literature of the penguins. He says that their poetry must be the most unearthly poetry of all since it is purely kinetic and purely silent. He has readers imagine the darkness and the frozen winds of the Antarctic, where the penguins cannot see or hear each other but must feel the warmth of each other as they cover their one egg with their bodies and brave the dangers of the frozen land. As Petri says, "in unutterable, miserable, black solitude, the affirmation. In absence, presence. In death, life" (173).

The last extract is an editorial by the president of the Therolinguistics Association. It is this editorial that really sums up the other two extracts and gives meaning to Le Guin's story. What is language? Language is communication. What is art? Art is also communication. So, why do therolinguists only study animals? Because animals are the only other beings besides humans that can communicate. But what if, the president speculates, there is an art that is non-communicative? What if there is an art form that is non-kinetic and passive, "not an action, but a reaction: not a communication but a reception" (175)? What about plants and rocks? Couldn't a consideration of these forms of nature be a challenge to our anthropocentric biases? The answer for the president, and for Le Guin, is that yes, there is a sacredness and a poetry in all things, human and nonhuman included. If our normative modes of perception are subverted through the employment of mythopoeic fantasy, then Le Guin's art has served its purpose.

"May's Lion"

Although the plot line in "May's Lion" is quite simple, what Le Guin wants to show the reader is how the power of mythopoeic fantasy can transform or re-vision a story that is told as a real event. In essence, there are two versions of the same story concerning May's lion, one factual and one fictional. The story was written when Le Guin was working on the novel *Always Coming Home*. She was trying to find a bridge to connect her experiences as a child in the Napa Valley with her fictional world of the Na valley. The story worked for her purposes but was not suited to be a part of the novel itself. Instead, Le Guin decided to publish the story on its own. Furthermore, the link between the factual account and the fictional account is made quite explicitly; there is a literal break between the two versions and it is the contrast between the two versions that readers must contemplate.

In the first version of the story, the narrator relates how May, a seventy-, eighty-, or ninety-year-old is relating her story to the narrator's mother as she sits on the edge of an irrigation well. May is in her kitchen, and she hears a strange noise from outside, a sort of gargling yowl that fades to a soft purr. She looks out her window and notices that it is a sickly mountain lion (or in another version a bobcat) that is lying underneath a fig tree. May believes that the lion is sick and has come to her yard to die or to offer her companionship, so she decides to do what she can for the lion. She brings out some water for the lion to drink, but she is careful not to get too close so that they scare each other. Thus, there is a respect for otherness shown by May, which Le Guin makes explicit.

May has a problem, though, in that she needs to milk her cow Rosie, and the lion is in her way. She doesn't know what to do, so she calls Miss Macy who warns her that the lion may have rabies, and that May should immediately call the sheriff. After some hesitation, May calls the county police who then come out in two carloads to meet what has now become a threat. May relates, "I guess there was nothing else they know how to do. So they shot it." (183). Sadly, May looks off to the field her brother, Old Jim, used to take care of, and she knows that in thirty years, this beautiful field of blackberry and wild oats will be replaced by "a rich man's vineyard, a tax write-off" (183). It is clear at the end of this version that May was never scared of the lion and knew it wasn't a threat. She didn't want the lion shot. She just didn't know what else to do.

Seven. "Yes. You can keep your eye"

It has been argued throughout this book that mythopoeic fantasy is a subversive mode of storytelling that transforms the readers' perspective so that the environment may be seen in a sacramental way. In the second version of May's story, Le Guin makes this explicit by giving the story of May's lion a bit of a twist, a way to revision the story, so that the narrator may give the story back to May. The narrator states, "I want to tell it as fiction, yet without taking it from her: rather to give it back to her" (183). In this version, May becomes "Rain's End" (which means end of May) and who lives in the mythical valley of the Na. One day, awakening from a nap in her nine-pole house, a frame of poles with a mat roof and floor, she spots the lion. He is, again, under a fig tree, and he looks at Rain's End with "yellow eyes that saw her in a different way than she had ever been seen before" (185). Again, Le Guin is careful to point out the otherness of the other; the two look at each other in difference. Rain's End begins to sing a song to the lion. She tries to remember the Puma Dance Song, but she can't; instead, she makes up her own song:

> You are there, lion
> You are there, lion... [185].

There is power in the simplicity of the song because it seems to reflect Le Guin's desire for the presence of the lion. The lion is "there," as an animal and as other.

Rain's End also speculates that the lion could be a messenger since lions are from the "Seventh House," the same place where dreams come from. Maybe he has a spiritual message he wants to give Rain's End or to her people. Although she can't quite figure out what it all means, Rain's End still has to milk her cow Rose. When she comes back from milking the cow, Rain's End offers the lion milk because she knows he has come to have company while it dies. The lion doesn't touch the milk and Rain's End realizes that he will never eat from the "House of Earth" again. As night approaches, all Rain's End can do is sing to the lion as it dies. Since she doesn't know any of the songs that lions sing when they die, she decides to sing what she knows—the five songs of the *Going Westward to the Sunrise*. When Rain's End wakes up before the sunrise, she realizes that the lion has died, and she sings the last of the five songs for him:

> The doors of the Four Houses
> Are open.
> Surely they are open

Later in the morning, Rain's End goes to get help to carry off the body of the lion where "the buzzards and coyotes could clean it" (188).

At the conclusion of the story, the narrator of the tale of Rain's End reflects on the meaning of the two versions of the story and offers this final message:

> It's still your story, Aunt May; it was your lion. He came to you. He brought his death to you, a gift; but the men with the guns won't take gifts, they think they own death already. And so they took from you the honor he did you, and you felt that loss. I wanted to restore it. But you don't need it. You followed the lion where he went, years ago now [188].

"She Unnames Them"

One of the most powerful examples of a perspectival shift occurs in the short story "She Unnames Them." It comes as the last story in the collection, but, as Le Guin mentions, it "had to" because it embodies her perspective and what side of the argument she is on, and "what the consequences (maybe) are" (191). Only three pages long, this story gives us a new perspective on the Eden myth because it is told from Eve's perspective. In the original Genesis story, Adam is made in God's image and is given the breath of life, while Eve is created as a "helper" or "partner" only after God has given Adam the animals and the power to name them (naming in the ancient world gave one power over that which is named). This myth sets up what was referred to in previous chapters as "mythic dissociation," where God is different from humans, humans are different from animals, and all are different from nature which is to be "subdued" or to be dominated. In contrast, what happens in Le Guin's version of the story is that all the animals willingly give up their names because, basically, they don't "fit." And what happens when these animals accept namelessness? Notice the beauty of Le Guin's language and how evocative and alive the animals become in losing their names:

> The Insects parted with their names in vast clouds and swarms of ephemeral syllables buzzing and stinging and humming and flitting and crawling and tunneling away [195].

Or the fish of the sea:

> Their names dispersed from them in silence throughout the oceans like faint, dark blurs of cuttlefish ink, and drifted on the currents without a trace [195].

Notice that in losing their names, Le Guin evokes the nature of the animals by referencing their physical features, their habitats, their behaviors or their vocalizations. As a result of their namelessness, Eve feels a closeness to the animals now that these barriers have been removed; so much so, that "my fear of them and their fear of me became one same fear" (195). What is left, of course, is for Eve to give up her own name because it doesn't "fit" her either. She turns to Adam, who is busy "fitting parts together," and gives him back her name. Adam is too busy to listen to Eve, so she parts with these revealing words: "Well, Goodbye, dear. I hope the garden key turns up" (196).

The use of the Garden metaphor is the key to the whole sense of the Eden story. Of course, gardens appear in mythologies all over the world connoting "oneness" between male/female, humans/nature, and the sacred/profane. As Karen Armstrong points out in *The Case for God*, the Eden story was never to be taken as a historical account, but rather as ritual. As she points out, Eden was metaphorical for how life was supposed to be. To Armstrong, Eden expresses a *coincidentia oppositorum* "in which, during a heightened encounter with the sacred, things that normally seem opposed coincide to reveal an underlying unity" (Armstrong 29). In the Garden of Eden, there is no difference between divine and human, and Yahweh walks in the cool of the shade. The story shows readers that, by "unnaming" the animals, Eve has re-entered the Garden of oneness while Adam, busy "fitting parts together," is still in the realm of the dual.

As Eve leaves Adam, it is difficult for her to express herself. Up until that point in time, language has allowed her to take things for granted; now, her words must be "slow" and "new," and as she walks down the path, she notices the trees as "dark-branched, tall dancers motionless against the winter shining" (196). Interestingly, this last line— if it is to be taken as her stance—is reminiscent of Tolkien's view of fantasy literature as discussed in chapter four. Recovery, for Tolkien, was a means of "regaining a clear view," of things in their newness, divorced from the possessiveness which language gives us. Le Guin differs from

Tolkien (and the other authors discussed), though, is that she is saying that the power to regain the original state of oneness is the purview of the feminine. Thus the Garden of Eden story has been subverted. This also ties Le Guin's story to the ecocritics' call for a paradigm shift, a shift from the obsession with the human perspective to the animal perspective.

The Poems: Animal, Vegetable and Mineral

Buffalo Gals and Other Animal Presences is a book that approaches nonhuman alterity from a number of directions—from stories to "thought experiments" involving perspectival shifts—and also from prose to poetry. Interspersed between the prose, there are sections devoted to poems that ask readers to question their notions of agency. While a comprehensive discussion of the poems would broaden our understanding of Le Guin's work, our goal will be to point to some of the basic themes of the sections of poems included in the book.

Three Rock Poems

The first section, "Three Rock Poems," presents Le Guin's views of rocks as both existing in time in a different way than everything else (they are *really* old) and also that they are place. They are literally foundations for everything and are under everything; therefore, Le Guin emphasizes that the rock is the center. This idea is made concrete in the poem "Mount St. Helens/Omphalos," where the first line is "O mountain there is no other where you stand the center is"; later in the poem, there is a reference to the moon landing in 1969. When the "children of the moon" look towards the earth, they see the large volcanic rock and immediately desire to come home, "Earth, hearth, hill, altar, heart's home, the stone is at the center" (57). Indeed, Le Guin's use of the word *Omphalos* in the title suggests that this center, or "navel" of the world, is also connected to a religious center (the most famous *omphalos* is in Delphi but exists in other places as well).

The other two poems, "Flints" and "The Basalt," also attest to the foundational nature of rocks. In the former poem, the age of rocks is emphasized. The last lines are: "that mean the world / "that mean the world is old." So, rocks literally do mean the world to us as they are foundations or sacred centers, but they are also indications that the world is old. As Le Guin says in her introduction to these poems, rocks are able to exist in their shapeless *thingness* beyond the count of human years. In the poem "The Basalt," Le Guin employs an interesting shift in perspective by implying that when one is holding a rock, one is holding a word and "you can pick up a word and hold it, / opaque, / untranslated" (56). The rock exists regardless of humans' need to know what it means (how it is translated), and the rock exists as an unchanging object for which the beauty is in its *thingness*, in its alterity.

FIVE VEGETABLE POEMS

In the second section of poems, "Five Vegetable Poems," the first four poems are about the fragility and strength, and the threat for survival of nature. "Torrey Pines Reserve" describes the silence and beauty a specific place, a "gentle wilderness," a "lizard place," where the fragility of the sandstone, carved away by the power of wind and water, is a lesson to humans: "one must walk lightly / this is fragile" (76). And further, "Hold to the thread of way. / There's a narrow place for us..." (76) that is both a direct reference to the Dao but also a reference to a holy, numinous way of being in the world, a way of being that recovers the sense of the sacramental vision. In "Lewis and Clark and After," the seemingly simple poem about the famous Lewis and Clark expedition of 1804–1806 goes on to become a paean against how we see the world. Traveling across a forest continent, the expedition doesn't notice the "solemn company" of the trees, due to the inability of the tribe (those on the expedition and humans in general) can only see trees with one eye. The reference to sight has resonances with other sight references in Le Guin's work (e.g., Myra losing her eye and then getting a new one from Bluejay). It also has resonances with my thesis: in order to see the world sacramentally, one must learn to see in a new way, a way that values alterity and sees all of nature as interconnected.

Perhaps the most mythopoeic poem in *Buffalo Gals and Other Animal Presences* is "The Crown of Laurel," a retelling or revisioning of the Greek myth of Daphne and Apollo. In her introductory comments on the poem, Le Guin stresses the importance of myth as a foundational technique for teaching us how to live in the world. In order to work, however, Le Guin reminds us that myths *must* be retold. This has been the thesis of the sacramental vision as well: revisioning myths in mythopoeic fantasy allows readers to rediscover a sacramental vision of the world, one that perhaps has been lost in our modern world. The Daphne and Apollo story is one that Le Guin revisions in order to show her readers the perspective of Daphne. The story as told by Ovid is well known. Cupid shoots Apollo with an arrow that makes him fall in love with Daphne, and Cupid shoots Daphne with an arrow that repels Apollo's love. When Apollo pursues his love through the forest, Daphne prays to her father, the river god Peneus, to help her in her flight from Apollo. Peneus responds by transforming Daphne into a laurel tree. Not able to have his love, Apollo honors Daphne by always wearing a crown of laurel as a reminder of his love for Daphne.

Le Guin gives readers an intimate view of Daphne's thoughts on Apollo. The poem starts with Daphne acknowledging Apollo's need to honor her by wearing the crown of laurel, but also adds that Apollo "seems to have lost interest" (78). She recalls that when Apollo chased her, it wasn't because she was trying to save her virtue that she ran (because that "belongs to men" [78]) but that she just wasn't in the mood; plus, she states, "he didn't care" (78). Daphne then reflects on the period of time before she was pursued by Apollo, a time shared with the satyrs, her sister nymphs, and her brothers of the streams. It was an idyllic time before the approach of the sun god. When he does show up, Daphne states that there was "no center but himself, the Sun. / A god is like that, I suppose; he has to be" (80). Daphne then laments, "But I never asked to meet a god, / let alone make love to one!" (80). What Le Guin introduces here is not only the problems with patriarchal domination systems and the need for a revisioning of this order by shifting the point of view to the female (as she did in "She Unnames Them" as well), but she also is conjuring up the Apollonian/Dionysian dichotomy. As a literary or philosophical concept, Apollo and Dionysus represent two modes of experiencing the world. Apollo represents the sun, reason, order, control, while Dionysus represents wine, disorder, revelry, and intuition. Throughout the poem, readers see a paradigm shift, from Apollo's bright world of the masculine and reason, to the world of Daphne, who prefers the Dionysian. At the conclusion of the poem, Daphne "gets dressed" or transforms into the laurel tree and lets the wind dance her. And even though Apollo still honors her by wearing the crown and singing her praises, Daphne ends, "My silence crowns his song" (80). And what a powerful silence it is.

Seven Bird and Beast Poems

The third section of poems is titled "Seven Bird and Beast Poems." In her introduction to these poems, Le Guin says that they are about "cominglings" of humans and other beings. The poem "What is Going on in The Oaks Around the Barn" is about one of Le Guin's favorite birds, the acorn woodpecker. One of the most unusual activities of the acorn woodpecker is that it bores holes in oak trees and stashes acorns in it that it can never get out. This, Le Guin, says, is a problem to be solved, but not by the woodpecker. It is the ornithologist who must try to understand the behavior; for the woodpecker, it makes perfect sense. And who is to say why a bird (or any other animal for that matter) does what it does? The point is made clear when Le Guin reflects on a barn she came across that had holes neatly bored in the walls with acorns in them. Was this a winter supply for the woodpeckers or a form of art? This same idea is central in Le Guin's story, "Author of the Acacia Seeds," as discussed earlier. Leaving our anthropomorphic biases behind, how can we approach the nonhuman on its on terms?

In "Totem," the narrator identifies the mole as a totem animal, totem being the word for a family or individual guardian from the natural world that guides one through life. In the poem, the mole is also seen as "mound builder" and "maze maker" and a "shaper of darkness" (134). As Richard Erlich points out in his discussion of the poem, the mole embodies the yin aspects of life: darkness, earth, femininity, water, aspects that Le Guin champions in many of her works.

"Sleeping Out" is what Le Guin refers to as a true ghost story. As kids camp out, strange noises are heard and there is something "crashing" in the darkness. The presence is so palpable that the crickets cease with their songs and the coyote giggles distantly in the hills. There is a command from one of the kids: "Don't turn on the flashlight." The reasoning for this is that the light will "make a hole in the air" and the strange presence will be more frightful as it encloses the area around the light. It is a fear that is literally coming from the brush but also coming from an "old dark mind." Again, Le Guin makes good use of Daoist images of old, dark and forests, and connects them with an experiential feeling of fear of the unknown.

Four Cat Poems

"Four Cat Poems" comprises the last section of poems in *Buffalo Gals and Other Animal Presences*. For Le Guin, cats are messengers of sorts, guides that exhibit the qualities of yin. A quick glance through the poems brings out words such a "dark," "silence," "sleep," and "negative" that underline Le Guin's comment that "all cats are yin enough" (151). In fact, Chinese references can be found throughout the poems. For example, in "For Leonard, Darko, and Burton Watson," the specific reference is to a parable in *The Way of Chuang Tzu* (and one of the best translations is by Burton Watson). The parable is the Butterfly Dream where Chuang, the Daoist sage, has such a powerful dream of himself as a butterfly that upon awakening, he doesn't know if he is Chuang Tzu dreaming he is a butterfly or a butterfly dreaming he is Chuang Tzu. The parable is a questioning about what exactly constitutes "reality" and how is it different from the reality of dreams. Is there such a distinction? How do we know what is real and what is not? The question is taken up in Le Guin's poem where the narrator is sitting in the "May grass" reading a "Chinese poet" with a "black and white cat" (154) nearby. The narrator notices that the cat is aware of the writing of the swallows in the air, and then she begins to write herself. As the cat falls asleep, the narrator has a question: Whose poem is it? The narrator's or the cat's? This is interesting not only because it asks readers to consider the relationship to the Chuang Tzu parable, but also the central question Le Guin has been asking throughout many of the stories and poems in her collection: what exactly is art? Who is doing it? Are there boundaries between humans and nonhumans? Can nonhumans have art?

"Black Leonard in Negative Space" is a complex poem, again, dealing with Daoist themes. Everything that surrounds the cat (the negative space) is what the cat is not, and in that space there is everything. It is only the cat that occupies space, and that space is responsible for the cat existing in time. Thus "time / is space for love and pain" (152) refers to the ordinary phenomenological time—that which separates all things and creates duality. When the cat dies, the poem speculates, it will rejoin space without a seam. And in that space all things will be one.

Although not her own poem, Le Guin translates and discusses Rilke's "Eighth Duino Elegy" because, as she says, it is the poem she has loved and learned so much from. It is an important poem for Le Guin as it addresses the need for a postantropocentric view of the animal. In Rilke's elegy, it is only the animal that sees openness; it "has its dying always behind it and God in front of it, and its way is the eternal way" (192). In contrast, only our eyes (the rational west) see things backwards, and we are taught this way of seeing the world as children. The world for us is always "never, nowhere-nothing-not" a negation of all the beauty inherent in viewing the world openly. Thus the animal, in Rilke, is superior to the rational human because our rationality (which we inherent from Greeks) is not our blessing but our curse. When our awareness is faced towards death and not away from it, "it overfills us. We control it. It breaks down. We recontrol it, and it breaks down ourselves" (193).

The fascination for the animal perspective is a critique of dominant/Western/human perspectives and a call for a revolution, a radical re-thinking of our relationship to otherness. This revolution in thinking constitutes what Mathew Calarco's states in *Zoographies: The Question of the Animal from Heidegger to Derrida* as a need to think "unheard-of thoughts." Science and philosophy are unable to deal fully with the issues of the nonhuman and alterity, so a full participation in all disciplines is necessary. Calarco asserts that "the human-animal distinction can no longer and ought no longer to be maintained" (3). What is needed are new languages, new histories, and finally new art. It is in many of Le Guin's works, but especially in *Buffalo Gals and Other Animal Presences*, that she delivers to her readers perspectives other than the human perspective. Whether it is Coyote, an acorn woodpecker, a horse, a cat, or even an oak, the stories and poems of Le Guin challenge the Western view of the nonhuman. In its place she asks readers to consider a radical de-centering of the human, a realization of what Thomas Birch describes as the universal consideration of all things, of putting a "face" on the nonhuman so that our humility towards the natural world allows for a fully nonanthropocentric thought to be developed.

Conclusion

In Coyote-like fashion, I've saved discussion of the introduction to *Buffalo Gals and Other Animal Presences* until the end; partly because Le Guin mentions the disabling effect of introductions (which she prefers to read at the end) but, perhaps more importantly, because many of the points made in my thesis are explicitly stated in her introduction and are applicable to all of our authors. The first point is that of mythopoeic fantasy's ability to have readers re-envision the world. "Civilization," by which Le Guin means a male dominated, Christo-centric and hegemonic system, has relegated anything that is not part of this system as "other," including women, children, and animals. By subscribing to this hierarchical system, civilized man has "become deaf," not hearing the animal cries of brotherhood, of community, of interdependence. Instead, all civilized man understands are "master" or "father," terms that reflect the hierarchical domination system that sees only itself. It is what Le Guin refers to in her essay "The Carrier Bag Theory of Fiction" as the "Killer Story," the story that is all about the swords and spears (and other long, hard things), but will ultimately bring about civilization's demise. According to Le Guin, what we need are new stories about "containers," that hold and carry things like berries, or oats, or even stories themselves. She believes the earth's survival depends on these stories and in the use of the voices of the others in *Buffalo Gals* (whether they be children, animals, rocks, or plants). She is offering readers new stories in order to change the way we see the world.

In order for the doors of perception to open, the myth of man's civilization (which Le Guin ascribes to monotheisms which assign a soul to man alone) must be subverted. It is this sense of subversion that Rosemary Jackson has given us as the central concern of fantasy. This subversion of the myth of civilization seeks to find an answer to one of the questions Le Guin poses: Where is the place that Coyote made? For Le Guin, it's certainly not the church, which she describes as "the dreadful self isolation of the Church, that soul-fortress towering over the bestial/mortal/World/Hell" (11). It's not Euclidean, it's not male, and it's not an Arcadia in the past. What it is, for Le Guin, is an engagement with the other, a seeking to find animal presence not by dominating nature but being connected to it. Echoing some of Coyote's subversive activities, Le Guin says it probably would look like a place Coyote made after having a conversation with his own dung. It is a place that is totally different from Eden. As Le Guin says elsewhere, "Driven forth by the angel with the flaming sword, Eve and Adam lifted their sad heads and saw coyote, grinning" ("Non-Euclidean" 90).

Perhaps the most important element of Le Guin's introduction is the sense of the numinous (or the holy) which she infused within all of her stories in this collection. In many of her essays, Le Guin laments the fact that we have no awareness of the "Sacred Now," we have a lack of meaning in our lives because we don't have a sense of "place," we don't quite know where, or even if, we belong. If we did, we wouldn't be destroying the earth's resources and our literature would celebrate the earth more than it does. This is the reason that the true introduction to *Buffalo Gals* is Denise Levertov's poem "Come Into Animal Presence." By beginning her collection of stories and poems with this poem, Le Guin seems to be saying that it is only when we view nature not in anthropomorphic terms as extensions of ourselves, but when we see the wildness of the other and respect it for what it is that we sense the holy. It is the space in between both human and nonhuman (where both love and cruelty occur) that is holy ground. "Those who were sacred have remained so," one of the lines of the poem states, "holiness does not dissolve, it is a presence / of bronze, only the sight that saw / it faltered and turned from it. An old joy returns in holy presence" (14). In *Buffalo Gals and Other Animal Presences*, Le Guin returns us to this old joy, this sense of the sacredness of all things, where our sight does not falter, but sees the interdependence of animal, vegetable, mineral, and all things in between.

CHAPTER EIGHT

The Sacramental Vision
Perceiving the World Anew

"The fantastic is a compensation that man provides for himself, at the level of imagination, for what he has lost at the level of faith"—Maurice Levy, *Le Roman Gothique Anglais* [617]

"Art and nature are more than just mirrors of each other; they are parts of the same biological impulse to life"—Don Elgin, *The Comedy of the Fantastic* [29]

Tom Shippey points out that the dominant literary mode of the twentieth century is the fantastic. Citing such texts as George Orwell's *Animal Farm* and *1984*, William Golding's *Lord of the Flies* and *The Inheritors*, and Tolkien's *The Lord of the Rings*, Shippey's claim is easily extendible into the twenty-first century. More and more authors are employing the fantastic as a mode that departs from consensus reality due to the fact that this "impulse" expresses the deepest experiences which humans may encounter in literature; this is in direct contrast to the mimetic impulse, which fails to encompass all the varieties of experience available to us. Moreover, the fantastic impulse is equally shared with the reader who embraces this mode of literature more so today than in any other century. As proof of its widespread appeal, one need look no further than the franchise of *Star Wars*, *Star Trek*, any recent superhero, or the recent literary resurgence of fantasy in the *Harry Potter* series or in Peter Jackson's adaptation of Tolkien's *The Lord of the Rings* and *The Hobbit*.

By employing Kathryn Hume's definition of fantasy as "any departure from consensus reality," we were able to intentionally cast our nets wide for the purposes of incorporating many works in order to understand their appeal. Given this inclusive definition of fantasy, we can now place our mythopoeic fantasists in a meaningful academic discourse

Eight. The Sacramental Vision

and specifically relate them to the field of religious studies. What is most interesting concerning these authors is that, although each is distinctly expressing the numinous, all advocate the use of the imagination as a viable means of *experiencing* religion without the overt use of any specific doctrine or dogma. It is this religious experience which transcends dogma that is the defining element of mythopoeic fantasy; it is also this element to which readers of the past hundred years have responded so enthusiastically.

In *The Secret Life of Puppets*, Victoria Nelson states that "the arts, now regarded as homocentric secular territories ruled entirely by the imagination, have come to serve as a kind of unconscious wellspring of religion instead of the other way around" (9). According to Nelson, nowadays we can locate our deepest religious impulses not in traditional religious practices but in the imagination itself. What this proves for Nelson is that our culture is undergoing a profound shift, from a previous emphasis on Aristotelian thinking, which embraces logic, to a Platonic idealism, where the deeper religious dimension is nonrational and underlies our basic assumptions concerning the reality of the world. For Nelson, the religious impulses of our modern culture are not to be found in churches but in the works of the imagination.

This shift towards Platonic idealism also underlies what has been a central focus of the present study: the nonrational. Concerning our present predicament, Nelson says, "The larger mainstream culture, via works of the imagination instead of official creeds, subscribes to a nonrational, supernatural quasi-religious view of the universe: pervasively, but behind our backs" (vii). This emphasis on the nonrational has been analyzed in detail by Rudolf Otto in his text *The Idea of the Holy*. I have extended Otto's discussion, which largely pertains to traditional religious forms, to the wider realm of the imagination. If Nelson is correct in her argument that works of the imagination offer a form of religious expression, then it is no wonder that readers respond so powerfully to the mythopoeic fantasists considered in this study. The nonrational factor contained within these works evokes a numinous consciousness, the unique feeling-oriented experience of divine reality which transcends our rational knowledge; it is that quality of "holiness" from which we experience a sense of "awe" beyond such concepts as good or evil. Being an apprehension of divine reality not covered by our rational knowledge, it is indefinable or indescribable; it may only be evoked through symbols which reflect the experience. The indescribable nature of the experience, as well as its sense of "awe" or "wonder," is acknowledged by fantasy critics and authors, so the application of Otto's concept of the numinous is effective in revealing the religious quality of these secular works.

What is the practical application of such an analysis of fantasy literature? My proposed answer is that it can contribute to the fields of ecocriticism, posthumanism and the larger discourses within cultural studies. Scholars in these fields are interested in how nature is constructed and how these constructions affect our worldview; however, such concerns have been largely relegated to nonfiction, works by nature writers such as Thoreau, Muir, Abbey, and Dillard. I have attempted to widen the field of ecocriticism and posthumanism to include imaginative literature as both reflecting and challenging how we *perceive* the natural world. I seek to expand the environmental applications of Don Elgin's *The Comedy of the Fantastic*, which discusses the literary modes of tragedy and comedy, to a consideration of the unique religious implications these fantasy works have for the way nature is perceived.

Concerning environmental problems, Elgin discusses an important point related to our failed attempts at avoiding environmental destruction. He says that these matters are not solved by an increase in technology, which merely shifts the problem. On the contrary, what needs to be challenged are our most basic assumptions about the environment itself. Environmental crises, he states, "are logical end results of the central attitudes western humanity has developed and propagated about the relationship between itself and its environment" (3). These attitudes about our separation from nature, Elgin claims, stem from three basic areas: religion, especially Western Christianity; the shift from a hunter-gatherer society to an agricultural society; and, the French and Industrial Revolutions. My concern is the effect that "religion" has on the authors examined in this book. By analyzing the religious dimension, specifically Otto's concept of the numinous, we are confronted with a basic problem which seems to be solved by mythopoeic fantasy.

In terms of religion, the most destructive piece of literature from an ecocritical perspective is in the biblical account of creation in Genesis. Many environmental critics argue that God's command to have "dominion" over the earth is a carte-blanche to utilize the earth for human purposes. As Roderick Nash points out in his article "The Greening of Religion," the Hebrew words in consideration are *kabash* and *radah*,

Eight. The Sacramental Vision

both of which are used in the Bible in a negative manner: *radah* meaning "to rule," "to tread down," and "to scrape out," and *kabash* meaning "to subject," "to force," and "to bring into bondage" (196).

The problem with Genesis is that it sets up what Joseph Campbell terms "mythic dissociation," a view of the universe that is shared among the Judeo-Christian religions. Ultimately, it sets up a differentiation between God, humans, and nature, where no sense of identity among the three is conceived. According to Campbell, once one subscribes to this particular view of the universe, the mystical function of myth, that which provides the sense of awe, disappears. As Campbell argues, this function of myth is the most important function; he states, "myth opens the world to the dimension of mystery, to the realization of the mystery which underlies all forms. If you lose that, you don't have a mythology" (*The Power of Myth with Bill Moyers* 31). If Nelson is correct, and we now find our deepest religious impulses in literature, then we ought to look in this direction to see if our lost mythology reappears there.

Similar criticism of Christianity is seen in activist groups such as Greenpeace and Earth First!, the latter of which has as its central priority "to protect and restore wilderness because undisturbed wilderness provides the necessary genetic stock for the very continuance of evolution" (Taylor 47). Many of the advocates of such groups look to other religious traditions for guidance, such as the American Indian, Buddhist, and Daoist, which espouse a sense of interrelatedness that they feel is not present in Christianity. Many within these groups are quite hostile to the Christian worldview; as Bron Taylor says of Earth First!, "Virtually all of today's Earth First!ers believe patriarchy, hierarchy, and anthropocentrism reflect related forms of domination that destroy the natural world" (54). As has been shown in the present study, there are mythopoeic fantasists who are working within the Christian framework and seem to have similar issues with environmental destruction (Coleridge, Macdonald, Lewis and Tolkien); and, there are those who are working outside the fringe of a specifically Christian dogma to explore other possibilities mythopoeic fantasy may offer (Blackwood and Le Guin).

The sense of Christianity's anthropocentrism has led to much controversy, instigated by Lynn White's famous essay, "The Historical Roots of our Ecological Crisis." Arguing that Christianity "bears a huge burden of guilt" for environmental destruction, White believes that since this anthropocentrism promoted our separation from nature, we must rethink how we perceive the natural world. He states, "since the roots of our trouble are so largely religious, the remedy must also be essentially religious, whether we call it that or not" (14). Contrary to the widespread belief that White was attempting to destroy religion, he concludes the essay by advocating a reform of its most basic premises. This leads us now to a fascinating possibility. If our culture is now looking for religious experiences in imaginative literature rather than in traditional religion, why not look at mythopoeic fantasies to see if they provide viable alternatives to the way we perceive the natural world?

Such a move, if successful, puts into question all the previous concerns about Christianity (or any other religion) as being at fault for environmental problems. In their own distinct way, each of the authors in the present study was deeply influenced by a religious worldview, but his or her fantasy betrays a concern for the way nature is perceived and a need for a revisioning or resacralizing of the world. In the introduction, this need for revision was discussed within the context of Kathryn Hume's *Fantasy and Mimesis*. She groups fantasy into four different modes—illusion, vision, revision, and disillusion—which are effective ways of understanding the concerns of the present authors. However, she fails to provide a thorough discussion of any of our present authors, and some, such as Tolkien, (it is my belief), she categorizes incorrectly. It has been my intention to locate *all* of our authors within Hume's mode of "revision," because they provide new ways of experiencing and ordering our reality and, in the context of ecocriticism or posthumanism, these new ways help resacralize nature.

More specifically, fantasy aids in the revisioning of the natural world due to its subversive function. According to Rosemary Jackson, in her book *Fantasy: The Art of Subversion*, fantasy allows for a total breakdown between distinctions such as animal, vegetable, and mineral; our normative modes of perception are undermined. As she argues, fantasy traces what is "unsaid" or "unseen" in a culture. Jackson's concern for the subversiveness of fantasy seems in close relation to Haraway's cyborg myth which has as its prime concern fusions between the human/animal/cyborg. In this sense, fantasy does not escape reality but attempts to make reality strange: "fantasy is not to do with inventing another non-human world; it is not transcendental. It has to do with inverting elements of this world, re-combining its constitutive features in new

Eight. The Sacramental Vision

relations to produce something strange, unfamiliar, and apparently 'new,' absolutely 'other' and different" (Jackson 8).

Jackson's concept of subversion helps to explain the need of the mythopoeic fantasist to depart from reality in order for a revisioning of the natural world to take place. In one way or another, these authors believe that they are not transcending this world for mere escapism; on the contrary, they are recombining elements of this world in order to help the reader see the world as it was meant to be seen, as an infusion of the numinous. Thus what fantasy really helps us escape is not this world but our perceptions of it as being devoid of any religious value. Coleridge describes this as an escape from the "lethargy of custom"; MacDonald believes art rescues us from our "weary and sated regards"; Lewis advises that "if you are tired of the real landscape, look at it in a mirror"; and, finally, Tolkien argues that the imagination relieves us from the "drab blur of triteness, of familiarity."

In terms of ecocriticism and posthumanism, this subversive element in fantasy is extremely important. Many of the environmental critics discussed in the introduction argue for a learning of a new language, or a new way of thinking about our relationships to nature. Mythopoeic fantasy is already a viable means of achieving this. By its subversiveness, through which it departs from consensus reality, it offers an imaginative engagement with that which is non-human. Thus art and nature reflect each other. As Don Elgin states, "the apprehension of beauty in art is built on the same principles as apply to nature" (28).

Employing the distinction between "inner" and "outer" divine reality, I have analyzed Coleridge's *The Rime of the Ancient Mariner* and MacDonald's *Phantastes* as concerned with the realm of the inner. Each of these works deals with the theme of the annihilation or death of the self in order for this divine reality to be perceived, a theme related to Otto's discussion of the numinous because the numinous can only be apprehended by a loss of identity. As Philip C. Almond says, "the recognition of the objective value of the numen is accompanied by a corresponding devaluation of the self, and existence in general" (75). In Coleridge's *The Rime*, the death of the self mirrors the biblical theme of fall and redemption. The Mariner shoots the Albatross and his fall is related to the first utterance of a sense of identity: "I shot the albatross." This action instigates his mythic dissociation, where once a sense of self develops as a result of the crime against nature, he is cursed. His redemption, however, occurs as he is able to experience the beauty of the water snakes; he blesses all of God's creatures because he has identified with a higher, more divine reality than his finite self allows.

In *Phantastes*, George MacDonald betrays the same focus on the inner dimension of the numinous but in a less allegorical manner. The death of the self theme occurs within the wider context of Romantic love. Through his many pursuits of his ideal lady, the figure who embodies the numinous or divine reality, Anodos must continually learn to give up his sense of identity in order to serve his lady. It is only when he finally gives up his life for his lady, literally, that he is able to experience the divine reality from which his self has excluded him. This overreliance on the self is similarly revealed with Anodos's encounter with the Shadow, the character who divorces Anodos from his many encounters with the wonders of fairyland which, in our argument, are encounters with the numinous itself. Again, it is only when Anodos realizes the importance of being humble or lowly that he is able to transcend his finite self to an experience of the higher reality of the numinous.

The annihilation of the self theme in both Coleridge and MacDonald's texts is relevant for the experience of the numinous as well as for revisioning the perceptions of the natural world. It has already been pointed out that the perception of the numinous is accompanied by a devaluation of the self; *The Rime* as well as *Phantastes* employs this theme in order to present the reader with a certain *experiential* mode of perception. This, in turn, helps in a revisioning of the natural world because the boundaries of the self are challenged, which is precisely the ideological goal of ecocriticism. In challenging the sense of identity, the boundaries of the self are enlarged and the whole world may be perceived as containing the sacramental vision. As Roger S. Gottlieb states in his article "Spiritual Deep Ecology and the Left: An Attempt at Reconciliation," "a spiritual perspective suggests that only with this discovery of a sense of selfhood beyond the ego can we become released from the ego's compulsions and inevitable disappointments" (521).

What is interesting is that this death or annihilation of the self is traditionally more characteristic of Eastern religions such as Daoism or Buddhism. In fact, many of the environmental critics who are hostile to Christianity's anthropocentrism look to Eastern religions for a new way of perceiving the world untainted by the self. Referring to this turn to Eastern religions, Roderick Nash says, "by advocating the submergence

Eight. The Sacramental Vision

of the human self in a larger organic whole, they cleared the way for environmental ethics" (215). It is, in part, for this reason that our study included authors such as Blackwood and Le Guin; although both have nods to the Christian worldview (if negative), they have also widened the range of possibilities for exploring the numinous and our relation to the environment in constructive ways. However, what is to be gained by the present study is the realization that the death or annihilation of the self which helps in perceiving the numinous is not the exclusive claim of Eastern religions; in fact, there are unique contributions to environmental revisioning by authors who are largely influenced by the Christian worldview. So, if Nelson is correct, and our culture is shifting to a more Platonic worldview via works of the imagination, we should widen Lynn White's suggestion of looking to St. Francis to a consideration of mythopoeic fantasists.

If Coleridge and MacDonald place their emphasis on the "inner" problems of perceiving the sacramental vision, then Lewis and Tolkien place their emphasis on the "outer," that is, the numinous as it exists on a more epic scale. Mineko Honda suggests the reason for this emphasis on the "outer" is that for Lewis, and by extension Tolkien, God is absolutely "other," and although the imagination is a means by which God reveals himself, God cannot be directly known. This is in contrast to the slightly different approach of Coleridge and MacDonald who, with their emphasis on problems of the self, tend to be a bit more mystical. Mystical approaches typically accept the possibility of full merging with the divine. However, the bridge that connects both sets of authors is that their fantasies are apocalyptic in the sense that their theoretical structures are meant to "unveil" or "reveal" the transcendent.

It is Lewis in *The Last Battle* who adheres most closely to traditional Christian thought when he allegorically portrays how present perceptions of the world, and in fact the world itself, must be ultimately destroyed in order for the sacramental vision to occur. Lewis's apocalyptic vision is more direct than the other authors because he structures the book around the biblical text of Revelation. By creating a fantastic context where the "old" Narnia is destroyed and replaced by a "new" Narnia, Lewis betrays a Platonic influence, where this world is a mere shadow or copy of a reality which is somewhere more real. It is only when the characters go "further up and further in" to this new Narnia that they are in a perfected paradise. Thus in Lewis's theological worldview, the sense of longing or *Sehnsucht* is what keeps this vision of the perfected world in the here and now. As Eliane Tixier has argued, the result of this longing is always accompanied by the ability of seeing the "footsteps of the divine" in this world. Therefore, even though Lewis's vision is much more epic than Coleridge and MacDonald's, it is still related to how the world is perceived here and now. This has been illustrated by the dwarfs, whose motto "the Dwarfs are for the Dwarfs," betrays an over-reliance on the self and keeps them from perceiving the wonders of the "new" Narnia. According to Aslan, they have been imprisoned in their own minds.

Tolkien's detestation of allegory is largely what separates his vision from that of Lewis. Tolkien believed that what was most important was "applicability" rather than strict allegory, so the numinous as it is perceived in Middle-earth tends to be more direct since it concerns itself with a sense of awe at the created world and not necessarily a transcendence of it. Nonetheless, as with Lewis, Tolkien projects his ideas of the numinous on the outward world with such characters as Tom Bombadil and Treebeard, and with such settings as Lothlorien and the Shire. These characters and settings are "applicable" because they are manifestations of Tolkien's theory of recovery; they represent how the world was *meant* to be seen. However, as awe-inspiring as these characters and settings are, they are subject to fading. Thus, in a similar manner, both Lewis and Tolkien's visions partake in the theme of ultimate loss, although the loss comes more gradually for the latter.

Algernon Blackwood's work is the most autobiographical of the works presented, and *The Centaur* was his most autobiographical work. Being raised in a strict Christian family (his father was a revivalist), it is no wonder that Blackwood turned to mystical traditions and organizations such as the Order of the Golden Dawn, the Theosophical Society and the Society for Psychical Research. Also, given Blackwood's appreciation for what his strict father did give him (a deep devotion to what was spiritual), it is no wonder that Blackwood also found this spiritual wonder in Eastern religions such as Hinduism and Buddhism. It is this that led Algernon to find a deity not just active on Sundays but every day, and everywhere. The overwhelming presence of nature was Blackwood's main influence, and he believed he could convey that only within a literature which opened one's eyes to the numinous. Blackwood's work also calls for an expansion of consciousness (which like MacDonald

Eight. The Sacramental Vision

involves a death of the self), and a questioning of what the distinctions between human and nonhuman actually are. Blackwood presages a posthumanist need for boundary questioning, boundary crossings and intimate connections, so much so that, as our broad definition of mythopoeic fantasy has stated (Hume's "any departure from consensus reality"), leads us also to question literary boundaries of "fantasy," "science fiction," "horror" or even those authors called simply "weird."

Ursula Le Guin is perhaps the most vocal of all the examined authors in her critique of the Western, hegemonic, dualistic, and aggressive worldview. Many of her works (most especially in her *Earthsea* books, *The Left Hand of Darkness*, and *The Lathe of Heaven*), Le Guin shows her indebtedness to Eastern philosophical traditions, in particular Buddhism and Daoism. In *Buffalo Gals and Other Animal Presences*, however, she is relying on characteristics of indigenous religions. Of course, many similarities exist between Eastern philosophical and indigenous traditions, most particularly respect for the environment and the view of the world as a connected web. Le Guin's use of nonhuman nature, including Coyote or rocks or trees or even "aliens," Le Guin, like Blackwood, calls for boundary questioning and boundary crossings. As with Blackwood, Le Guin is Haraway's cyborg author, a creator of myths which infuse a deeply spiritual awareness of the world. An author who employs in *Buffalo Gals and Other Animal Presences* mainly the animal fable, but also thought-experiments, retellings of ancient stories and science fiction. So, as we have traced, the imaginative formulations of Coleridge, which allows for authors to express the deepest religious/spiritual feelings, have led to authors such as MacDonald, Lewis and Tolkien to express these feelings specifically through Christian-oriented mythological systems, and finally to our more modern examples of Blackwood and Le Guin, two authors who question important boundaries in a postmodern, posthuman world.

Some environmental critics believe that to lose the environment is to lose our sense of God. However, all of the present authors, in both their theories and in their art, show that neither of these elements, the environment nor God, needs be lost. We can awaken our experience of both through the imagination, which seeks to resacralize the world. This approach is useful in that it attempts to interpret the world as a symbolic disclosure of the divine mystery which, in this argument, is ultimately nonrational and experiential. In their works, these mythopoeic fantasists advocate this experience through their imaginative forms because, for some, traditional religious forms are no longer adequate. For these authors, the experience of the numinous in the form of the sacramental vision is what transforms nature from an object which must be appropriated to a mediator of wonder. According to many fantasy critics, wonder is the defining element of fantasy and its greatest gift; it is a spiritual good which cannot be lost. Thus fantasy, by making the familiar seem both strange and wondrous, gives us a new language to encounter the natural world around us in a new way through experiences which awaken our sense of awe, humility, and respect for the mystery which finally transcends both ourselves and our world.

Bibliography

Almond, Philip C. *Rudolph Otto: An Introduction to His Philosophical Theology*. Chapel Hill: University of North Carolina Press, 1984. Print.

Armbruster, Karla. "'Buffalo Gals, Won't You Come Out Tonight': A Call for Boundary-Crossing in Ecofeminist Literary Criticism." *Ecofeminist Literary Criticism: Theory, Interpretation, Pedegogy*. Eds. Greta Gaard and Patrick D. Murphy. Chicago: University of Illinois Press, 1998. Print.

Armstrong, Karen. *The Case for God*. New York: Alfred K. Knopf, 2009. Print.

Ashley, Mike. Personal e-mail. 28 September 2011.

Attebery, Brian. *The Fantasy Tradition in American Literature: From Irving to Le Guin*. Bloomington: Indiana University Press, 1980. Print.

Barfield, Owen. *What Coleridge Thought*. Middletown, CT: Wesleyan University Press, 1971. Print.

Barth, Robert J. "Theological Implications of Coleridge's Theory of Imagination." *Coleridge's Theory of Imagination Today*. Ed. Christine Gallant. New York: AMS Press, 1989. Print.

Bate, Jonathan. *The Song of the Earth*. Cambridge: Harvard University Press, 2000. Print.

Bennett, Jane. *The Enchantment of Modern Life: Attachments, Crossings and Ethics*. Princeton: Princeton University Press, 2001. Print.

Blackwood, Algernon. *The Centaur*. 1911. Harmondsworth: Penguin, 1938. Print.

Blackwood, Algernon. *Episodes Before Thirty*. London: Cassell, 1923. Print.

Blackwood, Algernon. "The Genesis of Ideas." *The Writer* 50.2 (1937): 35–37. Print.

Burger, Douglas A. "The Shire: A Tolkien Version of Pastoral." *Aspects of Fantasy: Selected Essays from the Second International Conference for the Fantastic in Literature and Film*. Ed. William Coyle. Westport, CT: Greenwood Press, 1986. Print.

Butler, James, and Karen Green. "Introduction." *Lyrical Ballads and Other Poems*. By William Wordsworth. Ithaca: Cornell University Press, 1992. Print.

Cadden, Mike. "Le Guin's Continuum of Anthropomorphism." *Ursula K. Le Guin Beyond Genre: Fiction for Children and Adults*. New York: Routledge, 2005. Print.

Calarco, Mathew. *Zoographies: The Question of the Animal from Heidgger to Derrida*. New York: Columbia University Press, 2008. Digital.

Campbell, Joseph. *The Flight of the Wild Gander: Explorations in the Mythological Dimension*. New York: Viking, 1969. Print.

Campbell, Joseph. *The Masks of God: Creative Mythology*. New York: Arkana, 1991. Print.

Campbell, Joseph. *An Open Life: Joseph Campbell in Conversation with Michael Toms*. Eds. John M. Maher and Dennie Briggs. New York: Harper and Row, 1989. Print.

Campbell, Joseph. *The Power of Myth*

Bibliography

with Bill Moyers. Ed. Betty Sue Flowers. New York: Doubleday, 1988. Print.

Cavell, Stanley. *In Quest of the Ordinary: Lines of Skepticism and Romanticism*. Chicago: University of Chicago Press, 1988. Print.

Cirlot, J.E. *A Dictionary of Symbols*. New York: Dorset Press, 1971. Print.

Coleridge, Samuel Taylor. "The Friend 1." *The Collected Works of Samuel Taylor Coleridge*. Ed. Barbara E Rooke. London: Routledge and Kegan Paul, 1969. Print.

Coleridge, Samuel Taylor. "From Biographia Literaria." *The Portable Coleridge*. Ed. I. A. Richards. New York: Penguin, 1950. Print.

Coleridge, Samuel Taylor. "The Rime of the Ancient Mariner." *The Portable Coleridge*. Ed. I.A. Richards. New York: Penguin, 1950. Print.

Coleridge, Samuel Taylor. "Selections from the Statesman's Manual." *The Portable Coleridge*. Ed. I.A. Richards. New York: Penguin, 1950. 386–94. Print.

Collins, Adela Yarbro. *The Apocalypse*. Collegeville, MN: The Liturgical Press, 1990. Print.

Collins, John J. *The Apocalyptic Imagination: An Introduction to Jewish Apocalyptic Literature*. 2nd ed. Grand Rapids: Eerdmans, 1998. Print.

Collins, John J. *Daniel (a Hermeneia Commentary)*. Minneapolis: Fortress Press, 1993. Print.

Curry, Patrick. "Less Noise and More Green." *Mythlore* 21.33 (1996): 126–38. Print.

Curry, Patrick. "Magic Vs. Enchantment." *Mallorn: The Journal of the Tolkien Society* 38 (2001): 5–10. Print.

Elgin, Don. *The Comedy of the Fantastic: Ecological Perspectives on the Fantasy Novel*. Westport, CT: Greenwood Press, 1985. Print.

Erlich, Richard. "Ursula K. Le Guin and Arthur C. Clarke on Immanence, Transcendence and Massacres." *Extrapolation* 28 (1987): 105–129. Print.

Gaarden, Bonnie. "George Macdonald's *Phantastes*: The Spiral Journey to the Goddess." *Victorian Newsletter*. Ed. Ward Hellstrom. Bowling Green: Western Kentucky University Press, 1999. Print.

Galbreath, Robert. "Ambiguous Apocalypse: Transcendental Versions of the End." *The End of the World*. Eds. Eric S. Rabkin, Martin H. Greenberg, and Joseph D. Olander. Carbondale: Southern Illinois University, 1983. 53–72. Print.

García de la Puerta, Marta. "J.R.R. Tolkien's Use of Nature: Correlations with Galicians' Sense of Nature." *Mythlore* 22.1 no. 83 (1997): 22–25. Print.

Gilbert, Stuart. "Algernon Blackwood: Novelist and Mystic." *Transition* 23 (1935): 89–96. Print.

Glotfelty, Cheryll. Introduction. *The Ecocriticism Reader: Landmarks in Literary Criticism*. Eds. Cheryll Glotfelty and Harold Fromm. Athens: University of Athens Press, 1996. Print.

Gottlieb, Roger S. "Spiritual Deep Ecology and the Left: An Attempt at Reconciliation." *This Sacred Earth: Religion, Nature, Environment*. Ed. Roger S. Gottlieb. New York: Routledge, 1996. 516–31. Print.

Happold, F.C. *Mysticism: A Study and an Anthology*. New York: Penguin, 1963. Print.

Hein, Rolland. *The Harmony Within: The Spiritual Vision of George Macdonald*. Grand Rapids: Christian University Press, 1982. Print.

Hill, John Spencer. Introduction. *Imagination in Coleridge*. Ed. John Spencer Hill. London: Macmillan, 1978. 1–26. Print.

Holy Bible: New Revised Standard Version. New York: Oxford University Press, 1989. Print.

Honda, Mineko. *The Imaginative World of C.S. Lewis: A Way to Participate in

Reality. New York: University Press of America, 2000. Print.
Hooper, Walter. *Past Watchful Dragons: The Narnian Chronicles of C.S. Lewis*. New York: Collier, 1971. Print.
Hume, Kathryn. *Fantasy and Mimesis: Responses to Reality in Western Literature*. New York: Methuen, 1984. Print.
Huttar, Charles A. "C.S. Lewis's Narnia and the Grand Design." *The Longing for a Form*. Ed. Peter Schakel. Kent, OH: Kent State University Press, 1977. 136–58. Print.
Irwin, W.R. *The Game of the Impossible: A Rhetoric of Fantasy*. Chicago: University of Illinois Press, 1976. Print.
Jackson, Kasi. "Feminism, Animals and Science in Le Guin's Animal Stories." *Paradoxa* 21 (2008): 206–231.
Jackson, Rosemary. *Fantasy: The Literature of Subversion*. New York: Routledge, 1981. Print.
Jasper, David. *Coleridge as Poet and Religious Thinker: Inspiration and Revelation*. London: Macmillan, 1985. Print.
Le Guin, Ursula. *Buffalo Gals and Other Animal Presences*. New York: ROC, 1987. Print.
Le Guin, Ursula. "The Carrier Bag Theory of Fiction." *Dancing at the Edge of the World: Thoughts on Words, Women, Places*. New York: Grove Press, 1989. Print.
Le Guin, Ursula. *Cheek by Jowl*. Seattle: Aqueduct Press, 2009. Digital.
Le Guin, Ursula. "A Left-Handed Commencement Address." *Dancing at the Edge of the World: Thoughts on Words, Women, Places*. New York: Grove Press, 1989. Print.
Le Guin, Ursula. "A Non-Euclidean View of California as a Cold Place to Be." *Dancing at the Edge of the World: Thoughts on Words, Women, Places*. New York: Grove Press, 1989. Print.
Le Guin, Ursula. Personal letter. 30 January 2001.
Le Guin, Ursula. *The Wave in the Mind: Talks and Essays on the Writer, the Reader, and the Imagination*. Boston: Shambhala, 2004. Print.
Lewis, C.S. *An Experiment in Criticism*. Cambridge: Cambridge University Press, 1961. Print.
Lewis, C.S. *George Macdonald: 365 Readings*. New York: Collier, 1974. Print.
Lewis, C.S. Introduction. *Phantastes: A Faerie Romance*. Grand Rapids: WM.B Eerdmans, 1958. Print.
Lewis, C.S. *The Last Battle*. New York: Collier, 1956. Print.
Lewis, C.S. *On Stories and Other Essays on Literature*. Ed. Walter Hooper. San Diego: Harcourt Brace, 1982. Print.
Lewis, C.S. *Surprised by Joy: The Shape of My Early Life*. San Diego: Harcourt Brace Jovanovich, 1956. Print.
MacDonald, George. *A Dish of Orts: Chiefly Papers on the Imagination and Shakespeare*. Whitethorn, CA: Johannesen, 1996. Print.
MacDonald, George. "To Louisa Powell." *The Expression of a Character: The Letters of George Macdonald*. Ed. Glenn Edward Sadler. Grand Rapids: Eerdmans, 1994. 26. Print.
MacDonald, George. *Phantastes*. Grand Rapids, Grand Rapids: Eerdmans, 1858. Print.
MacDonald, George. *Unspoken Sermons, First, Second and Third Series*. Whitethorn, CA: Johannesen, 1999. Print.
Manlove, Colin. *Christian Fantasy: From 1200 to the Present*. Notre Dame: Notre Dame Press, 1992. Print.
Manlove, Colin. *The Chronicles of Narnia: The Patterning of a Fantastic World*. New York: Twayne, 1993. Print.
Manlove, Colin. "The Circle of the Imagination: George Macdonald's *Phantastes* and *Lilith*." *Studies in Scottish Literature*. Ed. G. Roy Ross. Columbia: University of South Carolina, 1982. Print.
Manlove, Colin. *Modern Fantasy: Five Studies*. New York: Cambridge University Press, 1975. Print.
McGillis, Roderick F. "*Phantastes* and

Lilith: Femininity and Freedom." *The Gold Thread: Essays on George Macdonald*. Ed. William Reaper. Edinburgh: Edinburgh University Press, 1990. Print.

Murphy, Patrick. "Voicing Another Nature." *A Dialogue of Voices: Feminist Literary Theory and Bakhtin*. Eds. Karen Hohne and Helen Wussow. Minneapolis: University of Minnesota Press, 1994. Print.

Nash, Roderick. "The Greening of Religion." *This Sacred Earth: Religion, Nature, Environment*. Ed. Roger S Gottlieb. New York: Routledge, 1996. 194–229. Print.

Nelson, Victoria. *The Secret Life of Puppets*. Cambridge: Harvard University Press, 2001. Print.

Niiler, Lucas. "Green Reading: Tolkien, Leopold and the Land Ethic." *Journal of the Fantastic in the Arts* 10.3 (1999): 276–85. Print.

Otto, Rudolf. *The Idea of the Holy: An Inquiry into the Non-Rational Factor in the Idea of the Divine and Its Relation to the Rational*. New York: Oxford University Press, 1923. Print.

Prickett, Stephen. *Victorian Fantasy*. Sussex: The Harvester Press, 1979. Print.

Rabkin, Eric S. "Introduction: Why Destroy the World?" *The End of the World*. Eds. Eric S. Rabkin, Martin H. Greenberg and Joseph D. Olander. Carbondale: Southern Illinois University Press, 1983. vii–xv. Print.

Richards, I.A. *Coleridge on Imagination*. New York: W.W. Norton, 1950. Print.

Sammons, Martha. *A Better Country: The Worlds of Religious Fantasy and Science Fiction*. New York: Greenwood Press, 1988. Print.

Sandner, David. "The Fantastic Sublime: Tolkien's 'on Fairy-Stories' and the Romantic Sublime." *Mythlore* 22.1, no. 83 (1997): 4–7. Print.

Schakel, Peter. *Reading with the Heart: The Way into Narnia*. Grand Rapids: Eerdmans, 1979. Print.

Seeman, Chris. "Tolkien's Revisioning of the Romantic Tradition." *Proceedings of the J.R.R. Tolkien Centenary Conference*. Eds. Glen Goodknight and Patricia Reynolds. Altadena, CA: Mythopoeic Press, 1995. Print.

Shippey, Tom. *J.R.R. Tolkien: Author of the Century*. Boston: Houghton Mifflin, 2001. Print.

Singer, Irving. *The Nature of Love: Courtly and Romantic*. Chicago: University of Chicago Press, 1994. Print.

Slochower, Harry. *Mythopoesis: Mythic Patterns in Literary Classics*. Detroit: Wayne State University Press, 1970. Print.

Taylor, Bron. "Earth First!: From Primal Spirituality to Ecological Resistance." *This Sacred Earth: Religion, Nature, Environment*. Ed. Roger S Gottlieb. New York: Routledge, 1996. 545–57. Print.

Tolkien, J.R.R. *The Fellowship of the Rings*. New York: Ballantine, 1954. Print.

Tolkien, J.R.R. *The Letters of J.R.R. Tolkien*. Ed. Humphrey Carpenter. Boston: Houghton Mifflin, 1981. Print.

Tolkien, J.R.R. "On Fairy-Stories." *The Tolkien Reader*. New York: Ballantine, 1966. Print.

Tolkien, J.R.R. *The Return of the King*. New York: Ballantine, 1955. Print.

Tolkien, J.R.R. *The Two Towers*. New York: Ballantine, 1954. Print.

Trixier, Elaine. "Imagination Baptized, or 'Holiness' in the Chronicles of Narnia." *The Longing for a Form*. Ed. Peter J. Shakel. Kent, OH: Kent State University Press, 1977. 136–58. Print.

Warren, Robert Penn. "A Poem of Pure Imagination: An Experiment in Reading." *Twentieth Century Interpretations of the Rime of the Ancient Mariner*. Ed. James D. Boulger. Englewood Clifs, NJ: Prentice-Hall, 1969. 21–47. Print.

Watson, Jeanie. *Risking Enchantment: Coleridge's Symbolic World of Faery*.

Bibliography

Lincoln: University of Nebraska Press, 1990. Print.

White, Jonathan. "Coming Back from Silence." *Conversations with Ursula K. Le Guin.* Ed Carl Freeman. Jackson: University Press of Mississippi, 2008. Print.

White, Lynn. "The Historical Roots of Our Ecological Crisis." *The Ecocriticism Reader.* Eds. Cheryll Glotfelty and Harold Fromm. Athens: University of Georgia Press, 1996. Print.

Williams, Anne. *Art of Darkness: A Poetics of Gothic.* Chicago: University of Chicago Press, 1995. Print.

Wilson, Keith. "The Quest for 'the Truth': A Reading of George Macdonald's *Phantastes.*" *Etudes Anglaises.* Eds. C. Cestre and A. Digeon. Paris: H. Didier, 1981. Print.

Wolff, Robert Lee. *The Golden Key: A Study of the Fiction of George Macdonald.* New Haven: Yale University Press, 1961. Print.

Wordsworth, Jonathan. "'The Infinite I Am': Coleridge and the Ascent of Being." *Coleridge's Imagination.* Eds. Richard Gravil, Lucy Newlyn, and Nicholas Roe. Cambridge: Cambridge University Press, 1985. Print.

Index

absolute reality 77
Adam and Eve 18, 45–46, 134; *see also* "She Unnames Them"
agency 121, 148, 151, 155, 163–164
Algernon Blackwood: An Extraordinary Life 136
Alice in Wonderland 8
Almond, Philip C. 183
"Ambiguous Apocalypse" 79
American Indian 146, 149, 181
Anodos 55–56, 58–69, 184
Anti-Christ figures 83
apocalypse 39, 69–71, 78–82, 82, 84, 89, 92, 104, 107, 109, 185, 199
The Apocalyptic Imagination 81
Ashley, Mike 136, 144
Aslan 80–89, 91, 186
Attebery, Brian 9, 14, 26, 54, 95, 198
"The Author of the Acacia Seeds" 162–165
Avatar 5
awe *see* numinous

Balder 76
Barfield, Owen 35, 43
Bate, Jonathan 27–31, 102
Bennett, Jane 25, 120
The Bhagavad-Gita 126
biocentrism 103, 106
Biographia Literaria 1, 32–37, 47
Blackwood, Algernon 2, 3, 9, 20, 25, 119, 122–144, 181, 185–187, 198–199
Blake, William 56- 57
Bombadil, Tom 25, 104–106, 112, 117, 186
The Book of Lost Tales 94
Brave New World 7
Brihadaranyaka Upanishad 20
Buddhism 19, 131, 134, 136–137, 139, 184, 186–187; *see also* mythic association

Buffalo Gals and Other Animal Presences 25, 145–177, 187
"Buffalo Gals, Won't You Come Out Tonight" 149–151
Burger, Douglas A. 115
Burnet, Thomas 34, 39, 46–47

Calarco, Matthew 19
Campbell, Joseph 18–22, 28, 31, 44, 79, 89, 102–103, 134, 138, 181, 198
The Castle 72
The Castle of Otranto 129
Cavell, Stanley 40
Cazotte, Jaques 10
The Centaur 25, 119, 123, 129–141, 143, 186, 198
Christ 41, 80, 133–134
Christian Fantasy: From 1200 to the Present 74
Christian mythos 119, 120
Christianity 2, 18, 21, 22, 25, 29, 76–77, 79, 119, 133, 139, 145, 180–182, 184; *see also* mythic dissociation
Chronicles of Narnia 5, 73–75, 80, 91; *see also* Narnia
The Chronicles of Narnia: The Patterning of a Fantastic World 73–74
"The Circle of the Imagination: George Macdonald's *Phantastes* and *Lilith*" 64
Cirlot, J.E. 41
Coleridge, Samuel Taylor 1, 20, 24, 27, 29, 31–48, 53, 56, 62, 66, 69–70, 73–74, 77–79, 86, 96–97, 100, 119, 131, 136, 139, 155, 181, 183–187, 198–202
Collins, Adela 82
Collins, John 81–83, 85, 87–88, 199
Crowley, Aleister 125
Curry, Patrick 102–104, 107

Index

cyborg 19–21, 182, 187
A Cyborg Manifesto 19

Daniel, Book of 87, 199
Daoism 2, 133–134, 184, 187; *see also* mythic association
Daphne and Apollo 171–173
"Le Diable Amoreux" 10
"Direction of the Road" 154–156
A Dish of Orts: Chiefly Papers on the Imagination and Shakespeare 48–54, 58, 200
Dr. Jekyll and Mr. Hyde 72
The Door in the Wall (H.G. Wells) 72
Dunsany, Lord 124

ecocriticism 6, 17, 19, 22, 29–30, 47, 78, 86, 98–101, 103, 170, 180, 182–184, 199
ecopoets 29–31, 102
ecospiritualists 122
Edwards, Jonathan 91
Elgin, Don 105, 113, 115, 117, 178, 180, 183, 199
enchantment 13, 15, 22, 258, 30, 37, 60, 97, 102–103, 120–122; *see also* wonder
The End of the World 86
Ents 12, 14, 24, 30, 72, 84, 108, 111–114, 116
environmental crisis 2, 17, 18, 21–24, 26, 28–29, 78–80, 83, 98, 102, 112–113, 119, 134, 138–139, 145–146, 180–181, 183–185, 187
Episodes Before Thirty 125–126, 130, 138
escape 7–8, 11–14, 30, 40, 99–101, 135, 182–183
escape and consolation 99
eucatastrophe 102
An Experiment in Criticism 72–73, 200

faerie 15, 37–38, 43, 95, 103, 142
fairy 5, 16, 24, 65– 67, 77, 94–96, 99–100, 136
fairy tale 48, 72–73, 102
"The Fantastic Sublime" 99
The Fantastic Tradition in America 26
Fantasy and Mimesis 6, 182, 200
Fantasy: The Literature of Subversion 10
Fechner, Gustav Theodor 131
The Flight of the Wild Gander: Explorations in the Mythological Dimension 20
Freud, Sigmund 12
Frodo 106, 108–111, 117
"From Joy to Joy: C.S. Lewis and the Numinous" 75
Frye, Northrop 88–89

Gaarden, Bonnie 62
Galbreath, Robert 79, 199
The Game of the Impossible 23
García de la Puerta, Marta 109
Garden of Eden 19, 39, 45–46, 133–135, 139, 141, 143, 159, 169, 170; *see also* "She Unnames Them"
Genesis 18, 28, 79, 168, 180–181, 198
George MacDonald: 365 Readings 61
Gilbert, Stuart 126, 129
Goethe 57
Golden Age 28; paradise 28, 134–135, 139, 143; *see also* Garden of Eden
The Golden Key 66, 72, 202
Gottlieb, Roger S. 184
"Green Reading: Tolkien, Leopold, and the Land Ethic" 103

Happold, F.C. 127–128, 133–134, 136, 139
Haraway, Donna 19, 182, 187
Hargrove, Gene 105
The Harmony Within 59, 199
Harry Potter 5, 178
Heaven 77, 187
Hein, Rolland 59
Herbert, G.B. 105
Hill, John Spencer 34
Hinduism 19, 131, 134, 136, 139, 159–160, 186; *see also* mythic association
"The Historical Roots of our Ecological Crisis" 2, 18, 181
The Hobbit 5, 106, 115–117, 178
the Holy 15, 73–74, 76, 105, 112, 121, 177, 179
"Horse Camp" 152–161
Hume, Kathryn 2, 6–11, 13, 16–17, 22–23, 25, 52, 130, 140, 178, 182, 187, 200
Hutter, Charles A. 91
Hymns to the Night 58

The Idea of the Holy 1, 15, 75, 94, 104, 108, 179, 201

Index

"Imagination Baptized or 'Holiness' in the *Chronicles of Narnia*" 75
Imagination in Coleridge 34
immanence 79
In Quest of the Ordinary 40
The Inheritors 8, 178
Irwin, W.R. 80
Islam 79
ISLE: *Interdisciplinary Studies in Literature and Environment* 17

Jackson, Rosemary 6, 10–13, 16–17, 23, 25, 109, 130, 140, 148, 176, 182–183
James, M.R. 124
Joshi, S.T. 123, 126, 130, 135, 140
J.R.R. Tolkien: Author of the Century 93
Judaism 79

Kafka, Franz 7, 72, 121
Kant, Immanuel 34, 40
Keats, John 56–57

The Last Battle 25, 71, 80–92, 117, 185, 200
Last Judgment 83
Le Guin, Ursula K. 2, 25, 119, 122, 145, 187
Leopold, Aldo 103, 106, 201
Lewis, C.S. 1–3, 5, 7, 8, 9, 12, 20, 25, 29–30, 40, 52, 53, 61, 70–101, 104, 107, 109, 117, 119, 131, 136, 139, 171, 181, 183, 185–187, 187, 199–200
Lilith 48, 58, 63–64, 72, 200–201
The Lion, the Witch, and the Wardrobe 80
Longfellow, Henry Wadsworth 76
Lord Dunsany 124
The Lord of the Rings 5, 8, 12, 25, 71–72, 84, 93–94, 96, 103–104, 106–108, 110–111, 113–115, 117, 178
Lothlorien 104, 107–112, 115, 117, 186
Lovecraft, H.P. 124
Lucy 86, 202
Lyrical Ballads 32–34

MacDonald, George 1, 2, 20, 24, 29, 31–32, 40, 43, 47–79, 86, 100, 119, 136, 139, 142, 147, 155, 183–187, 200
Machen, Arthur 124
"Magic vs. Enchantment" 102

Manlove, Colin 51–52, 54–55, 58, 64, 69, 73–74, 200
Mariner *see The Rime of the Ancient Mariner*
marvellous 10–12
The Masks of God: Creative Mythology 18, 21
"May's Lion" 166–168
"Mazes" 152–154
McGillis, Roderick 63, 69
Middle-earth 8, 11, 25, 93–94, 107, 109–111, 114–115, 117, 186
mimesis 6, 10, 72, 98, 103, 178
Mitchison, Naomi 104, 107
Modern Fantasy 51–52, 200
The Mysteries of Udolpho 129
mysticism 56, 69, 125, 127–128, 133, 136, 138, 142, 199
myth 8–10, 18–22, 28, 31, 41, 46, 72–74, 76, 79–81, 84, 89, 92–94, 101–103, 110, 119, 131–134, 138–141, 147, 149, 151, 156, 159, 164, 168–169, 172, 181, 183, 187
mythic association 20, 79–80, 103, 131, 134, 164
mythic dissociation 18–20, 31, 41, 89, 102–103, 131–132, 147, 164, 168, 181, 183, 188
mythopoeic fantasy 1, 2, 6, 8–30, 32, 39, 40, 43, 45–48, 50,–55, 65, 69, 71–72, 74, 77–81, 89, 91–92, 94, 99, 101–103, 105, 119, 129–131, 140, 142, 145, 147–148, 150, 155, 165–167, 171–172, 176, 178–183, 185, 187

Naked Lunch 8
Narnia 7, 11, 71, 75, 80, 82–92, 109, 185–186, 200–201
natural world 5–31, 36, 38, 43, 47, 50, 54–56, 65, 69–71, 80, 84, 90–92, 99–110, 121, 131, 135, 138, 148–156, 180–184
The Nature of Love 56, 201
Nelson, Victoria 38, 179
Niiler, Lucas 103, 106, 108
1984 7
Novalis 49, 55, 57–58
numinous 1, 2, 9–10, 15–17, 20, 22, 24–28, 30–34, 36, 38–48, 50, 52, 54–58, 60, 62, 64–82, 84–92, 94–96, 98–112, 116–122, 124–140, 142, 144–150, 152, 154, 159, 177, 179–180, 182–186, 188; *see also* awe

197

Index

O'Malley, Terence 123, 131–132, 134, 143
"On Fairy-Stories" 5, 8, 12–15, 24, 95–99, 101–102, 108–109
"On Myths" 72
On Stories and Other Essays on Literature 12, 71–72, 74, 77, 89, 93, 101
One Earth One People: The Mythopoeic Fantasy Series of Ursula K. Le Guin, Lloyd Alexander, Madeline L'Engle, and Orson Scott Card 9
Otto, Rudolf 1, 15–16, 22, 26, 30–32, 50, 54–55, 69, 72–73, 75, 77, 94–96, 99, 104, 107–108, 112–113, 121, 129, 134, 138, 142, 147, 179–180, 183, 198, 201
Oziewicz, Marek 2, 9

paradise 39, 41, 66, 80, 82, 85–86, 88–91, 110–111, 113, 135, 185; *see also* Garden of Eden
pastoral 7–8, 115, 117, 172
"Pearl" 110
Penzoldt, Peter 126
Phantastes 24, 48, 52–53, 55, 58–59, 61–69, 72, 76–78, 183–184, 199–200, 202
"*Phantastes* and *Lilith*: Femininity and Freedom" 63
Plato 56, 90
Platonic tradition 53, 76, 81, 90, 91, 179, 185
posthumanism 2, 19, 119, 155, 180, 182–183, 187
postmodern 2, 26, 120, 148, 150, 187
Potter, Beatrix 76
Power of Myth 19
Prickett, Stephen 53
primary imagination 34–36
primary world 25, 95, 98, 102, 109

"The Quest for 'the Truth'" 68

Rabkin, Eric 71, 78–79, 86, 199, 201
Radcliffe, Ann 129
Reading with the Heart: The Way Into Narnia 88
recovery 12–13, 30–31, 33, 39, 41, 43, 46, 53, 56, 66, 68, 70, 99–101, 103, 105, 107–108, 115, 117, 139, 169, 186
Revelation, Book of 25, 80, 82–85, 87–88, 90, 92, 140, 185

revisioning 9, 12, 17, 21–31, 39, 43, 55–56, 62, 69–71, 80–84, 89–90, 95, 97, 103, 123, 133, 139, 171–172, 182–185
The Rime of the Ancient Mariner 1, 24, 27, 32–34, 37–47, 62, 69, 136, 183, 199–201
Risking Enchantment: Coleridge's Symbolic World of Faery 37–38, 41
romantic love 56–60, 62–64
Romanticism 40, 56–60, 62–64, 73–74, 77, 91, 96–97, 99–100, 184, 199, 201
Rowling, J.K. 5
Ruekart, William 18

sacramental vision 2, 13, 17, 36, 39, 45–46, 50, 53, 66–90, 99–119, 135, 142–143, 155–160, 171–172, 178–188
Saga of King Olaf 76
Sandner, David 99–100, 201
Saruman 111–116
Schakel, Peter 88–89, 200–201
"Schrödinger's Cat" 162–165
secondary world 11, 14, 16–17, 25, 48, 79, 96–97
The Secret Life of Puppets 38, 179
Seeman, Chris 97–98, 201
Sehnsucht 25, 52, 74–75, 91, 186
the Shadow 48–70, 77, 82, 84, 87, 90, 184–185
Sharkey *see* Saruman
"She Unnames Them" 168–170
Shelley, Percy Bysshe 56
Shippey, Tom 93–94, 104, 110, 113, 178, 201
Shire 25, 104, 110–111, 115–117, 186, 198
"The Shire: A Tolkien Version of Pastoral" 115
The Silmarillion 94
Singer, Irving 56
Slethaug, Gordon E. 105
Slochower, Harry 46
The Song of the Earth 27, 29, 31
Space Trilogy 7, 8
Squirrel Nutkin 76
Star Wars 5, 178
Stevenson, Robert Lewis 72
sub-creation 13, 96
sublime 99–100, 109, 142
subversive function 94–103, 108–109, 117–121, 133, 140, 148–155, 164–167, 170, 176–83

198

Surprised by Joy 71, 75–77, 91–92, 200

Tales of Terror and the Unknown 128
Thomas, Jesse 75
Thoreau, Henry David 121, 148, 180
Tixier, Eliane 74, 186
Todorov, Tzetan 10, 11
Tolkien, J.R.R 1–3, 5, 8–9, 12–16, 20, 24–25, 29–31, 40, 53–54, 70–72, 74, 78–79, 84, 93–119, 128, 131, 133, 136, 139, 142, 155, 169–170, 178, 181–183, 185–187, 198–201
"Tolkien's Revisioning of the Romantic Tradition" 97
transcendent 9, 10, 17, 18, 20, 21, 24, 29, 36, 38, 69, 70, 79, 81, 82, 97, 98, 99, 100, 102, 109, 138, 146, 164, 185
Treebeard 25, 111–114, 117, 186; see also Ents
trickster figure 149

Unspoken Sermons 48, 50, 56, 200
Upanishads 126
utilitarianism 112–113
utopia 113

"Vaster Than Empires and More Slow" 157–159
Victorian Fantasy 53, 201

Walpole, Horace 129
Warren, Robert Penn 44–46
Watson, Jeanie 37–38, 41
We 7
The Weird Tale 124, 135
Weiskel, Thomas 99
Wells, H.G. 72
What Coleridge Thought 35–43
White, Lynn 2, 18, 22, 28–29, 79, 139, 145, 181, 185
"The White Donkey" 159–162
"The Wife's Story" 152–154
Williams, Anne 41–43
Wilson, Keith 68–69, 78
Wind in the Willows 7
Wizard of Oz 7
Wolff, R.L. 66, 68
wonder 1, 7, 14–16, 25; see also numinous
Wordsworth, William 33–34, 77

Yeats, William Butler 125
Yoga Aphorisms 126

Zoographies: The Question of the Animal from Heidegger to Derrida 19, 175

www.ingramcontent.com/pod-product-compliance
Ingram Content Group UK Ltd.
Pitfield, Milton Keynes, MK11 3LW, UK
UKHW021845140426
5217IPUK00022B/1606